Persimmon Apricot Gunfighter

Jason S. Litz

Black Rose Writing | Texas

ISBN: 978-1-68433-511-4
PUBLISHED BY BLACK ROSE WRITING
www.blackrosewriting.com

Printed in the United States of America
Suggested Retail Price (SRP) $18.95

Persimmon Apricot, Gunfighter is printed in Chaparral Pro

*As a planet-friendly publisher, Black Rose Writing does its best to eliminate
unnecessary waste to reduce paper usage and energy costs, while never compromising
the reading experience. As a result, the final word count vs. page count may not meet
common expectations.

This work is dedicated to my mom who is the greatest champion of my writing and who's persistent prodding is the reason you are able to enjoy Persimmon Apricot or any of my other novels.

In memory of my dad, Larry E. Litz, who always wanted the best for us and who kept us on the straight and narrow. While he was not a writer, he was a fine artist. It was he from whom I inherited my wry humor which permeates my stories.

Persimmon Apricot Gunfighter

I
MEETING PERSIMMON

By now, I am sure you have heard iniquitous rumors about Persimmon Apricot—how he killed a man for laughing, or how he cut out a man's tongue, or how he set fire to a saloon full of people and shot anyone who dared burst from the flames. Unfortunately, I can only attest to one of these but what I do offer you in these pages are first-hand accounts and eyewitness testimony. The problem with rumor is it becomes embellished for the sake of entertainment and its context lost. Whether this effect is good or bad, it is unfair to its subject. Regarding Persimmon Apricot, if it is entertainment you want, the truth is sufficient.

No doubt you will ask yourself how the likes of me came to ride with such a notorious gunman or at least wonder how I lived to tell about it—I almost didn't. To begin with, that is not my real name on the cover. These pages hold the complete and truthful story of my brief stint with Persimmon Apricot and some of the facts are not the sort a free man wants known. I tolerate life and enjoy not being in prison. Though I consider myself fairly innocent, a court might rule differently.

After graduating from a rather prestigious college in Carolina, I begrudgingly took a job with the editorial staff of a major newspaper. Forgive me for my vagueness. I withhold some of the details for aforementioned reasons. Suffice it to say, the job was mundane and a leech on my soul. I admit I had a lazy streak which I inherited from my maternal great-grandfather's branch of the family tree. Like my grandfather, I fought it and did not shirk my responsibilities because, more than work, I hated ridicule and ridicule is the only thing a vagabond earns.

It was supposed to be fate that I would be a great writer, but fate sat back on its haunches and refused to budge like the stubborn jackass it is often known to be. Deciding that I would have to take a firmer grasp of the reins, I saved my money, quit my job, and bought a train ticket. One is not a vagabond with a year's wages in his pocket.

I was a lover of the dime novel and since I fancied myself a writer; I set out to go west and earn an exorbitant living writing them. Instead it became brutally obvious my literary skills had been dulled by, and were suited only for, the blandness of newsprint. In that I found steady though meager wages as a traveling reporter. I established connections with big town papers to which I telegraphed or mailed articles on topics of interest that I stumbled upon as I worked a sweeping circuit through the West. When I entered a small town, I sold what I could from my catalog of articles to the local rag, playing up the fact that all... well, most... eh, a good number of them, had been featured in big papers in Chicago, San Francisco and the like.

It was while sulking in a slow shuffle along one such small town's planked sidewalk that I first laid eyes on Persimmon Apricot. I was lamenting the puny sale I had made to the resident single-sheet newspaper and was wishing for a story of sufficient size to be fleshed out into a novel and compelling enough to be successful despite my skill, when I noticed several well dressed men clumped at the corner ahead of me. One was a sheriff's deputy with a grey beard and a belly. Another I recognized as the local mine owner. The other two I assumed were town founders, one of which had a burly, callused right hand he was using to scratch his chin, contemplatively. I assumed he was the local blacksmith. The group had evidently adjourned a regular meeting in the aptly named *Saloon* behind them.

As I drew closer, one of the unfamiliar men took notice of me and turned to greet me. He was the local pastor and head of a vigilance committee of sorts, a body of God-fearing townsfolk who made their assistance available to the sheriff. I gathered from the heated conversation which had spilled out onto the saloon porch, that the men had been meeting on whether or not the town could afford to hire a full-time marshal. The town's dilemma was that it shared the same county as Leadville and anyone who knows anything about Leadville knows the raucous town consumed most of the sheriff's time and that of his deputies.

"You new in town?" the pastor asked as he thrust out his hand to greet me. "Planning to stay on with us? You don't look like the mining type, what's your trade?"

The pastor's demeanor was inviting, even if his questions were tiresome, but I answered each in turn as I tried to eavesdrop on the tense discussion behind him regarding whether or not the mine should foot the bill for the new town marshal. The mine owner made assurances that the mine would pay its share of the salary but another committee member could not make the mine owner commit to a figure.

The bickering abruptly ceased and the unexpectedness of it jolted the pastor's attention. He looked to see what could have prevented either of his headstrong cohorts from forcing the last word. When the pastor turned, my curiosity followed.

It was not the stranger riding into town that captivated everyone's attention; it was the massive draft horse he rode. It was a majestic animal with hulking muscles which rippled under its dark brown coat. Had the stallion been drawing a coach, no one would have paid him any mind, but a saddled rider was noticed. The stranger's broad shoulders were draped with an oilcloth duster and he wore a black hat with a wide brim turned down in front and what I believe Mr. Stetson calls a telescope crown which is round with a flat top.

The behemoth strode up to the railing in front of our little crowd, its muzzle looming over the tallest of us, even as we were elevated by the plank sidewalk. The stranger flung the right side of his duster around his back in preparation to dismount and when he did, I caught a glimpse of the Smith and Wesson in a shoulder holster tucked under his left arm. With his left foot holding his weight in the stirrup, he brought his right leg over the horse's rump, pivoting with his belly on the saddle and holding himself there long enough to dislodge his left foot before sliding off the beast and dropping onto the damp road with both feet.

I expected him to tie off his horse, but when he did not, I realized it would have been pointless. For, what post would have held the animal if he took a notion to pull free? The crowd exchanged pleasantries with the stranger who seemed cordial. Clearly, he was not a talker, but he was not shy about answering questions, the answers of which included that he was not a miner and was only passing through. Being naturally suspicious and realizing that everyone but the stranger had introduced themselves, the deputy pleasantly asked, "What was your name again? I didn't catch it."

The stranger reared his head to cast a firm eye on the deputy, then took a step back to make himself room. With his left hand, he pulled aside his duster as if it were a curtain, purposefully exposing the grip of his Schofield, before answering in a dark and deliberate voice, "My name is Persimmon Apricot." Then, as if to indicate shooting the deputy was not his preference, he added, "Pleased to make your acquaintance."

The saloon porch was silent. The sheriff's deputy was contemplating how to react while everyone around him held their breath, anxious to see the deputy's reaction and praying they did not get shot. Though I never heard him tell it, I know the deputy understood that Persimmon's posturing was to head off any foolishness about his name. I have often wondered what would have happened if a man among us had simply cleared his throat wrong? To everyone's relief, the deputy showed himself to be a prudent man and chose to address Persimmon as if he had offered an open hand rather than a threat.

"Likewise," was the deputy's reserved reply.

With no offending party to shoot and the pleasant discourse dampened, Persimmon removed his duster, shook it off, and draped it across his saddle then began to loosen his saddle bags.

The town was strung along the step formed by a ridge at the foot of a mountain. There was plenty of downhill behind the row of buildings jammed together along the side of the street where we stood. Across the road a sheer cliff rose up, growing taller as it moved south along the road toward us until it collided with a rocky crag jutting out from the mountain. Tucked in that niche was the Bansheen Saloon with a pair of windows facing our group and a door bobbing off its corner. The rest of the cliff's length was dashed at its base with boulders, rock heaps, and the odd building where the rocks allowed.

I heard the committeeman, who I had yet to identify himself, say, "Yonder comes the ugly one now."

Up the far side of the street strode a man with a revolver on his hip and a mean look on his face, not unlike Persimmon's visage a moment earlier. The man was on the downhill side of homely. There was no prominent feature to his face, but those he had were mismatched. In his hand, the gunman carried a coach whip. I assumed he did not want to leave it with his wagon and have it walk off when he was not looking.

"I think he's in charge of the hired guns," came a voice from the committee.

Another chimed in, "Name starts with a J I think… James… Jameson… or something like that."

"Well, I can't arrest him for being ugly, so until he's done something—" the deputy began, obviously continuing the group's earlier conversation to which I had not been privy.

The reverend broke in. "The problem is they never seem to *do* anything, especially when a deputy is in town, but things happen, and several men have lost their land and their mining claims to Ugly's boss."

I listened intently hoping to get a story out of it and, being a guest to the conversation, I felt obliged to stare at the whip toting man as long as this cadre of town fathers did. I glanced over to be sure I was not the only spectator and found that even Persimmon had taken an interest.

Turning back, I saw the gunman step from the planking in front of one building and into the gap between it and the hardware store ahead of him. About the same time a Mexican boy of eight or nine years exited the hardware store with a metal pail. The boy carried it around to the side of the store to dump its murky contents into a rivulet which ran off the rocky slope before cutting a groove across the road.

The boy longed to play in the stream and he almost bent over. Thinking better of it, he only paused to toe in a leaf and watch it be swept away by the swift current. Heading back inside, the boy was still watching his leaf catch on pebbles and spin as it washed across the road, not noticing the man with the whip until he slammed face first into the ugly man's thigh. The bucket bounced off the man's knee. The ugly man cursed and kicked at the boy, catching the child in the shoulder and spinning him to the ground. Cussing as he walked past the boy, the man noticed that a few drops of muck left in the bucket had splashed onto his pant leg. Furious, he swiped at it with his hand, accomplishing nothing, but cursing all the more. The boy had scrambled back to his feet, tears in his eyes, hesitating whether to reach for the pail or run inside without it.

The horrid man turned back in a rage. Heaving obscenities at the child, he loosened his whip, drew back and struck at the boy. The whip cracked across his left eye and cheek bone. Grabbing his eye with both hands, the child staggered and fell across the store porch.

The predator now had the taste of blood and he ripped the whip behind him through the air but before he could lash out at the boy again there came a thundering, "HEY!" which echoed down the street.

The commanding bellow stunned the ugly man and he glanced back to find all eyes on its source, Persimmon Apricot. Quickly our attention returned to the man with the whip and, being under scrutiny, he began to coil the whip, yelling, "somebody ought to get the vermin out of the street."

Those were prophetic words and, as the ugly man continued his strut up to the Bansheen Saloon, one of the committee turned to the deputy, "Well, now you have something to arrest him for."

A heavy-set man with a beard and white apron emerged from the hardware store. He looked up the street to see that the ugly man entered the saloon before he felt it was safe to sweep the sobbing boy up off the planking. The boy grabbed at the man's apron and smeared it dark with blood. We all watched as the store owner carried the poor child down the street to the doctor's place, all of us that is, except the deputy who stood staring at the Bansheen Saloon across the street and Persimmon who stared expectantly at the deputy.

Until that day, I had never seen the sort of vile hatred in a man's face like I saw grow on Persimmon's as the deputy failed to act. He glared at the deputy and I could not help but to think that someone was about to die.

It was the reverend who spoke next. "Well, deputy? Guess you need to be paying that fella' a visit?"

"Getting shot ain't going to help nobody," the deputy replied, not taking his eyes off the saloon across the street. "He's not alone in there. I saw three or four of his men go in earlier whilst we were meetin'. One poor Mexican kid ain't worth dying over."

"So, you're just going to stand there?" Persimmon seethed with contempt. The deputy only raised a rhetorical eyebrow in response which lit Persimmon's fuse. "Worthless sack of..." Persimmon trailed off in a growl as he stomped over to one of two saddle holsters and yanked free a 10-gauge side-by-side.

"Go on, get yourself killed," the deputy called out as Persimmon marched across the road.

Persimmon snapped the back of his hand by his ear in scornful dismissal.

I heard both hammers of the shotgun cock a few steps before Persimmon reached the Bansheen's door. Now, I could lie to you and say that it was my heroic duty as a newsman that possessed me to dart across the street, but the truth is, the grubstake of a year's wages with which I had come west was long gone and I had had nothing to sell the big papers for weeks. I had milked my satchel for all the stories the small-town papers wanted and I was broke. It was self-preservation that launched me across the road before Persimmon entered the saloon.

At first, all I could see in the window glare were the reflections of the clouds and treetops behind me. Pressing my face to the glass with my hand cupped around my right eye, I saw the ugly man facing me from the opposite side of a pool table. His whip was on the bar to his left and he was bent over preparing to strike a ball with his cue when Persimmon approached the table. The ugly man stood upright, eyes wide with terror as Persimmon let go both barrels from across the pool table into the man's midsection, smearing him on the back wall.

Expecting retaliation, Persimmon slammed the shotgun down hard and fast on the felt and snatched his Schofield from under his arm to defend against one of the ugly man's compatriots as he brought his pistol to bear. The man fired, but not before Persimmon's bullet struck him in the ribs. The man's bullet missed Persimmon and broke through the window a single pane from my head. Some of the glass shards collected in the folds of my sleeve. My body jerked from head to boot and I jumped to my left behind the solid wall. Shaking, I cautiously exposed only what I must to see inside.

Another combatant thought he would out flank Persimmon from the front corner of the saloon. I could see the man's forearm and the revolver in his hand. Persimmon was already in motion, sweeping his muzzle across the thin crowd until it came in line with the attacker in the corner. Persimmon was facing me as flame streamed from his barrel. The wall, behind which I hid, shook with the thud of the dead man falling against it. Persimmon scanned once more across the room, the Schofield cocked and ready in his hand. When he was sure there would be no more challengers, Persimmon backed up to the pool table, retrieved his shotgun with his left hand, and then backed out the saloon door.

Not liking the idea of crossing the road with two windows and a door to his back, Persimmon continued to retreat backward across the street. When he noticed me still at the window he called out, "Holler if they move." When he got to his horse, he holstered the shotgun in its scabbard then went inside the competing no-name 'Saloon.'

I jogged back across the street in time to hear the deputy say, "I guess I've got to arrest this feller now."

"You were afraid of those men yonder and didn't do your job. I think maybe you ought to be more afraid of the one man who killed three of them," came the reverend's retort.

Admonished, the deputy quietly steeped in the reverend's logic while I followed the reverend into the Saloon. Persimmon was sitting at a table where he could see the street but was not exposed to the windows or doors of the Bansheen. His hat was upside down on the table and he was holstering his revolver after having reloaded it. The barkeep set a glass and a bottle of whiskey in front of him and out of appreciation said, "It's on the house."

I have to give the reverend credit, he was gutsy. The man of the cloth walked up to Persimmon's table and removed his own hat and held it across his abdomen. "We do appreciate your efforts, we truly do, but it's hard to save the souls of men once they're dead."

"Don't cast your pearls before pigs, Reverend," was the Biblical counter made by Persimmon.

"Yes, perhaps, but just the same—"

"Hold it right there!" came a cry from outside, cutting short the reverend's sermon and warning Persimmon of danger.

Persimmon grabbed the grip of his pistol as heavy boot steps crossed the planking outside. Persimmon rose straight up, overturning the table while swinging the aim of the Schofield to rest on the doorway. The reverend and I clamored to get out of the way as one of the men from the Bansheen Saloon burst in, brandishing his weapon. It was a foolish act of vengeful bravado because he had not the time to lay eyes on Persimmon in the gloom before Persimmon fired a shot dead into the man's middle.

The wounded man dropped his revolver as he stumbled backward out of the doorway and off the planked walk, falling supine onto the street. Persimmon glanced over to me and the reverend whose expression seemed to scold, "Didn't we just have a talk about this?" Persimmon raised his brow, sighed and crept cautiously outside, weapon at the ready.

Gazing down on his squirming prey, Persimmon asked, "Have you given thought to Jesus as your Lord and Savior?"

"You go to hell," spit the unrepentant through the pain.

"Well, you think about it while you lay there and bleed to death," Persimmon instructed and walked back to the saloon door where the reverend stood. "See there, Reverend, if a man won't repent when he's gut shot he won't repent at all."

II
WITNESSES

I righted the table Persimmon had pitched over. The barkeep grabbed the bottle and glass off the floor. The bottle was still corked and full, but a large shard had been snapped from the lip of the glass. He paused to stare at the perfect half-oval missing from an otherwise pristine tumbler, then looked around at his feet for the missing bit. The broken piece failed to present itself and the bartender became bored with the chase after glancing left and right. Besides, Persimmon was about to return and he would be hunting a container in which to pour his whiskey.

The bottle went onto the table and the proprietor rushed to fetch a new glass. For a few moments the saloon was completely still. Men had just been killed, shouldn't there be a commotion? Was this eerie silence mourning, reflection, or simply disinterest? The room was empty, save for the bartender and I. The few other patrons that had been there before the shooting had all ducked out through the side door to ogle the scene from the perceived safety behind the next building over.

Bending down, I swept Persimmon's hat from the floor and in the process found the illusive glass shard. As I righted myself, the quiet was broken by the heavy beat of Persimmon's boots. The expression of irritation on his face was one of someone having been forced into an inconveniently scheduled chore. Noticing Persimmon's hair was slicked down unevenly about his head reminded me that I held his hat. I offered it to him as he approached the table. He took it and rested it, crown down, on the table then pulled the chair into position and sat as he had before the ruckus.

The barkeep hurriedly returned with a shiny new enameled tin cup in his hand. "I'm sorry Mr. Apricot, that was the last glass I had. Can I get you anything else?"

An abbreviated shake of Persimmon's head released the bartender to go about his business. After a sigh, one which I took to be of resignation, Persimmon pulled the cork and poured the cup half full.

So, here is the part of the story that you might not believe. I have a difficult time believing it myself, but when I analyze it, it makes sense. Sure, I had a story to write based on this incident alone but how long would that keep me before I would again be a broke peddler of plagiarized newsprint? I still longed for a story that could flesh out the pages of a novel and captivate the hearts and wallets of readers. Persimmon was an unapologetic killer, but those he killed were scum, or so it seemed. Also, my confidence was buoyed by the earlier actions of the reverend. He had a disagreement with Persimmon, but he was still breathing. No, I was not a clergyman, but I was not going to strike up a disagreement with Persimmon either.

Letting out a soft, shaky sigh myself, I stepped up to the table and made my introduction then asked in as respectful a manner as I could, "Mr. Apricot, may I sit and talk with you a few minutes?"

Half to my surprise, Persimmon stretched out his upturned palm toward an empty chair in a gesture for me to sit. My respectful manner and winning charm is what I would like to believe won me a seat at his table, but I know in truth, all I had to do was not make him mad with me. Any reasonable conversation was welcome to a man who has spent enough lonesome days between outcrops of civilization.

First, I explained that I was not part of the committee, nor a resident of the town. When I came to the part where I told him I was a writer, I was not sure which approach to my story would better serve me, embellishment of my talents or the pitiful truth. It was then when the bartender brought me an enamel coated tin cup. Its rim was chipped and rusty but the interruption evened my keel and also reminded me that I was still holding the broken chunk of glass. I handed it to the bartender who appeared happy not to have to hunt it later. Persimmon poured me a drink of rye so I paused, took a large sip, and decided to take my story somewhere down the middle, avoiding lies and inopportune details.

Coming to the portion where I asked Persimmon if I might follow along with him and write his story, I assured Persimmon I would strike any deal with him he thought fair and added that he would be doing me a great service. Though truthful, the statement was a pitiful attempt at winning his sympathy but I hoped it would lend weight to my request. Persimmon had shown he would fight for the underprivileged and I was certainly the most hapless individual with which I was acquainted.

Not a word, Persimmon did not accept or dismiss my request. He did not ask for clarification or call me a fool, nothing. I knew he understood everything I said, but he was also listening to the latest uproar outside. Contemplatively, he leaned back in his chair and stared at me. Without expression change, he reached up and slowly drew his pistol from under his left arm.

My heart pounding was all I could hear, but I feel confident in saying that I did not show fear. Reminding myself that nothing I had said should get me shot, I was determined to appear nonchalant though my gut was tight and my toes clinched in my boots. Persimmon never pointed the muzzle at me. Instead, he lay the revolver on the table, pointing it toward the door.

Immediately, two of the committee members burst through the open door and marched up to us, heedless of a dangerous man's nerves. Despite having felt the need to place his weapon on the table to afford him a quick response to whatever trouble entered the saloon, Persimmon did not flinch at their abrupt entrance but he did turn his attention to the two men. Silently, I welcomed their distraction because I melted in my chair from the relief I felt from not having been shot and I did not want Persimmon to notice.

"We had an impromptu meeting and, well, what would you say to being our town marshal?" asked the committeeman I did not recognize.

"Yes, how about it?" seconded the other man.

The reverend entered next, and knowing the question, waited to hear Persimmon's response.

"Nope," was all Persimmon replied.

"Despite my desire to save the souls of the denizens in this hard-bitten town, I can't will salvation upon them. If you could refrain from shooting first for every possible infraction, then a gunfighter is probably what this town needs for a marshal. What with drunken miners, no nonsense ranch hands, and the latest trouble brewing." Though intent in his duty to God, clearly the reverend was a practical man.

Would not that be perfect for me if Persimmon would take the job? A marshal in a town like this one was bound to have one scrape after another and in no time, I would have my novel. Persimmon's continued refusal of the position disappointed everyone.

"I'm not a gunfighter," was Persimmon's stern reply.

The change of mood was palpable. The committee was cowered by Persimmon's gruff tone. Excitement in the men's eyes softened to caution and, though I did not consider myself a part of this conversation, I felt my body tense again. Rather than watch the committee members squirm, I turned my focus to what held theirs, Persimmon's gun hand resting loosely on the grip of his revolver.

"Um, pardon me for asking please, but how can you not be a gunfighter? We saw—" but Persimmon cut short the committeeman with blacksmith hands.

"I don't hire out my gun and I don't do any marshallin'."

The reverend was bolder, as often are men with God on their side. "So then, what is it you do?"

Irritation at the impertinence of the question manifest as a twitch in Persimmon's fingers. I glanced at his face, expecting him to return a volley of hellfire, but there came another interruption from outside.

The pudgy sheriff's deputy strode through the door followed by a man in an apron. The bottom corner of the apron was soaked in crimson where his knee had pressed it into a puddle of blood and the center was muddled where the man had wiped his hands of the same. Though I did not recognize his face, I knew he was the barkeep from the Bansheen Saloon.

"Mr. Apricot, this man here—" respectfully began the deputy, but he was drowned out by shouting from across the room.

"What are you doin' in my place, Peabody? You best be gettin' back to the Bansheen if you know what's good for you," cried McLaglen, our otherwise subdued bartender.

"Hush up McLaglen, this don't concern you," was Peabody's vicious retort.

"Well, if it don't concern me, then it doesn't belong in here so get the hell out!" screamed McLaglen, much to the annoyance of the deputy.

"Hey! Quiet down," commanded the lawman, crossly.

"Perhaps, if you had been this perturbed at the whipping of the boy…" I thought as I watched the fat deputy bluster, but what was done is done and I supposed there was no point in speculation. The barkeep from across the road began to fuss again, but the deputy threw his hand up, closed his eyes and shook his head in disgust. I think it was loud noises that riled him.

"Just go back outside," the deputy ordered Peabody with a sweeping motion of his hand at the wrist.

"But—" Peabody started.

"Nope, out! I don't need you in here anyway… go." The deputy's hand was still sweeping the air as Peabody backed sheepishly out of the doorway, stopping to lean on the outside door casing.

Our bartender, McLaglen, found the arrangement satisfactory enough not to push his luck with the deputy. He went back to what he pretended to be doing and the deputy got back on point.

"This fella' here claimed you busted in his place and shot that other man without warning. He said that ugly fella'—"

"His name's Lizard Johnson," interrupted Peabody.

The deputy blew a sharp sigh followed immediately by, "Shut up! The court can care about his name. I don't… what kind of name is that anyway? Never mind. You keep quiet out there." The deputy looked at the floor a few seconds, his right hand stuck out to his side as he tried to regain balance of thought. "So, he says you put both barrels of that shotgun into his ribs and he never went for his gun. And before you tell me it is Peabody's word against yours, there are two other witnesses outside who will back him up."

I got the feeling that this was the confrontation for which Persimmon had placed his weapon on the table. His hand was still resting on its grip. I was surprised when the deputy did not tell Persimmon to back away from his gun, but perhaps the deputy was more insightful than I gave him credit. Why push a dangerous point unless you were prepared to get shot backing it up?

"We're witnesses. I'll testify on Mr. Apricot's behalf," vowed the committeeman with blacksmith hands.

"Me too," came another voice.

The reverend did not volunteer for perjury. He remained quiet, waiting to see how it all played out—another prudent man.

"You men can't claim to be witnesses. You were over here with me watching from across the street. None of you were in the Bansheen at the time," scolded the deputy.

A number of thoughts raced through my mind as I am sure they did the other men. It looked as though the deputy was going to arrest Persimmon.

What would Persimmon have to say about that? Was I about to be shot in the crossfire? Either way, it looked like the town would not get its marshal today. Was I about to get shot? Where in the world did Ugly get the name Lizard Johnson? Yes, I know I have said this before but it was weighing more and more heavily on my mind the longer the silence prevailed—was I about to get shot?

Before I could devise an escape route the reverend, of all people, said, "These men might not have been in the Bansheen but he was. Rather, he was looking right through the window at the whole scene."

I looked up to see the reverend's finger pointing my way and every eye in the room on me, including Persimmon's. No one had yet thought to ask me what I saw. I know the truth should always prevail and I generally prescribed to that statement but several points of argument hit my mind at once, not least of which was—was I about to get shot?

A deposition either way could get me shot. If I claimed a result in Persimmon's favor, I was not sure the survivors from the Bansheen Saloon would not hunt me down. Then again, it was Persimmon whose fingers were slowly flicking back and forth on the grip of his Schofield within arm's reach of me. I did not know what sort of man Persimmon truly was, but it was my impression at that moment that he had no intentions of being arrested and was biding his time to see how the situation played out.

I looked to my left at the deputy who was staring back at me intently, waiting for my answer. The expression on his face should have been the impatient expectation of a man who wanted to get his job done, but instead his eyes expressed feelings of hopeful longing. Every other man in front of me held a similar gaze except for two, the Bansheen's bartender who glared hatefully from the doorway and Persimmon whose visage was perturbed.

Would justice be served if Persimmon was arrested? Clearly the ugly dead guy was bad. No, I had never met him but what sort of man takes a coach whip to a small child? I can tell you what kind, the kind that needs killing. Maybe my attitude was that of proverbial judge and jury but I had seen worse things done to better people and I did not have any sympathy for ugly ol' Lizard Johnson.

Also, there was little chance the committee would convince Persimmon to be the town marshal but there was no chance if the prospective marshal was hung. Persimmon might deserve to swing from the end of a rope. As the saying goes, I did not know him from Adam, but what violence I had witnessed Persimmon commit was perpetrated against those who would harm him or the innocent and I hoped that was always the case.

This was a good bit to process while an expectant crowd was staring at me, but the mind grinds such chunks into manageable bits far quicker than it can describe them. You might think I also had the selfish notion that helping Persimmon could help me gain his trust and his story for my financial gain, but honestly, that never crossed my mind. The only selfish thought I had was—can I keep from getting shot?

"I have to say, it all happened pretty quickly but Ugly..." I caught myself and glanced to Peabody standing in the doorway. His sneer had not changed, but I corrected myself for safety's sake and continued, "I mean, Lizard Johnson locked eyes with Mr. Apricot as soon as Mr. Apricot approached him." I was unsure of where my story would end, but I liked the way it was headed—maybe I wouldn't get shot.

I continued, "I couldn't hear if anything was said but I could see in Johnson's eyes that he knew Persimmon was there for him, either to arrest him or shoot him. I don't know what Johnson was thinking, but he looked as though he felt threatened. I saw his hand go down. I'm sure he was going for his gun."

"So, was he going for his gun or not?" the deputy demanded.

I knew what the deputy wanted. He wanted me to give an emphatic, "Yes." Now, I am not a liar. I do not lie. I have been known to steal from others' articles but I never resold someone else's article as my own. I simply stole the content and wrote my own article so, in that sense, I used the original article as an eyewitness account and I knew other newsmen had done the same. Thief? If you wish, but a liar I was not. In my defense, I was not certain that the story I had just told was not fact. The Bansheen Saloon Gunfight, as it came to be called, did happen fast and I think maybe Ugly did drop his arms. Definitely his arms moved, I just could not picture in my memory if it was before or after two barrel-loads of buckshot hit him.

When up against all other considerations that I have mentioned, the timing of his arm movements seemed like splitting hairs. I knew in another western locale, perhaps elsewhere in this county, the issue would not even be a factor in the case and Persimmon would be a free man. I elaborate on my methods here to provide the reader an explanation for my answer to the deputy's question.

"Yes," I said firmly.

Persimmon's demeanor held. The only differences were that he was now watching the door and had stopped stroking the grip of the revolver. Instead he had his hand around it with his fingertips resting on the table but with his index finger through the trigger guard and his thumb on the hammer. The committee was celebrating amongst themselves as if the victory had been theirs. They had not noticed the change in Persimmon's hand but I had and rather than be relieved I began to worry more earnestly, accidentally or not— was I going to get shot?

The deputy nodded sharply at my answer, as if punctuating the end of the matter, then turned to leave.

The Bansheen barkeep, Peabody, was dissatisfied and blocking the doorway. "That's it? Ain't you going to arrest him?" Peabody grilled the deputy.

"What for? He's got a witness that says Johnson went for his gun," the deputy answered but Peabody did not budge.

"I've got two witnesses out here that say he didn't," Peabody reminded.

Oh, the witnesses! I had almost forgotten about Lizard Johnson's friends, otherwise known as witnesses. I was likely going to get shot and it was not going to be Persimmon who would do it.

"Those men were friends of the deceased but this fella' here," the deputy made sure to point me out again, in case anyone wanting to shoot me had forgotten where I was, "he is from out of town. He didn't know either party so the court is going to figure he didn't have an ax to grind with either. It will be their word against his and that will leave reasonable doubt. No jury is going to convict him, so arresting him is a waste of my time and county money."

"So, what you're saying is if he didn't have that witness, he'd hang." It was a statement, not a question, and from my point of view it sounded like a threat.

The deputy must have taken it the same way I did because he responded more forcefully to Peabody, "I suggest you leave the witness alone."

"Hold on a minute, deputy, I never said I—"

"I know what you said. Just keep in mind that even if that man walked off a cliff while taking a leak, we have several people here that would attest to what he claimed he saw so it wouldn't matter."

What the deputy said next was low and hushed, but I saw him jab his thumb in Persimmon's direction and saw his raised brow. My guess was that he gave to Peabody the same advice the reverend had given to the deputy, be afraid of Persimmon Apricot.

I was glad the deputy had given an explanation of how my death would not change things. Rather than being shot, I was now more afraid of intimidation and beatings to get me to change my story.

Peabody stormed off in disgust and I could see out the window that the opposing witnesses followed him back to the Bansheen Saloon where another man was fidgeting about outside. It was the undertaker and I recognized him because he was also the local wheelwright. He had dragged the dead men from the Bansheen and was busy loading dead Lizard Johnson into a wagon.

Instead of leaving, the deputy turned back and announced, "Well, Reverend, I am going to be taking my leave of you. I am due in court on another case."

"You're not just going to leave us with dead men in the street and ill will in their friends' hearts, are you?" the reverend guilted the deputy.

"Can't be helped, but Jim will be coming in with the 10:30 stage. I'll wait for him and have him stay over a night or two until things settle. Your friend there said earlier that he intended to move on soon. He can take his trouble with him."

"But Jim's just a kid," the reverend worried aloud.

"Jim's a capable deputy. You be sure to give him the respect the badge deserves. He might look a little green, but he's brave. He volunteered to ride along with the stage. Someone's held it up twice this month. I doubt they'll hit it again. I think they figured that no one would expect it to be hit twice so they had an equal chance at surprise both times but we're taking extra precautions now." The pudgy deputy's confidence in his fellow deputy failed to reassure.

"Are you sure all is well because it's a quarter to two now," the reverend asked.

The deputy stuck his head out the door and looked northward, up the street. "Yep, yonder he comes now. Don't know who that fella' is with him though."

With the immediate threat over, Persimmon holstered his revolver and topped off his drink. The committee had set in to try to sweet talk him into the marshal's position. I listened, thinking that all things considered, it seemed to me letting Persimmon go his way was the wisest option. Persimmon did not appear to be paying them any attention. His gaze was still fixed on the door.

There came a new voice from outside which asked, "What's all this?"

Persimmon heard the voice and must have recognized it. He sat back in his chair, threw what whiskey remained in the tin cup to the back of his throat, and grimaced, "Let me be."

The committee got the message and promised to check with him later as they retreated. I leaned forward to get my weight right to stand, but when Persimmon pulled the cork, he poured whiskey in my cup first. It wasn't much, a splash atop the whiskey already in my worn tin, but it told me to sit and stay a while to which I obliged.

All I could see of the men talking outside was the occasional flash of a hat brim on the edge of the doorway. I could tell it belonged to the pudgy deputy because I could make out that it was his voice speaking and the hat brim bobbed with the story of what had taken place. Only a word here and there was discernable, but what else would the deputy be telling? Then the story stopped, there was a pause, the two voices exchanged a few words, another pause, then boot clops on the planking approached the door.

The deputy entered, followed by a much younger man I took to be Jim, the second deputy. He was followed by an older man, weathered, maybe five years Persimmon's senior, though it was difficult to get a bead on either man's age.

"That's the man," the deputy announced, nodding in Persimmon's direction.

The weathered man's face puckered in disdain. "I might've known it was you," he growled.

Persimmon sat, leaning back in his chair. The tin cup was in his left hand, not his right as before. His right hand, his gun hand, was draped across his chest within an inch of the Schofield.

There were a few agonizing moments of silence in which all I could hear was the same frightful question repeating in my head—was I about to get shot?

III
JENSEN BROTHERS

Out of concern for my own safety I should have excused myself and slipped away. I had never met the marshal and had only known Persimmon an hour, but the disdainful scowl of each man made it clear they had a history and not a pleasant one. Yet, something kept me seated. One might suggest it was logical that a U.S. marshal would not open fire on a man without warning. Nor would a man who had barely avoided being arrested for murder fire upon a U.S. marshal and consequently two sheriff's deputies. Therefore, I was probably safe where I sat. Nonetheless, I do not think anyone who witnessed either man's glare at the other would have agreed.

After he felt he had glowered sufficiently, the marshal held his right finger out in front of the deputy to draw his attention then broke the silence. "If he killed those men in the street, why haven't you arrested him?"

"The last fella' attacked him and I saw it. As for the men in the saloon across the street, that man yonder is an eyewitness that says it was in self-defense." Again, I found the deputy's finger pointing in my direction.

The marshal's glare did not change, but it did come to rest heavily upon me. Now I was on his blacklist too. It is amazing how quickly a man can dig himself a hole from which there is no escape, and without the least intention. My spirit rebounded a bit when the marshal lifted his condemning stare from me and put it back on Persimmon.

"I ought to take you in—" the marshal began but was cut short by the deputy.

"What's the point? You'll just be wasting your time," the deputy advised. If the marshal would concede the point, it would bolster the deputy's judgement.

"Maybe, but he could sit in jail until the circuit judge comes around. It would keep him from killing anybody else for a time," the marshal replied before turning his threats back to Persimmon. "But as much as I would like to see you in a cage, or on the end of a rope, I've got other mongrels to hunt down today."

I was surprised at Persimmon's silence and when I noticed it, I looked to Persimmon. A feeling of panic swept over me like that of a man standing next to a boiler that could explode at any moment. I wanted to push back from the table but felt as though the scrub of my chair leg across rough sawn floor could be enough to trigger the explosion.

The marshal turned to face the deputy. "I'm going to need you to take me up to the Dead Horse Mine. I hear the Jensen brothers have a hideout near there and I aim to take them in."

"I hadn't heard the Jensens were in these parts, but that could be who's hit the stage recently. Sorry, but I am due in court tomorrow. If not for that, I would be glad to oblige. The mine is south of town a piece. I'm sure someone can point you in the right direction." The deputy tipped his hat and walked outside, followed by his fellow deputy, Jim.

"Hold on..." the marshal chased after the pair and the conversation continued outside, somewhat heated but muffled to my ears.

Soft footsteps approached from behind me and both Persimmon and I turned to see the reverend. With all that happened, I had not noticed him standing by the bar, watching.

"Sounds like trouble follows you," the reverend commented in a tone of repentance to Persimmon.

"Seems that way sometimes," was Persimmon's resigned reply.

"It's never too late for forgiveness." The reverend thought he saw a crack in the door of Persimmon's soul and if he pushed a bit, it would open. He did not understand that for Persimmon, a cracked door was for a spying eye and slipping a pistol barrel.

"Will you check on the boy for me?" Persimmon asked the reverend, deftly changing the subject.

"Certainly... For all I have witnessed today, your humanitarian concern for that boy gives me hope," the reverend said as he walked hat in hand to the door.

Persimmon replied inquisitively, "That gives you hope for humanity?"

"No, for you."

As I watched the reverend exit the saloon, I caught a glimpse of the older deputy heading down the street, no doubt to collect his horse at the livery. Deputy Jim came inside, tipped his hat pleasantly at our table, then called for a beer as he headed to the bar.

"Hanging around a few days, are you?" McLaglen asked as he fumbled under the counter for another tin cup.

"One or two, but first I have to help the marshal catch those Jensen boys. Maybe that will put a stop to the stage holdups too and I will get a night in my own bed," the young deputy explained.

He must have chugged his beer because I immediately heard McLaglen ask him if he wanted another.

"No, the marshal is chomping at the bit to head out," answered the deputy.

Persimmon had turned an ear to the conversation behind him and I was startled when his chair rocked forward and launched him to his feet. Adjusting his holster strap, he wriggled his shoulder and pulled the shirt wrinkles from underneath the leather. Then he grabbed his hat from the table, glanced at it quickly for any debris, brushed his hand across a spot on the brim, then placed it on his head and lumbered to the door. I stayed put, not wanting to get shot. I figured whatever Persimmon was up to could be witnessed from afar.

"Hey, Edwards, are you seriously planning to take on the Jensen gang with just this kid?" Persimmon called out through the doorway to the U.S. marshal who was fidgeting with his saddle.

"I didn't figure you for someone who would give a damn about my welfare," replied U.S. Marshal Edwards, half-jokingly.

"I don't. Getting yourself killed is your choice, and a welcomed one, but getting this kid killed so you can collect a bounty isn't right and you know it," Persimmon scolded.

"It's his job," snapped the marshal.

"Being a lawman doesn't mean throwing out good sense," Persimmon began.

"You never seemed to care about that before," the marshal growled.

"And good sense shouldn't be used as an excuse for cowardice either," Persimmon bit back. His hands hung by his sides and I watched as he clinched and ground his mighty fists in indignation.

Deputy Jim could hear everything I heard. I noticed when he passed me he walked all the way to the window and then approached Persimmon along the front wall which was as head on as he could. It was a cautious move and it showed the young deputy had at least some good sense.

"I appreciate your concern, but I reckon it is my job," Jim said to Persimmon.

It was not a fatherly look Persimmon gave Jim. It was more one of a senior man on the same job. Either way, it was difficult to identify that expression behind the still gritted teeth and flared nostrils. However, Persimmon's tone of voice when speaking to Jim helped me discern one from the other.

"Those Jensen boys aren't up there alone. You need to take a posse with you. At least then the Jensen gang would have more targets to shoot at and give you time," Persimmon advised.

Jim squeezed past Persimmon in the doorway, headed to his horse, then over his shoulder he replied, "Ain't anyone in this town going to help."

Jim mounted his horse and rode for the edge of town. Marshal Edwards sat on his own horse in the middle of the street. I could just see him through the window and I expected him to goad Persimmon once more before he left, but instead he turned and followed Jim's lead to the Dead Horse Mine.

Persimmon returned to the table, picked up the bottle of whiskey and poured himself a swallow then corked it. After throwing back the shot, he wrapped his huge hand around the neck of the bottle and toted it to the bar where McLaglen stood doing nothing. It was a slow time of day in a small copper mining town.

"What do I owe you?" Persimmon asked.

"It's on the house. Some of the men you shot scared off a lot of my business these last few months. An enemy of theirs is a friend of mine," was McLaglen's morbid reply.

Persimmon nodded in gratitude then placed the bottle on the bar. "Hold this for me. I'll be back directly."

"Yes, sir. It'll be here waiting for you," promised McLaglen.

Persimmon sauntered back to the door, his mood lifted by whatever internal revelation or resolution had struck him. Pausing, he scanned the road outside. I assume he was watching for trouble. Then he turned back to me, "Well, come on."

I was not sure if it was an order or an invitation. I think it was the latter dressed like the former but either way I was caught off guard. "Me?" I half-gasped.

"You wanted to follow me around for a story, didn't you? Well, you're likely going to get one if you come ahead on."

I stood and threw back the bulk of the whiskey I had been sipping as I figured I needed any courage I could muster. Then, gathering my hat, I timidly made my way to the door. I had gotten what I had asked for and I was not sure I wanted it.

"You got a horse?" he asked. I suspect Persimmon half expected me to say no.

"I do… down at the livery getting fed and watered."

"Well, go fetch him. I'll meet you down there," instructed Persimmon.

We left by the north end of town but once we were out of sight, Persimmon detoured down the gradual base of the mountain and through the thin forest. I could see the Arkansas River snaking along the broad valley floor below us. We circled back below town and then climbed back up to the southerly road. Rarely did our gait fall below a gallop. When we came to a fork of the main road and two muddy ruts alongside a mountain stream, Persimmon followed the ruts.

I knew where we were headed but wanted to confirm it. "You're headed to help the marshal against the Jensen boys, aren't you?" I asked, breaking the silence for the first time since we left town.

"Hell no! I'm going to make sure he doesn't get that kid deputy killed. Granted, the boy has a sense of duty but duty without good planning is suicide and does no one any good."

So, Persimmon was a bit of a philosopher. I was making a mental sketch of his personality for my novel. Maybe, finally, I would succeed at something meaningful.

Below me I noticed the occasional hoof print in the mud between the rocks. It was the rainy season and the day was overcast but dry so far. We crisscrossed the creek several times. Its babbling spoke nothing of the violence ahead. After nearly an hour of riding Persimmon stopped, then plied his way up a rock-strewn hill, away from the rutty trail. I followed but when I began to ask what we were doing, Persimmon shushed me with a brisk wave of his hand.

At the top of the rise, Persimmon eased his huge horse up until he could see over into the small valley below, then returned to me a few yards behind. He dismounted so I did too, then he handed me his reins.

"Stay here with the horses," Persimmon directed, assigning me both an important job as well as a generally safe one.

After rummaging in one of his saddlebags, he pulled from it an older Smith and Wesson Model Three and held it out for me. "Don't fire it unless you need to and if you need to, mean it."

Now, I was not a fool to go into the wilds of mining camps unarmed and I wanted Persimmon to know it, so I spoke up as I put a hand on the Smith and Wesson. "I have a Colt in my saddlebag."

"Oh," Persimmon said with surprise, taking back the pistol. He paused a moment in thought then asked, "Cap and ball?"

I nodded.

"When was the last time you fired it and refreshed the powder?" Persimmon inquired, reminding me of a contemptuous old schoolmarm I had as a child.

To my shame, Persimmon's suspicions were right. I bet I had not removed the Colt from my bag in six months and I could not remember when I shot it last. Its presence gave me a false sense of security but I never took it into saloons with me. In fact, I did not have a holster for it.

"That's what I thought." Persimmon handed me back the Model Three. "Tuck it into your belt and hang onto these horses."

Humiliated, I nodded but did not say a word. Persimmon reached for the second of the two scabbards he had stacked and hanging from his saddle. Instead of a shotgun, Persimmon pulled from it what I was sure to be a long-barreled Winchester 1876. I say that due to the rifle's heft and to a short stint where I worked as a sales clerk in a small store in a one-store town which I didn't have the money to get out of fast enough—but I digress.

As he had in town, Persimmon tossed his duster across his saddle, then cocked the lever-action rifle and cautiously approached the rise of the hill. After scanning all that he could see, he eased himself over the crest and down the other side, out of view. He must have known that there was no story to be gained, standing there holding horses. I had not ventured this far to play stable boy. I tied his massive plow horse to a sapling followed by my own pony which looked like a toy in comparison.

When I topped the hill, pistol in hand, I was nearly overwhelmed by the conscious realization that outlaws lurked somewhere nearby. I distinctly recall thinking that I would be glad when this day is over because I wanted to get through it without being shot.

Below was a clearing scarred by the creek we had traced to get here. On the far side sat a weathered cabin with a tiny cord of smoke rising from the chimney. Persimmon was watching from his position, tucked in behind a rock, downhill and to my right. I began to wonder if we were in the correct location. Where were the marshal and deputy? Then I saw them. The two lawmen figured to be stealthy and had done much the same as we had except, they had gone around our hill and over to the next to avoid approaching the cabin by the road. The two of them were slipping down the hillside to my left. After pausing to regroup in the cottonwoods by the creek, they headed up the sloping pasture toward the cabin.

I'm not a lawman but it seemed like a foolish thing to do. Where was everyone? The only sign of inhabitation was the rope of smoke from the chimney. Deputy Jim stopped not too many feet from the cottonwoods. Marshal Edwards was the hunter who approached the cabin. When he reached the door, he found it unlocked and, on what looked like a private count of three, the marshal burst into the cabin. No shots were fired and in less than a minute the marshal emerged from the cabin door, puzzled and I think a bit frightened that he did not know where his prey had gone or if they were hunting him.

The hair on my neck was upended and I began looking about for anyone who might be creeping behind me when there came the crack of a rifle. I winced and turned toward the sound. The bullet kicked up dust near the marshal's feet and he and Jim dove back into the cottonwoods for cover. A firefight ensued between the two lawmen and multiple assailants which I could not see for the tops of the cottonwoods. I don't think Persimmon could see them either. Rather than trying to get to a new position, he patiently waited and watched the tree line around the perimeter of the small meadow. His instinct proved to be sound when two men broke from the trees on the backside of the cabin and rushed down the meadow. They disappeared behind the cabin for a few moments but then I saw a hat poke above the roof's ridge. One or both of the outlaws was using the cabin as a parapet. The outlaw slung his left elbow over the ridge for support. Next came his rifle as he bore down on the marshal and deputy but, before he had a chance to aim, there came a blast much closer to me. It was Persimmon.

Persimmon's bullet struck the outlaw in the cheekbone, bowling him over. I watched his hand disappear as he slid out of sight. Deputy Jim heard the report of Persimmon's rifle and spun around, searching frantically for the adversary who had flanked them. I held still; I did not want to be mistaken for one of the gang. Persimmon had had the sense to put the large rock between him and the lawmen.

Jim was scanning between the hill below me and the cabin as he reloaded his pistol. He did not have to hunt long for an attacker. The second outlaw on the cabin roof had not seen the shooter who killed his friend or from what direction the bullet had come. Rather than settle into a position on the roof's ridge, the second man popped up and fired quickly into the cottonwoods, then ducked for cover. Deputy Jim scrambled to get a bead on the roofline but when the bandit rose for a second shot, Persimmon fired again, knocking the outlaw from his perch.

Jim again scanned the hillside below me for the shooter. I do not know if he had an idea who it was that was behind the rock but he knew it was someone who was shooting the men who were trying to shoot him so it must be a friend.

Two more men broke from the tree line, this time with the cabin between them and Persimmon. I could see them only a moment before the cabin obstructed my view but to my surprise, both men rounded the far front corner of the cabin, headed for the door. Neither man appeared to be armed but considering that they hung out with a gang of thieves and murderers and considering they both ran into a gunfight rather than away from it, it was safe to assume they were part of the gang. Persimmon was of the same mind and managed to put a bullet squarely through the sternum of the lead runner. The second man never slowed. The door was not latched and he tumbled through it then slammed it shut.

Not a minute later a rifle muzzle peeked from the cabin window. Persimmon saw it too and fired. The bullet merely splintered the wood at the base of the window but it was enough to drive the rifle's owner from view. Deputy Jim was understandably fearful and I saw him slap Marshal Edwards on the shoulder to get his attention and then point to the cabin.

As best as I could tell from the ruckus there were at least four men wedged in the rocks and trees on the far hill, raining lead down upon the two lawmen. As far as Marshal Edwards was concerned, his troubles lay uphill and to that end he was doing his best to aim and fire with the rhythm of his opponents' fire, only exposing himself when there was slack in the shooting, which was not often. Jim squirmed until he managed to turn toward the cabin and still be covered by a cluster of small trees from the volley raining from the hill to his left.

Several shots were fired from the interior of the cabin, striking the cottonwoods surrounding Jim. One splintered a trunk next to Jim's cheek, spraying his face with wood chips and slivers. The deputy wiped at his eyes and tried to hunker down further but there was no place to go. The marshal did not draw fire from the cabin because to do so meant the outlaw had to approach the window to get a clear view. The orange glow of the muzzle blast was faintly visible against the gloom of the cabin's interior as three more shots were fired from inside, the last of which threaded the cottonwood trees and hit Deputy Jim in the left shoulder. The bullet knocked him backward onto a clump of roots where he lay motionless except for the agony twisting his face.

My teeth clinched in dread that the next shot would rip through Jim's middle. I wanted to scream out, to draw the outlaw's attention, to prod Jim to move, to get the marshal to save Jim from the peril in which he had placed him, but no one would hear me over the cacophony of gun blasts from the hill. Then came the rifle barrel through the window and I knew the outlaw felt free to take careful aim on the lawmen. I glanced below me to see what Persimmon was doing but he was gone.

The outlaw in the cabin fired. The bullet splashed into the creek, beyond the marshal. The marshal took notice, but instead of turning to fire at the cabin, he only scooted his body nearer the incline of the creek bank to take himself out of the outlaw's line of sight. That left Jim as the sole target for the gunman in the cabin. Where was Persimmon?

Though I did not want to draw fire, I could not live with myself if I did nothing. I cocked the hammer on the Model Three and took aim on the cabin. There was no point in trying to shoot through the window, the assailant was behind the wall. Besides, I was a poor shot trying to shoot long distance with a short-gun, the broadside of a barn was the best I could hope for. I aimed high, at the bottom edge of the roof, and fired. A second later, I heard the pop of the bullet hitting the cabin wall. Where on the wall it hit, I don't know, but it was sufficient to rattle the outlaw and he ducked back inside.

When the rifle barrel emerged again, Jim was ready. The hammer was cocked on his repeater and as the barrel of the outlaw's rifle tipped forward through the window to point down at the deputy, Jim raised the rifle with his right arm, rested it on his knee and fired. Instantly, the muzzle of the outlaw's rifle pointed skyward and the gun fell with a clatter and slid to a propped position in the window. Jim gripped his left shoulder and rolled to his stomach. With his good arm, he kept low and drug himself alongside the marshal, turning his attention back to the attackers on the far hill.

Not knowing if I had been discovered, I dropped to my belly behind a dead log. Where was Persimmon? I looked behind me to the horses and they were there but he was not. It was a minute or two before I heard the crack of his rifle and traced the sound to the far edge of the meadow. Persimmon had flanked the outlaws. Until now the battle had been a stalemate with all parties well protected. Persimmon's first flanking shot quieted one gun on the hill and forced another to turn on him, leaving what I estimated to be two men still firing down at the marshal and young deputy.

You might ask why I did not spring to action and flank to the left? Well, I am sure by now you have a good idea as to why. There was still a good chance that if I stayed put, with the horses as my escape if needed, I would not get shot.

Besides, while I was pondering the idea and also whether or not my firing blindly through the tops of the cottonwoods would be of any help, Jim made a break from the line of fire and dashed out of the creek bed and through the woods to the left. Soon the outlaws came under gunfire from three directions. The fight continued a couple more minutes but then I heard Jim yell out, "I got one!" After that the shots on the far hill became scarce and higher up the mountain until the remaining outlaws fled entirely.

There was a pause, everyone held their positions, then Persimmon called out, "Edwards! I'm coming down. Don't you dare shoot me."

Edwards was still in his original position, half sunken into the muddy bank behind the log, and I watched as he drew a bead on Persimmon and held it. I thought he was going to fire and I almost cried out but again, Jim beat me to it.

"Mr. Apricot, I am damn glad to see you!" Jim yelled as he traipsed down to the cottonwoods, cradling his left arm in his right. It was plain his wound was beginning to hurt him now that the rush of excitement was waning.

I was standing in open view now and Persimmon motioned for me to join them at the bottom of the hill. Edwards saw the gesture and looked over his shoulder to see me. I have often wondered if he did not blow a deep sigh of relief that he did not take the shot at Persimmon with me watching. I gathered the horses and led them along a more gradual, roundabout way to the meadow.

Marshal Edwards had not said a word before I got to the three of them standing in the shade by the creek. I imagine he would have just as soon been shredded by bullets than to be rescued by Persimmon. Despite his wound, Jim was all aglow, shaking Persimmon's hand and recounting the scene from his perspective.

"Why didn't you light out after those other two? You were closer and already afoot. You let them get away," scolded Marshal Edwards, thanklessly.

"The hell you say! I didn't come here to earn you a bounty, I don't give a good damn if you ever come out of these mountains. I came here to keep you from getting the kid here killed." Persimmon nodded in Jim's direction. "He's an honorable lawman but too green to have the sense not to get himself killed following you. Although, I suspect that has changed a good bit as of today."

"Look here, you might have fooled that jury in New Mexico that you shot that man in his pajamas out of self-defense but one of these days I'm going to catch you in a position you won't wiggle out of," the marshal seethed.

"I suggest you don't corner me," was all the reply Persimmon gave and his eyes backed up the threat.

I wanted to tell the marshal what an ungrateful son-of-a-bitch he was and I don't think I would have gotten shot doing so, considering the company, but I did not need an enemy, especially one as vicious as Marshal Edwards. He had yet to show concern for Deputy Jim and though the wound might not have been life threatening, the young man was clearly in pain. Despite my disgust I remained quiet, as inconspicuous as I could be, but I'll be damned if the marshal did not take notice of me anyway.

Perhaps he knew the argument with Persimmon was unwinnable and needed to change the subject to save face but he looked at me, turned back to Persimmon, jabbed his thumb in my direction and asked, "Who the hell is this anyway?"

"That's Pete," Persimmon answered as fast as if it had been the truth.

Pete is not my name and I did not introduce myself to Persimmon as Pete. However, the remainder of Persimmon's answers gave me the impression that one or both of two possibilities was true. Option one, Persimmon felt that Edwards did not deserve the truth, and I am certain this was the case. Option two, Persimmon was protecting me by giving Edwards nothing.

"Does Pete have a last name?" the marshal snapped.

Persimmon ignored the question. He was having a grand time deceiving the marshal. "That's Pete from St. Louis. Big newspaperman back there. He just came out looking for a story worth tellin'... It sure ain't yours."

"Mind your tongue you insolent..." the marshal held his own amidst the fussing, then turned to me to get the upper hand. "What's your name, Pete from St. Louis?"

I glanced at Jim who was just as stunned as I was, with his brow raised. Persimmon's irreverence was contagious and it is funny what will pop into your head for no good reason. Where the pirate Blackbeard came from, I do not know. Maybe the marshal's last name touched on a memory which led me to Blackbeard's real name. However I got there, I ran with it and answered, "Teach."

"Pete Teach. Your name is Pete Teach, huh?" the marshal sounded dubious. "I recommend you mind the company you keep, Mr. Teach."

Saying the name and knowing the joke was one thing but to have the marshal doubt me and be at a loss to prove it made me feel more in control. My chest rattled as I exhaled the tension.

Harassing me was a stall while the marshal decided what to do next. I do not know if he believed he would get what he demanded or not, but the next words out of his mouth were, "I'm going to need to commandeer your horses to take these bodies back."

Persimmon laughed indignantly, took the reins of his horse in his left hand, grabbed a hunk of mane, stuck his left boot in a second stirrup that hung lower so that mortal man could mount the huge beast, flung his right leg over the saddle, sat upright and said, "The hell if that's so."

With that, he and I rode back to town.

IV
A PIECE OF PAPER

It was late afternoon when we entered town by the south road, passing between the saloons. A man I recognized from earlier was propped against a post outside the Bansheen, glaring at us as we trotted by. Persimmon did not appear to take notice of him but I knew he must have. Persimmon had been pleasant company on the ride back to town. He had not ranted about the marshal as I thought he might and I did not prod. I think getting the upper hand on the marshal lifted Persimmon's spirits. To my surprise, we did not stop at McLaglen's saloon; I guess that is what I will call the place even though the sign above the porch simply read "Saloon." Instead we rode through town, past the store, a law office, an assayer, the local smithy and his clinking hammer, the livery stable and a variety of small cabins.

With any fledgling mining camp, the influx of riches sprouts an air of permanence. Canvas tents become wooden buildings, bare shanties are painted, saloons are joined by theaters and fine restaurants and if the lode holds out long enough, wooden structures are exchanged for stone and masonry. This town was at the beginning of the paint stage and some of the homes were painted. One such cottage was very pleasantly colored with light blue walls and a white porch railing and window trim. I took it to be the reverend's home due to its proximity to the church.

The church was not much larger than the cottage. It was dressed in all white and donned with a squat steeple complete with a small bronze bell which strained to do its best to ring out to the mines and saloons and summon poor sinners to come home. I was a bit amazed when it was in front of the church's roofless stoop where Persimmon came to a halt. At the same moment, the door opened and a woman came backing out of it, bent over as if she was helping someone. When she stood upright and turned, I saw the boy with a bandage over his left eye. It was the child ugly ol' Lizard Johnson had whipped. My gaze gravitated back to the boy's mother; how beautiful she was! She was not the fat and haggard working mother I had imagined.

Startled to see us and having no idea who we were, she pulled the boy close to her and began side stepping away. It was then that I noticed Persimmon's face, it was stoic but his eyes burned with an emotion which I could not quite read. Passion, sadness, longing, pity, I could not tell but when I realized I was staring at him as he stared at her, I became uncomfortable and not knowing what to do, I shifted my eyes from him to her to the church door to the ground and back to him.

Persimmon made no move to dismount. Rather, he sat there and watched the woman walk away as did I. Every few steps the woman would look back over her shoulder at us. As the distance from us grew, her expression softened from worry to curiosity. She had not yet slipped from our view when the church door opened again. This time it was the reverend who seemed astonished but pleasantly so.

"Gentlemen, I'm very glad to see you did not get yourselves shot. Please, won't you come inside?" the pastor invited.

The big man's mood had turned sullen. Quietly, Persimmon slid down the side of his great animal, dropping to both feet simultaneously as he had before. In contrast, I was able to dismount my modest pony in the same average way as anyone else.

Inside, the church had long wooden benches for pews. The benches were backless but at least the seats were sanded and splinter free. Persimmon straddled one and sat down and I, still feeling more like an audience member than a player, sat straight on a bench two rows behind. The reverend set astride the bench opposite the aisle from Persimmon and spoke first.

"So, you're here for salvation, I hope, or have you reconsidered the job of town marshal?" the reverend asked Persimmon, occasionally glancing at me out of obliged acknowledgment.

"How's the boy?" was Persimmon's dismissive but curious answer to the reverend's presumptuous meddling.

"Doc says it is too early to tell. He'll have to wear a patch for a few weeks. His brow tempered the blow, but it still struck the side of his eyeball hard. It is up to the Lord if he sees again," the reverend shrugged, wishing he could paint the boy's condition in a better light.

Persimmon grunted a sarcastic, "Hmm," then laid back on the bench.

"Do you believe in the Lord?" pried the reverend.

Persimmon lay there in silence for a moment, then began to speak in a groan as he strained a bit to sit upright. "I believe in Him. I just don't see Him come to town that often." It was the sort of wry statement that would prove indicative of Persimmon.

The reverend was taken aback I think, but he recovered and quipped, "Maybe you and He are just crossing paths. Perhaps you should try meeting Him at the station."

Persimmon changed the subject again, "We saw the boy and his mother leaving. Was the doctor here?"

"No, Mrs. Sanchez came by to thank me and repay me because I had paid the doctor for her. I didn't accept the money, of course. That poor woman doesn't have enough now," the reverend lamented.

"Where's her husband?" Persimmon asked, clearly perturbed.

"No one knows. Some say he ran off and left her. Most think he's dead. Either way, she was left taking care of the boy and trying to hold on to the ranch for his sake."

"Why not sell the ranch and use that money to take care of the boy?" was the common-sense question from Persimmon.

"Because thanks to her husband... late husband, she owes almost as much on it as it is worth. If she sold it, she would have nothing. At least on the ranch she can grow her own food and have a roof over her head without depending on the charity of others. Although it is through the charity of the church that she has been able to make her last few payments." The reverend's explanation prompted more questions.

"Why not sell her herd then?" I chimed in.

"She has no herd, just a milk cow and a bull... Let me give you the entire story rather than have you piece it together. You see, there's a railroad about to come up from Buena Vista. When it does, her ranch will double in value, maybe more. She needs to hold out until the track is laid and the train is running to get the most for her land but if she can hold out that long, she could then take a loan against the new value and hire some hands and build a herd and get the ranch going again. She can build something worth passing down to her son. So, in short, she has it all, or she has nothing."

"Sounds like a loan is what got her in this shape in the first place," Persimmon interjected.

"Well, that is the other side of this story," the reverend continued. "No one knows why Mr. Sanchez took the loan in the first place and he disappeared shortly thereafter. Speculation runs from paying off gambling debts to him taking the money and running. One thing everyone agrees on is that the Sanchez family was fine, with a small but profitable ranch before Jenkins arrived."

"How do the Jenkins brothers tie in?" I asked.

"I think you are thinking about the Jensen brothers that the marshal was after. Those are the outlaws the marshal and deputy Jim went after when you two followed them. Jenkins is a rich fella' from back east. He came to the area with a box full of money, buying up land and mines. Some of his dealings definitely have the taste of being shady but those who sold to him left town right away and without much to say. In the case of Sanchez, we know he took a loan from the bank and sold his meager herd. The rumor is that the money was given to Jenkins rather than the ranch. If that is the case, and Sanchez was trying to hold onto the ranch for his family, then why would he abandon them? This is why I suspect he was murdered." The reverend paused, either out of guilt for the accusation or to let Persimmon and I soak it in, or both.

Beginning to pace up the aisle, he continued, "Jenkins purchased various loans from the bank which conveniently made him Mrs. Sanchez's landlord. As soon as she gives him reasonable cause, he is going to foreclose on the ranch. There is no way Mrs. Sanchez can continue to pay the note from now until the railroad gets here and no bank is willing to loan her money before those tracks are a sure thing. Even then, she's going to have a fight to get a bank to loan a single mother that much money and with another lien holder on the property. She was selling the few remaining cattle and her furniture, some horses, and whatnot, and the boy was working at Freeman's dry goods store. All that to make the note. She managed to make the last two months' payments only because of help from the church. Meanwhile, Jenkins patiently waits to score a great piece of land for nothing."

The weight of the tale was evident as the reverend held his head in his hands but there was one more misfortune to add. "The problem now is that the church coffers are about empty. I could give her everything I have but it wouldn't be enough."

"Surely she would pay it back when she gets the ranch up and running again?" I blurted. I had become emotionally vested in her plight and was a bit embarrassed at my outburst.

"Sure she would, tenfold, but I don't have it to give her. I have tried to get Mr. Fortson, the mine owner who is also on our committee, to help out, but he claims he has his own troubles to deal with. I think he, and many others, fear Jenkins. Although, to be fair, I've heard rumors the mine's vein of copper might be playing out." The reverend's troubled pacing snaked back and forth between the half dozen rows of pews.

"What is her payment each month?" Persimmon asked in a resolute tone.

"Better than two-hundred dollars," answered the reverend, despairingly.

Persimmon sat there for a moment, then reached into his vest pocket and pulled from it a folded piece of paper. Unfolded, I could see it was a telegram but I could not read it from where I sat. Persimmon stared at it for a while, as if it were a photograph, before folding it and returning it to his pocket. Then he dug into another pocket and brought forth a thick bundle of cash. After counting out four-hundred dollars onto the bench in front of him, Persimmon stuffed the remaining few bills back into his pocket before handing the counted stack to the reverend. "Use this to supplement her payments as needed. I should be back in a few weeks."

The reverend's eyes widened in astonishment, not at the money but at the generosity of a stranger, and not any stranger—Persimmon Apricot. "Thank you very much. Out of curiosity, may I ask what drives you to make such a benevolent gesture?"

"Don't concern yourself with that, just make sure it gets where it's needed." Successfully dodging the reverend's questions seemed a natural talent of Persimmon's.

"I will," the reverend said as he stuffed the folded bills into his coat pocket. "You know, I have been a pastor for twenty-three years and much of that has been in rougher mining camps than this. I've come to know men's hearts. I don't know what burdens yours but you have a good heart, Mr. Apricot. Why don't you lay down your troubles? Christ can shoulder a far greater load than man."

Persimmon stood and stared through bitter eyes at the reverend. I cringed, imagining the tongue lashing about to be unleashed from

Persimmon's mouth but he said nothing. Instead, he pivoted on the heel of his boot, marched three paces to the door, then turned back to me. "You comin'?"

I had no idea where that piece of paper was taking him but yes, I was coming. Likely, I would have a novel in a week's time. I bid the reverend goodbye and apologized for being so nearly destitute that I could not add something to the cause. The reverend forgave me. Despite Persimmon's coarse response, the reverend's expression was one of hope.

After leaving the church I had expected to ride out of town. Instead, we rode to the telegraph office where Persimmon handed me a dollar and asked if I would ride up and fetch his bottle from McLaglen. He added that I was to pay for it, despite McLaglen's objections. Apprehensive is a mild way to describe how I felt about the task, but I was not ready to prove myself a coward.

I left Persimmon as he entered the telegraph office. Nearing the saloons, I ducked between two buildings and approached McLaglen's place from the back alley. Not seeing the man on the porch of the Bansheen was a relief. I slipped into McLaglen's Saloon, grabbed the bottle, threw the dollar and a thank you at McLaglen then rushed back to my horse. Through the Bansheen's window I could see several men inside. The one I had seen when we entered town came back outside and leaned against the post with a cigarette. The end of it glowed red hot from his long draw. Nervous, I clamored ungracefully into the saddle while my horse pranced away from me.

Now that I was under scrutiny there was no need to take the back alley. Guiding my horse onto the main street, I watched the man slowly blow a great cloud of smoke in my direction. I took it for what it was intended to be, a threat. No one chased after me but his presence unnerved me. My fear was being the easy outlet for the frustrations of gutless men.

When I returned to the telegraph office, Persimmon was waiting with a pleased expression, as if I had passed his test. Indicating our direction with a sideways nod of his head, we rode north out of town. Though I was glad to leave behind those men in the Bansheen and was equally glad to have fodder for a novel, one thing nagged at me. Perhaps it was not the smartest thing I had ever done, following this killer to who knew where.

The sun was about to rest briefly atop the Rockies to our west. Darkness would engulf us as soon as it rolled off the back side of the mountain but Persimmon made no sign of pitching camp. Instead, he turned up a wooded trail along a creek which only hastened the gloom of twilight. Persimmon's mood had been somber the entire ride which had not boosted my confidence to prod him with questions. Nevertheless, my angst over our intended destination was about to push me into asking him where we were going when I smelled something cooking.

A few feet farther Persimmon turned uphill, off the trail, and soon the forest parted into a clearing around a cabin. Out front, two men sat by a fire, rifles in hand, with a hunk of meat on a makeshift spit.

"That you Persimmon?" one man hollered.

"Yeah," Persimmon called back.

"I figured as much when I saw that monster of a horse a comin' but the other fella' wasn't expected." I had yet to fully clear the branches on the edge of the meadow so I was not sure which of the men was speaking.

The two men stood. One of them rested his rifle against the wooden chair where he had been sitting then both approached to greet Persimmon.

"You made it just in time for supper. We've got a nice leg of venison that's about ready. Who's your friend?"

I was going to introduce myself when Persimmon, again, introduced me as Pete.

"Well, why don't you and Pete take the bunks inside? While y'all are getting settled, me and Henry will get things ready. I hope you like your food spicy. Henry tends to get carried away with the red chilies."

I pulled from my saddle the bedroll I tried not to have to use and entered the small cabin, apprehensive of my mouth soon to be ablaze. I could only hope my newfound alter ego, Pete, was tough enough to handle the heat of red chili peppers better than I.

The interior of the cabin was as stark as the outside, save for a small stove in the center and one shaky table against the back wall. On it sat a small pewter-framed mirror, an oil lamp with its font painted in large tulips and a photograph of a beautiful woman with a parasol in a frame similar to that of the mirror. The layout of the table was almost shrine-like and I wondered why Henry or his talkative friend would ever leave such a beautiful woman to dig anything out of these cold hills.

I had my back to Persimmon when he entered the cabin. When I was done spreading my bedroll on the rickety cot, I turned to find Persimmon doing the same but I noticed the picture of the woman was now lying face down. I was too tired and too worried about my pending agony over those chili peppers offending anyone to ask about the picture. Instead, I went back to my saddle to pull it from my horse and to find out how much water was in my canteen—it was not enough.

Supper consisted of a slab of deer steak and coffee. I ate the steak from the inside out but there was no avoiding the crushed peppers. The hot coffee exaggerated the burn and my water supply was fast dwindling but I did not want to offend, or worse, be the butt of jokes. So, in a vain attempt to take my mind off of the hide being stripped from my tongue, I tried desperately to pay attention to the conversation.

"Looks like our vein of silver has dried up so me and Henry are going to move up the creek a ways and see if we can find anything. There's another mining shack up that way that was abandoned so we're going to move our operation up there. It's not as nice as your place but it will save us the trek. We sure do appreciate your letting us use your place all this time. What do we owe you?" the man explained.

I later found out his name was Robert. I could not imagine what sort of hovel it was he spoke of if it was not as nice as the shack behind me. There was nothing to this one but board and batting and a small stove.

"You don't owe me anything but there is one thing you could do for me. How 'bout check on the place for me, maybe stoke a fire in the stove now and then? If anyone wanders in, I don't want them thinking the place is abandoned. Everything I have in the world is either in my saddle bag or in that cabin." Persimmon's request sounded as though he was the one indebted. What surprised me was his comment on the contents of the cabin. Clearly, the items on the table were Persimmon's and of sentimental worth.

The last drop of water from my canteen hit my tongue and my mouth was still aflame. I had to find more water to quench the fire so I got up and walked back behind the shack. The horses were tied under the roof of a makeshift stable off the back of the cabin and I hoped the other men would assume I had gone to check on my horse. Surely there was a well or cistern or something as a source of water. On the side of the cabin I found a wooden bucket but no well. There was an inch of water in its bottom and I raked some into my cupped palm and drank it. A temporary cooling effect it gave, but it tasted like a skunk. I dumped the rest and carried the bucket around front, back to the fire.

"Where do you fetch water around here?" I asked, holding the bucket up to emphasize my quest.

"Down the hill at the creek you followed to get here, but don't use that bucket," Robert warned.

Warily I asked, "Why? What's wrong with this bucket?" assuming the bucket must be used for sluicing ore or something.

"Well, Henry here is too delicate for Sears and Roebuck—"

"Awe, hush up," Henry interrupted.

Robert only gave a wide grin and continued, "so he takes that bucket half full of water with him to the woods and that's what he uses to wash his ass."

Persimmon let out the first laugh I'd heard him make and Henry chuckled out of embarrassment. When I dropped the bucket they noticed my eyes, wide with horror. I spun away and doubled over, first with the dry heaves, soon followed by the return of Satan's flaming chili deer. It reinvigorated the agony in my mouth, accompanied now by a blaze in my throat and sinuses.

Persimmon let out a guffaw which echoed across the valley and then fell into such a laughing fit that he could not catch his wind and tumbled off his chair with a thud. Robert almost did the same.

Feeling as if my soul was fully engulfed, I repented the vanity which drove me to eat those chili peppers. I knew I had to quench the flames before the devil took me. Standing, my feet tangled with Henry's toilet bucket, nearly throwing me to the ground. A second wave of laughter filled the valley. Everything was a blur through tear-filled eyes as they watered from the burn in my nose. Ahead of me I could see undulating gold and knew it was the fire. Blindly, I tore past the hysterical laughter and desperate gasps for air. Had the tail end of a tree branch not hit me in the face I would have run off the three-foot embankment, at the edge of the meadow, and broken my neck. Grabbing at branches and trunks I stumbled my way down the embankment and dropped to my knees in the wet sand along the creek. I washed my face, blew my running nose and drank all the water I could stand. When I could see and breathe again, I climbed out of the creek bed and staggered back to the campfire.

Robert held a bottle of some sort of liquor; I did not care what it was. I hobbled over to him and snatched the bottle from his hand and took a big slug from it. Between the rotgut whisky and all those chilies, any germ in that bucket did not stand a chance, but neither did my mouth. I retrieved my canteen and returned to the creek to fill it. When I got back to the fire, the trio was still breathing hard and chuckling at my expense but I did not care. I went to bed.

V
UNPREDICTABLE

The next morning, I awoke to find Persimmon snoring in the other cot. I sat up slowly, my back stiff from the thin mattress and hard plank bed. Something felt funny to my stocking feet and I looked down to find under them a brown rug I had not noticed the night before. There were two of them, one beneath each bed. Nothing fancy, just four-foot rectangles of the cheapest floor covering available but I figured they were a grand addition to the paltry little shack when I considered how the bare dirt floor would feel on a cold morning.

Rubbing my eyes, I smelled coffee. Either Henry or Robert had a pot cooking on the fire outside and I dearly hoped they had plenty to share. In many ways, I felt inadequate around Persimmon but rising before him gave me a little superiority to latch onto, even if it was due to no longer being able to contort to a semi-comfortable position. I do not know why I felt the least bit superior about rising first but that is the way it was and I was determined to see it through. When Persimmon woke, he would find me bright eyed and saddle ready.

Quietly, I tied up my bedroll and was about to slip outside when I noticed the picture on the table had been moved again. It lay on the table but this time face up and about to fall off the edge. Carefully, I pushed it to a sound position, but I dared not wake Persimmon. Outside, Henry had a tin cup waiting for me. I assumed he and Robert slept around the fireside but there was nothing to indicate that they had done anything other than sit all night.

My plan was fully executed by the time Persimmon emerged from the cabin. I even handed him a cup of coffee which he accepted, blurry-eyed and indifferent to the world. He sat next to the fire, clothes disheveled, with a sunken expression I glimpsed briefly due to his low hanging head. He sipped at his coffee gradually. I suspected that my triumph was lost on him but it meant something to me, though I thought it best not to brag.

Forty-five minutes and three cups of coffee later, Persimmon seemed more like his old self, at least as far as my twenty-four hours with him had led me to believe. He stood and stretched and rather lazily stumbled behind the cabin to saddle his horse. When he returned, he called Henry and Robert over to him to give instructions that struck me as odd at first.

"I appreciate you boys watching my place for me and feel free to stay here any time. If anyone comes looking for me, *be sure* you tell them that I have gone to South Pueblo."

Since we had traveled north from town, I was certain we were heading to Leadville. South Pueblo was down the valley in the opposite direction. This puzzled me for a few minutes but before I asked about it, the notion dawned on me that Persimmon was probably expecting some of the men from the Bansheen to follow us and he was trying to mislead them as to where we were headed. That made good sense and made me feel safer too.

As we traced the creek back out of its ravine and down into the river valley, it was not long before I realized we were breaking south, not north. Were we really going to South Pueblo? I told myself that Persimmon was only confirming the ruse for anyone who might be watching and that once we got to the river we would turn north, but we never did. Finally, I got up the courage to ask where we were headed, as if I had not overheard him tell Robert and Henry.

"Going to catch a train," was the abrupt reply.

Catch a train? Where were we going by train? I wanted to ask but Persimmon's mood was dour and I thought it best to hold the remainder of my inquiries for later. The closest town with a train, as the crow flies, was Denver, but that was a hard ride over mountains. In contrast, to get to South Pueblo, all we had to do was follow the Arkansas River out of the valley.

I was along for the ride to get a story and a good story needs detail. After a bit, I began to slip a question into the thin conversation here and there but I was cautious to not crowd Persimmon's mood. Before I got to the point about our ultimate destination, I thought I would test the waters with simple questions which did not pry too far into his personal life. Gradually, I would ease into intimate topics, gauging his mood along the way. The first question I had on my mind, the one which had nagged me since I first watched Persimmon ride into town was, why did he ride a huge plow horse?

Another man in my line of work might travel by stage and steam but I had always had my own horse, even as an older child. A horse meant freedom. Though other means of travel were often faster than riding the same horse long distances across country, speed never struck me as a good trade for that freedom. Besides, horse travel was cheaper.

Next to Persimmon I felt like a boy again riding my pony alongside my father. Persimmon's horse was massive, the sort one would expect to find drawing a heavy wagon or plow. I strained to fit the breed with one in my memory and was ashamed to realize how poor a knowledge I had for horseflesh. Though I had not grown up on a farm, my close cousins had. When I stepped out of the front door of my home, to my left rose the spires of the churches downtown and to my right, the street confined by rows of houses soon spilled into a bucolic setting of pastures and barns. One of those barns lay on my cousins' place and it had always stabled horses. I was disgusted with myself.

I recalled a pair of Percherons I once saw. They were about the right size and build but some unknown memory told me that the dark brown color of Persimmon's beast was not right for a Percheron. At a loss for the breed, I still needed a way to phrase the question. Calling this magnificent animal a plow horse was likely to offend. Having already been embarrassed over the maintenance of my cap and ball Colt, I did not want to sound ignorant again.

"It's a beautiful horse but let me ask, why do you ride that cold blood?" I thought the compliment would temper the question.

Persimmon reached out and rubbed the horse affectionately behind the ear for a moment. "Samson is my friend. Besides, he's big enough to tote me all day and he doesn't get skittish if I fire a round between his ears."

Samson? It was the first time I had heard the horse's name and a fitting name it was but the answer had not satisfied my curiosity on the subject. "Please don't take offense but Samson is a huge horse and I assume not the fastest, what if you have someone chasing you?"

"I shoot 'em."

The blunt reply was not what I was expecting. I hesitated, searching for a sign that he was joking but Persimmon did not crack a smile. He was serious. I felt like I was testing my luck but I could not resist pressing the matter.

Testing the conviction of his answer, I asked, "Well, what if it is a large group of men and you fire your last shot, what would you do?"

"Reload."

Persimmon's response was as quick and just as matter-of-fact as before but this time it carried a slight sting of insult for my having asked a stupid question.

Uncomfortable, I decided to be quiet and let Persimmon start the next round of conversation, remembering a carriage my father was very fond of but seldom ever used. Once, when I was about eight, I was helping my father saddle his horse and he commented to me that his butt was wishing he was taking the carriage instead. So I asked him, if the plush seat of the carriage was more comfortable, why didn't he use it? Characteristically, he said if he took the carriage, invariably a woman would want to ride along and the incessant talking was worse than the hard saddle—I did not want to be that woman.

With no one to talk to but myself, I pondered Persimmon. What drove him? He was generally pleasant but reserved and he definitely did not suffer fools. He reminded me of an old man I once met in another raucous saloon. If I may digress briefly, finding something worth writing about was, more often than not, a soul gnawing task but every once in a while luck smiled kindly upon me. I do not recollect which mudhole of a mining town it was or the name of the saloon but I recall that I was sitting at a table near the wall, sipping a beer and making notes of what went on. I should specify I was making a mental note of what I witnessed because I had learned long ago that a writer in a saloon was asking to be picked on and I always tried to blend in as much as possible.

It was not long before two trail-bitten cowboys with bad reputations started getting rowdy. One shoved his whiskey-brave buddy into an old man standing at the bar, spilling beer on him. The old man wiped suds off his arm and scolded the cowboys for lack of manners. The cowboy who collided with him replied that he would shoot the old codger dead. The other cowboy cried out mockingly to his friend, "Manners! Don't forget your manners. You can't just shoot him down, you've got to have a duel, that's the gentry way."

The slightly inebriated belligerent latched onto the idea, eager to humiliate the old man with the challenge of a duel and certain the old man would decline sheepishly. To everyone's surprise the old man yelled out, "Come on then," as he stormed out the door into the street. The joke was now on the cowboy whose confidence was shaken by the old man's unexpected boldness. The only way to save face was to meet the old man on the muddy, hoof-plowed field of honor or be branded a coward. Spewing obscenities in an attempt to boost his courage, the cowboy brashly marched outside.

The old man was stoic, his hand resting on the grip of his revolver. Mock bravery, fear, embarrassment—I do not know what made the cowboy grab for his gun but the old man did not give him the benefit of the doubt. He yanked his six-gun from his hip and fired into the cowboy's chest. A crowd huddled over the wheezing man lying in the street while the old gunman went back to the bar and ordered a fresh beer. I slipped up to the bar cautiously, aware the old man's nerves were still raw. I placed both hands on the counter and eased down to him where he could see I was no threat and then, as politely and unassuming as I could, I interrupted his first sip of beer by asking him what it was that made him go outside?

Slowly, the old man took another swig of beer, set the glass on the counter, wiped his open hand down the suds on his whiskers, repositioned the beer glass, and then finally answered, "When I was their age I would have because I was immortal… young and stupid. Then I grew up a bit, had my mind settled on family responsibilities and I wouldn't have gone out there. Now that I'm old, I just don't give a good damn."

Like the old man, Persimmon had ample, "don't give a good damn," in him and I was learning that not giving a damn made for a dangerous man.

Waiting for Persimmon to strike up a conversation was a long wait, but I was determined not to be the one to break the silence. When he finally spoke he said, "We'll make camp up there," and pointed to a cluster of big rocks at the top of a rise. We rode into the shade of the mountain and up, out of the flood plain. The boulders created a natural fort and within them we found an open spot large enough for two men and a campfire.

I offered to tend the horses but Persimmon was particular of Samson's treatment. He gave the distinct impression that Samson was all he had in the world. Instead, I was given fire duty and three tins, one of potatoes, one of beans, and one of meat.

A master of the culinary arts I was not, but I managed to heat what we had and feed the two of us. Persimmon did not complain. Afterward, we lay on our bedrolls, on opposite sides of the fire. Persimmon had retrieved the whiskey bottle he carried from McLaglen's. It was still full which meant he had been drinking Robert and Henry's booze at the cabin.

I still had questions for Persimmon but I thought I would let him get a little further into his bottle which I hoped would mellow him. While I waited, I contemplated why a sympathetic father and loving mother would name their son Persimmon, especially when the family name was already produce. Could they not foresee the taunting that their son must surely have suffered? It might seem strange but I started to worry Persimmon might hear my thoughts. I tried not to think of it further but he must have really heard me.

Persimmon lay propped against a rock with his head balanced on his chin atop his chest. From under his down-turned brim he groaned, "You want to ask me, don't you?"

I wanted to ask him a number of things but which one he had in mind I could not fathom. "Ask you what?"

"About my name." Persimmon must have taken my continued silence as guilt and answered the question, despite my not asking it. "I was named after my great-grandfather who fought in the Revolution. It's a good name and nothing to be ashamed of."

My thought was, it might be a good name from a good man but not one for a man who already has a droop in his moniker. Of course, I did not say that to Persimmon nor did I think it a second time for fear he might again hear my thoughts. I only told him the other part of what I was thinking, "Well, it might be unusual but I think it is a strong name." I meant it. Persimmon did sound like a strong name but between the reader and myself, I am glad I did not have to defend it all my life.

The glow of the moon told me it was about to peek above the mountains and Orion was wading through the horizon. A cold breeze whooshed overhead, but the boulders shielded us nicely. The bottle rested on Persimmon's leg, his hand wrapped around its neck, and when he sloshed it, I could make out it was about a third empty.

Perhaps now Persimmon was prime for my questions, after all, he had asked one of my questions for me. Thinking that if I made my inquiries in a low voice, they would seem less intrusive, I softly said, "I do have a question that has been on my mind all day..."

Persimmon grunted acknowledgement.

"Who is the woman in the picture at the cabin?"

Persimmon did not answer at first so I followed with, "Is she a relative or—"

"Let it be," came a sharp warning from under the hat.

"I'm sorry, I just thought that—"

Persimmon cut me off again, only this time he shot to a sitting position and growled at me, "I told you to let it be!"

"I thought if—" I began but there was no explaining.

Appearing to levitate to his feet, Persimmon jerked the revolver from beneath his arm and lunged across the fire at me like a rabid dog. His toe raked the coals, kicking up a devilish curtain of embers behind him. Viciously, he shook the revolver at me, "What the hell don't you understand?"

Unwittingly, I had lit a match next to a proverbial powder keg. The hulking fiend loomed menacingly over me. Though the flame's undulating light reflected dimly off the rock behind me, in its gloom I could see Persimmon's eyes burning with rage, his chin quivering, and hear his teeth grinding together. His bark was deep and explosive and I could feel the words hit me in the chest.

His thumb wrapped over the hammer and I heard the clacking as he snatched it back, "I'm going to shoot you and you're gonna bleed! Then maybe you'll leave me be!"

VI
SECOND THOUGHTS

Here I was again, believing that being shot was imminent. I was making quite the habit of it in a mere two days. Persimmon hovered over me ominously for several terrifying moments. In his face shown a clear battle of conscience, whether to kill me or not. I kept quiet, afraid any noise might shove him over the edge as I watched his eyes flicker from burning rage to sadness and back again, his jaw clenching then slacking in repetition. There came over me the distinct impression that it was not I who Persimmon saw as his glare bored a hole through me. This seemed to be confirmed as his eyes drifted up the rock behind me and he stood and stumbled from the glow of the coals.

After a few minutes without any indication that Persimmon would return, I sat up to contemplate my next course of action. Several options played out in my head but they all agreed on the same sensible outcome; I needed to get the hell out of there!

Persimmon was clearly unpredictable, at least when he had been drinking. I could try to examine him, try to find what made him do what he did and in so doing, try to stick with him for my story's sake. Then again, there is no accounting for crazy. If Persimmon was not right in the head, there was no telling what he would do or why. Believing the actions of such a person can be rationalized, and thereby predicted if not controlled, was a good way to get one's self killed.

It was a moonlit night. If I slipped out of camp, I might be able to find my way in the dark. Then again, I risked being discovered while retrieving my horse before I ever cleared the boulders. Persimmon was certainly deeper into his bottle by now and it was unlikely his mood had changed, only worsened. I decided to sit tight. I would stay awake, keeping vigil as if that would save me from Persimmon's wrath but I fooled myself with the off-chance notion that in his inebriated state I might be able to flee if I felt threatened.

From the dull glow of the few coals peaking beneath a shroud of ashes and the blackness of what was now a moonless sky, I figured it to be around 5am. I do not know how long I had sat awake against the rock before fatigue drug me under but the cold night air had driven me back down into my blanket at some point. I lay there half asleep, occasionally cracking an eye, wondering what pulled me from the ethereal plane. I began hearing boots shuffling which played into my dreams as I dozed. I dreamt I was standing on the sidewalk of an unknown town, watching people pass in the streets as I waited on Persimmon to come out of a saloon nearby. Something tapped the top of my head and in my dream, I looked up to shoo away a large bumble bee but when it bumped me again, it drove me from the dream.

I lay there with my eyes closed, pondering what was real and what had been unconscious imagination when I received another boot toe to the forehead, hard this time, which jolted me awake with the fear that Persimmon had come to finish me. I snapped my eyes open to see the silhouette of boots and the muzzle of a shotgun bearing down on me.

"Where is he?" its owner barked in a hushed, smoke-scratched voice.

I squinted against the darkness to where Persimmon's bedroll had lain but it was gone. In its place stood a second man whose face was obscured by the night, but whose anxious sway in his stance declared he was not Persimmon.

The man with the scratchy voice darted his eyes nervously about the rocks, knowing he stood in the lion's den. "Where is that scoundrel you was ridin' with? He killed Lizard Johnson and now I aim to kill hgh—"

The grotesque gurgle of his last word was drowned out by the crack of a rifle echoing through the rocks. The bullet slammed into the base of the would-be assassin's throat, sending him reeling backwards. The shotgun fell from his hand and clattered on the hard ground. One hammer dropped and its barrel fired, kicking up a load of dust and sending a swarm of shot screaming past my head.

The shotgun lurched with the blast then came to rest as its wounded owner was shuffling through the coals. He soon lost what remained of his balance and collapsed, clutching his throat at his friend's feet. In the disturbed ashes a flame flickered to life and in its light I could see the panic in the second man's eyes. Frozen at first, the man jerked his head about, frantically searching for his attacker in the darkness. Finding no target, the terrified man fired his revolver threateningly, wishfully, into the night. His second bullet ricocheted and its hum was still trailing off when the man regained his faculties and turned to run. He had not gone two steps when the sharp report of an unseen rifle tore through the jagged rocks, its bullet hitting the fleeing outlaw mid-stride.

The shot struck him broadside in the ribs, shoving him sideways, leaving his fearful momentum to drive him headlong into the dirt where he lay crumpled and still before the last echo of the shot that killed him.

Soon I heard footsteps outside the light and worried what other compadre of this filth might lurk in the darkness, waiting to take revenge. I squinted into the dimness of the flickering shadows, straining to determine enemy from scrub. Panic lodged in my throat as the footsteps quickened and I swallowed hard as Persimmon broke into the light and stomped angrily across our campsite.

Persimmon drove his heel into the ribs of the first man he shot but he was no longer squirming. Satisfied the dead men were no more a threat, Persimmon grasped his rifle in both hands, as though he was going on a hunt, and walked out of camp. Did he think there might be others lying in wait for us? My saddlebags lay at my feet and though it was a little late, I dug into them and retrieved the Model Three Persimmon had told me to hang onto. I was glad Persimmon was too occupied to remind me how much good to me that pistol was in my saddle bag.

Blanket wrapped around me, pistol in my lap, I sat with my back against the rock staring at the sprawling figure of one dead man and the twisted silhouette of another in the emerging twilight. By the time dawn broke I had grown accustomed to them, and the cold. Raking together what coals still smoldered, I stoked them with dry grass and the remaining firewood I had collected the previous evening. I sat closer to the flame, still wrapped in the blanket, letting the soft heat of the small fire warm my chest and wondering what had become of Persimmon. It had been a restless night, to say the least, and my eyes stung a bit from fatigue and ember smoke. I had the makings for coffee so I decided to take comfort in it and worry about Persimmon after I had drunk my fill.

I suspect it was the aroma of fresh coffee that lured Persimmon back into camp. He strolled in, as if there were no dead men strewn about, produced a tin cup and filled it. I watched him when he was not looking at me. Once I was warm, I stood and stretched my legs while having another cup. Morbid curiosity drug me to the dead men. The one who had kicked me lay blood-soaked. His shirt and neck crusted in magenta which ran thick in the creases of his neck. The ground below his head looked like red clay I had seen on a visit to Georgia, except for a rivulet of excess which had trickled down hill and puddled under the back-cut edge of a boulder.

I recognized the man from the Bansheen Saloon but his partner lying in a heap behind him I had never seen before. Persimmon seemed almost relieved, completely unshaken. It puzzled me until I remembered his instructions to Henry and Robert. "If anyone comes looking for me, *be sure* you tell them that I have gone to South Pueblo." Persimmon had expected to be followed all along. Had he purposely left me in camp alone, as bait?

Perturbed with no reasonable outlet for my frustrations, I took the last of the coffee without offering it to Persimmon. I had had twice as much as he and really did not want it but I was going to take what little satisfaction I could get, no matter how petty.

After picking up the shotgun and stripping the gun belts from each dead man, Persimmon commenced to rifle through their pockets, taking any coins he found. One man had a silver watch, but it was engraved inside and Persimmon tossed it back onto the man's chest where it landed with a thud. This seemed to be a reminder to him and the next thing Persimmon did was to run his eyes and fingers over every inch of leather on the gun belts and then examine the pistols themselves. One belt had initials carved on the inside and he tossed it back to its owner after stripping it of a few bullets. I thought he was going to take the other belt, having not found any marks on it, but after a few moments he decided against it. He stripped it of its contents and then held it out from him, dangling it from one hand as he compared its length to my waist. Deciding I was not as portly as its former owner, he tossed it atop the blood covered corpse.

"Let's be on our way then," Persimmon suggested as if we had stopped for a picnic.

My animosity over being used for bait was tempered by my fear of the man. I was agitated enough to speak up but mindful of my tone of voice. "Don't we at least owe them a Christian burial?" I asserted as much as asked.

"These two would have killed you in your sleep if they had found me here with you. They certainly weren't Christian men and I don't owe them a damn thing. Let them feed the buzzards and dogs," Persimmon growled.

Pressed by the weight of Protestant duties and the proprieties of civil society with which I grew up, it felt wrong not to at least bury the men. "Whether it is the right thing to do or not, it isn't the wrong thing," was the last I would say on the matter if he vetoed it again.

Persimmon stood in silence, looking over the rocks at the valley below with the barrels of two Colts in his right hand and the shotgun in his left. No matter what he would say next, I was surprised he took the time to contemplate my words at all. After a minute, he turned and headed in the direction of the horses, "You want to bury them, go ahead, but I'm riding on as soon as I am ready."

Whether he intended to call my bluff or sincerely offer for me to live up to my words, I could not back out now. In my saddlebag I carried a small hand spade. I retrieved it and set to digging in the middle of our campsite but after fifteen minutes of scratching about I stopped to wipe my brow and survey the pitiful impression I had made. Persimmon had not returned so I crawled up the side of a boulder and peered out toward our horses. His saddlebags were on the ground near his horse but Persimmon was mulling about aimlessly. He could have been long gone if he had meant what he said. I was still afraid of him but oddly comforted that he was allowing me the time without leaving me.

I declared the shovel defeated but unwilling to allow Persimmon victory in the argument, I decided to cover the dead men in the abundant stone which littered the ground. I grabbed the crumpled man by the boot and dragged him alongside his partner. The stench of death was already present and stretching the body out produced a burp from the corpse which gagged me almost to vomit. After recovering a few feet in the clear, I set to hurriedly cover the bodies with rocks, tossing what I could from a safe distance upwind.

Curiosity brought Persimmon graveside where he watched me for a while. Whether he relented the point or the loss of trail time, I do not know, but he eventually kicked over a few rocks himself. When we were done, I did not presume to pray over them. After all, Persimmon was right, they would have killed me over nothing. I had given them enough of my sweat, saving them from the vultures and wolves. That was plenty.

We were two hours on the trail without a word. I rode several yards behind Persimmon, irritated, afraid, and unwilling to offer conversation freely. I thought of the night before as little as possible which meant it was on my mind almost constantly. I wondered what happened to the dead men's horses as I never saw them. My eyes gravitated to the dead man's shotgun poking from either end of Persimmon's bedroll. Every time I remembered how close the load of shot came to my head, a chill would run down my spine and my blood boiled. I contemplated how I was going to break with Persimmon. Would it anger him if I left abruptly? The better plan was probably to leave secretly in the night once we got to South Pueblo.

Entering a brushy patch of the valley, Persimmon began to 'gee' and 'haw' at his horse as if he were plowing. The big equine took directions better than most men and that is when I noticed that Persimmon did not wear spurs.

We stopped a couple of times to stretch, pee, and pull something from our bags to eat, but I do not remember saying a word. Our first glimpse of South Pueblo was a string of lights in the dark. There is also a town of Pueblo which sits on the opposite side of the Arkansas River and as I understand it, when the railroad came, rather than pay taxes to Pueblo the railroad started its own municipality.

Upon entering town, it was no surprise that the first place we went was a saloon. Feeling unable to make a break from Persimmon and with an honest taste for a shot of whiskey for the first time in my life, I sheepishly followed Persimmon inside. At the bar stood a fellow leaning back on his elbows, watching the door with a beer in his hand. A few feet down the bar from him wobbled a pair of drunks, laughing their heads off at whatever fool thing one of them had slurred to the other. I noticed the fellow on his elbows locked eyes with Persimmon and shifted his weight in Persimmon's direction as Persimmon threaded the space between him and the drunks.

"Persimmon," the man with the beer dispassionately greeted with a nod.

"Deacon..." Persimmon trailed in response before asking the bartender for a top-shelf bottle, a room for the night, and someone to tend the horses.

I took a position down at the far end of the bar where I figured I was most welcomed and could watch the room. Persimmon pocketed his room key and took his bottle and a glass to a table tucked under the stairs which led to the rooms above. The bartender walked to the back door, opened it and called to someone, then returned to what he was doing. In a moment, a young lad of about thirteen entered. The bartender leaned toward him and spoke something softly and pointed to Persimmon. The young man nodded and went to Persimmon's table where Persimmon gave him some instructions and a gold dollar, one I had seen Persimmon pull from a dead man's pocket that morning. The young man nodded again with a big smile on his face then headed out front.

Meanwhile, the barkeep slid a towel down the counter to where I stood and handed me a second room key. "Your room is down the hall from his," he said, then asked me what else I wanted but before I could answer there came a sharp whistle. I turned to see Persimmon staring at me as he pushed a chair with his toe from underneath the opposite side of the small round table. I suppose it was Persimmon's way of apologizing and I must say I was happy to know I was still wanted. Then again, what if Persimmon simply wanted to keep me nearby since we had buried two men and Persimmon clearly had no intentions of reporting the incident?

I wondered if I was a fool for keeping such dangerous company rather than hightailing it to safer environs but there was something about Persimmon that was equally comforting as he was discomforting. The barkeep handed me a glass and I cautiously walked to the chair and sat down, unwittingly holding the glass close to my vest.

Without protest, Persimmon made the reach and filled my glass. He then filled his own halfway, threw its contents to the back of his throat and filled the glass again. I have never been a whiskey drinker but my first swig turned out to be a full swallow. From then own I sipped the second half, desiring to soothe my nerves but keep my wits about me.

"You're wondering if I'm the devil... aren't you?" was the unexpected conversation starter Persimmon chose.

As I said, there was a comforting side to Persimmon which drew you in, however, remembering the night before made me unsure of my response. Granted, I learned I should never push a point with a dangerous man, especially when his faculties have been loosed with drink but I had not pushed that hard before and Persimmon was again drinking. Unable to accurately gauge my best response, I fell prayerfully back to the old adage that honesty was the best policy and I hoped not to prove it wrong by getting shot.

"The thought crossed my mind," I said, before retreating behind my glass.

"It was not my intention to dangle you out there as bait," he said, then paused and took a drink. "I wouldn't have liked it if someone did that to me and I wanted you to know I didn't purposely do it to you."

The moment was interrupted when the young teen returned with our saddle bags. Persimmon gave him a nod of approval and the young man laid the bags on the table then headed back out front, presumably to take our horses to the livery.

So far, Persimmon's actions were gracious. An apology was not what I had expected. Our silence on the trail had not been unproductive and Persimmon was not the unreflective wild animal he had appeared. I was still angry about the entire incident though; after all, I nearly had my head blown off.

"You could have told me we were being followed," I reprimanded, immediately wishing I had not.

Persimmon glared at me as I sipped at my drink nervously. One eye squinted a bit as his nose crinkled up in contemplation then his eyes softened and he answered as if comforting a frightened child. "I didn't know we were being followed, but I assumed we would be because it's the sort of thing cowardly men do. I should have given you fair warning. In the future, I will."

In the future? How often were we going to be followed by killers? It felt good to be wanted, but I wanted something too and I made my desire plain to Persimmon. "I don't want to get shot."

A smirk briefly crossed his lips and then in the same reassuring voice he said, "I won't let anybody shoot you."

"What about you?" I blurted my honest but impertinent reply.

"I promise not to kill you..." His tone grew dark, even sinister and his eyes distant. "Just don't ask me about certain things."

Certain things? What things? How could I know what things if I couldn't ask about them? Obviously, the woman in the picture at the cabin was off limits but he said "certain things," plural. Maybe it was best to apply that to mean anything not in the here and now.

Persimmon sat, staring out the door, his mood having turned somber. Remembering the man who had called him by name, I turned my attention to the bar. The gentleman had taken a fresh beer and moved down the bar to an empty table, away from the two drunks. Our stares met, each curious about the other. Was the man friend or foe? I got the impression he fell somewhere in between.

The taller of the two drunks was the least obtrusive, only cackling half the time and generally swaying in place. The shorter one was far more obnoxious, flailing his arms with inebriated gestures that somehow related to a story about a chicken and a raccoon with which he was struggling to regale his friend between fitful bouts of laughter. Persimmon sat staring at the door, motionless except for the occasional sip of whiskey. Now and then his eyes moved, darting between things only he could see.

Bored, I sat quietly, finishing my whiskey one drop at a time and contemplating what I would do, when a whoop burst through the relatively low hum of the room. It came from the large bellows of the tall drunk and it led right into an admonishment of disbelief for his short partner's latest tale, of which I had paid no mind.

"Ain't no way you said that to Wild Bill... you ain't ever even met Bill Hickok and if you had you'd've wet your pants."

"I did so meet him! I was in Deadwood the same year he was killed," the short drunk claimed in a weak defense, indignation smoothing the slur in his tongue.

"So now you're telling me you was there when Wild Bill was shot?" the tall drunk asked, accusingly.

"I didn't say that. I said I was in—"

"It doesn't matter, Deadwood would have chewed you up and spit you out. I don't know why you're always telling such stories as—"

"It ain't no story, it really hap—"

The pair continued to talk loudly over each other. I glanced back at Persimmon whose expression had turned from sadness to anger but his gaze still transcended this earthly plane and I knew he was oblivious to the drunks' argument or to my presence and I had a good mind to slip away when I heard the drunks' conversation take a dangerous turn.

"I bet you wouldn't say that to anybody, much less Wild Bill," the tall one goaded.

"And why not? I'd say it to any fella' you choose and—"

My soul cried out, "Damnit!" when the tall drunk whipped his long arm and boney index finger in Persimmon's direction. "That fella right yonder."

VII
DAMNIT!

Fear entered the short drunk's eyes and he swallowed hard as he swept back the last of his beer. His partner had thrown down the gauntlet and the short drunk was full of enough pride and alcohol to drown out any good sense he might otherwise have mustered. I did not know what the controversial words were that he claimed to have spoken to James Butler Hickok and lived to talk about it, but I knew he did not want to repeat them to Persimmon Apricot.

"Hey you, big fella'," the short drunk called out.

Persimmon's scowl had hardened as he sat steeped in memory. Whatever was on his mind made him grit his teeth and oblivious to everything around him. I put my hand out, trying to wave off the drunk but his friend prodded him in the shoulder.

"Hey, stranger... hey, answer me," the drunk was now becoming agitated at what he perceived as ill manners. "Hey, I'm talking to you. You deaf or somethin'?"

"I guess he don't think you're worth payin' any mind," the tall drunk laughed, which made his short friend indignant.

"I'll get his attention," the scorned inebriate exclaimed as he dug in his britches' pocket for a two-shot derringer. "Hey fella' you best answer me," he yelled at Persimmon then fired.

The report from the short barrel was deafening within the planked walls of the room. The bullet hit the table top just short of my hand and buried itself, heaving the splintered wood beneath my fingers. My reaction was far too slow to have saved me but instinctively I snatched my hand from the table and scrambled with my feet to shove the chair back and stand. Instead, the back legs of the chair hung against the uneven floorboards and it tipped backwards, pitching me onto the floor. Having some wits left about me, I used the momentum to roll for safety, behind another table.

The calamity of it stung Persimmon, jolting him back to the present. His eyes boiled with hate and his right hand reached for the Schofield under his coat. He rose to his feet with the whiskey bottle in his left hand, revolver in the other, pivoting clear of the stairway above him as he spun to face the shooter.

The short drunk realized Persimmon meant to shoot him but did so too late to bring the derringer to bear before Persimmon could fire. Persimmon's bullet shoved the poorly balanced drunk against the counter but one shot did not satisfy Persimmon, it merely opened the floodgate of his rage. Stomping toward his prey, he fired twice more before the man's corpse hit the floor and then a fourth time before his head bounced on the planking.

Seething, Persimmon swept the Schofield across the room and back, searching for any additional assailants before bringing the muzzle to rest on the tall drunk. A dark spot appeared on the front of the man's pants and stretched down his pant leg but the tall drunk did not notice that he had wet himself. Panicked, he stood frozen, staring down the barrel of Persimmon's pistol.

Once Persimmon felt secure, he holstered his revolver and walked back to his table. He was pouring himself another drink to wash his nerves when the sheriff burst into the saloon with his gun drawn and a deputy by his side.

The sheriff reviewed the scene. Persimmon took a drink and poured another while I stared at the dead man and wondered if perhaps, I was partially responsible for what just took place. Had I stirred painful memories that night in the rocks? Would Persimmon have taken a more measured approach to the drunkard if I had minded my own business? Any one of us might lash out impulsively when struck amid painful or infuriating thoughts but with a man like Persimmon the results are deadly.

The derringer in the dead drunk's hand was visible from where the sheriff stood, as was the Schofield peeking from under Persimmon's coat. Everyone in the room was fixated on either the sheriff or Persimmon.

"You shot him then, I take it?" the sheriff bellowed his question at Persimmon.

Persimmon nodded and took a sip of his whiskey.

"We have a no-carry ordinance in this town, so hand over your pistol," the sheriff calmly demanded.

"I see that's working really well for you," Persimmon smugly replied.

Knowing what I did about Persimmon, I was certain he would not be surrendering his pistol. The sheriff waited a moment and when Persimmon poured another whiskey and made no show of disarming, the sheriff reminded him, "You best comply. I've got my sights resting square on your midsection."

Persimmon downed the whiskey in one gulp and set the glass on the table. With a raise of his brow and his voice dripping with resolve, he shook his head slightly and said, "I don't care."

I knew what was coming when the sheriff waved the deputy to go and strip Persimmon of his gun. I wanted desperately to move away from the sheriff but the air in the room was thick with tension and I was afraid that if I made the least of movements, the sheriff would feel it and mistake me for a threat.

It was the tall drunk who unwittingly saved lives. Still standing over his dead friend, sobering and beginning to smell of urine, it was not until the deputy took a step toward Persimmon that the tall drunk noticed the sheriff was in the room. Feeling protected by the presence of law enforcement, the tall drunk rushed toward the sheriff, nearly falling over a chair.

"Sheriff, sheriff, do you see what he done? He shot him four times! He ain't done nothing to this fella, but he shot him four times," clamored the tall drunk.

The deputy stopped, startled by the cry of the drunk. The sheriff instinctively swung his revolver to the perceived attacker but quickly realized the drunk was no threat and trained his aim back onto Persimmon. Persimmon stood staring at the deputy, motionless except for a fist he slowly balled. When the drunk was within one stride of Persimmon, Persimmon spun to his left and jabbed his big right hand into the drunk's jaw.

The drunk's chin buckled followed by his knees and as they struck the floor, the rest of him fell backward over his feet. The sheriff, his deputy, and I were all transfixed on the urine soaked inebriate, watching his chest intently to see if it heaved with life. The blow had been so powerful that I am sure everyone in the room was convinced the man was dead until finally his ribs rose and settled in a breath of deep sleep.

"What the hell... Why did you do that and why did you shoot that man four times?" the sheriff demanded answers as he turned back to Persimmon.

"Dead is dead, what does it matter?" Persimmon asked in reply, avoiding a reason for either act.

The demand for Persimmon's weapon was about to resume and I knew I needed to change the subject before there was a bloodbath.

"Excuse me… sheriff, if I may…" I began. Both the sheriff and his deputy looked at me as though they had not known I was standing three feet from them all this time. "My name is Pete and I was sitting at the table with Mr. Apricot when the incident took place."

"You don't look like a gunfighter," the sheriff remarked, insultingly.

"No sir, I am a writer and it is my job to be a keen observer in moments such as these so that my eyewitness testimony is factual for our readership." My occupation of roving reporter could be deemed relevant so I played it up to my advantage and laid it on thick. "The dead gentleman fired upon us without provocation. I saw him aiming and his eyes were clearly set on Mr. Apricot. I believe it was his drunken sway which kept him from hitting his intended target."

I had no idea what the drunk intended to shoot but as tippled as he was, he could have easily wounded one of us, with or without intent. I pointed to the splintered table top, "As you can see the shot was close, in fact he nearly took my fingers off."

The sheriff seemed pleased that he was finally getting to the bottom of what had taken place and he addressed his questions to me. "Why did the dead man want to shoot this fella' and why did this fella' shoot him four times in return?"

"I don't know what these two were arguing about," I swept an index finger in the air, across the two drunks, one dead and one dead asleep. "Whatever it was, this one here was goading that one to prove it and chose Mr. Apricot for him to do so but Mr. Apricot was lost in thought and not paying them any attention. I don't know what he intended to do with that derringer but it looked like he was trying to graze Mr. Apricot. In Mr. Apricot's defense, it did appear as though the shooter was still trying to bring his weapon to bear on Mr. Apricot when Mr. Apricot shot him. The second and third bullets struck him as he fell. I believe the fourth was just residual from the heat of battle."

I used my explanation of the four shots as an excuse to work my way over to the body as if I was reviewing it and then to the bar where I slowly slipped down its length in the direction of the man who had spoken to Persimmon when we arrived. From this new position, I felt I could drop to the floor and be safe when the shooting started.

"Is that what happened? Anyone see it differently?" the sheriff asked the room as he scanned the saloon patrons for a rebuttal. Everyone nodded in agreement. "Well then, that's fine but you—"

"Look here sheriff, I'm going to take this bottle up to my room and I am going to go to sleep and head out of town in the morning. Keep that fella' away from me and there probably won't be any more trouble." Persimmon pointed to the floor in the direction of the drunk still breathing, then he turned toward the stairs and began walking way.

The sheriff's face was perturbed but contemplative. I stood, propped against the bar on one elbow with my fingers clenched around its palm-polished edge in anticipation of the sheriff's next words and whether or not I would be dodging gunfire.

"Hey!" the sheriff barked. Persimmon stopped but made no effort to look back. "You be gone first thing in the morning like you said."

Maybe it was the blood settling in my ears as my heart fluttered in relief but I swear I heard an audible sigh from the room. Persimmon made no reply, only continued to the stairs and up to his room. The sheriff kept his eyes on Persimmon until he was out of sight then holstered his revolver and directed the deputy to fetch the undertaker. Before the deputy could get out of the door, the sheriff nudged the tall drunk's leg with the toe of his boot and said, "Guess you better take this one down to the jail to sleep it off."

The deputy nodded and knelt beside his unconscious prisoner, lightly patting his cheek with the back of his hand. The drunk came around enough for the deputy and a patron, volunteered by the sheriff, to scoop him up and shoulder him as he staggered to the jail. I had no idea how the sheriff usually dealt with drunks but I was sure that this one would "sleep it off" until Persimmon left town the next day.

Once the undertaker had the dead man loaded in his hack, the sheriff scanned the room one last time, stopping his cold glare on me before turning to leave. If he saw me as a threat it could only have been a threat to justice but what I told him was the truth. At least it was the truth about what happened a few moments before. I did not mention Persimmon's threat to kill me around the campfire. Whether or not I had jabbed a demon with a stick the night before was an irrelevance best kept to myself. The way I figured it, so were the two men Persimmon had killed a few hours later. They would have murdered us in bed. I am certain a court would have found in our favor, what with witnesses of the Bansheen Incident and the fact that those men pursued us. Telling this sheriff about them would have served nothing but to complicate matters and guarantee a fight.

A deep breath relaxed my ribcage a bit, but I turned to the bar, reached for an upside-down stack of shot glasses and righted one which the barkeep promptly filled. I emptied it and as he poured me another, I noticed the stranger who had spoken to Persimmon. He was still at his post near the end of the bar, watching me, trying to size me up, probably wondering how Persimmon came to be in the association of a fellow like me.

The barkeep left the bottle near me so I grabbed it and found a seat on the far side of the saloon, away from the blood. I sat there, letting the first dram soak in before sipping the next, wondering how I came to be in the company of a man who appeared to live every day on the edge. No, he had not provoked the drunk but with a man such as Persimmon living in a country where civility was often a novelty, it was easy to see how every day could mean kill or be killed.

I was exhausted both physically from the long ride and lack of sleep, and worse, emotionally from the terror of nearly being killed twice in one day. One thing I could say for it, I had the makings of a story. The second shot of whiskey I took in two big sips while I pondered what to do next. Getting what I needed to finish the story was not worth dying over. Then again, Persimmon promised not to shoot me or get me shot. Was that promise his to keep? A train ride to a new location might take us out of the local unrest but trouble clung to some men like mud to their boot heel.

The second shot of whiskey settled the rattle in my chest and shakes in my hands. One more for good measure but I wondered if I might ought to stop after the third one because a fourth might pitch me over the brink. The strain was evident in my hunched shoulders.

After determining I was no threat, the stranger approached me and spoke. "You're friends with Persimmon, are you?"

Despite the dubious tone of the stranger's question I nodded faintly and answered, "Sort of."

"I get the sense that you know him well enough to know he's dangerous but you haven't decided how dangerous or why," the stranger remarked of his observations.

I laughed a bit more than the comment warranted as the nervous tension broke through and tickled my gullet, forcing me into a spell of coughing before I could answer.

"You're half right. I can assure you that I know how dangerous he is… well enough anyhow. As for the other half, I learned not to inquire about the why."

The stranger held his hand out, "Deacon Jefferson." Looking at my hand he gauged my handshake, how it fared in his estimation I do not know, but he continued, "I used to live in the same Kansas town as Persimmon and I can tell you the why."

VIII
WHAT AILS HIS SOUL

Deacon Jefferson sat down at my table, leaned back in his chair and eyed me for a minute. It was clear he wanted to talk but was not sure if he should. It was a surprise when the first question he asked me was if Persimmon was the best gunfighter I had ever seen? The question sounded like braggadocio from an admirer and Deacon did not seem to me as a devotee of Persimmon's. The question also struck me as odd and out of place in the conversation which gave me pause long enough to remember Persimmon's own words.

"Persimmon says he is not a gunfighter," I answered triumphantly.

"I see you know him better than I suspected. How long have you been riding with him?" came the next query into my credentials.

Sheepishly I replied, "Three days."

"Well, I bet they were an eventful three days. I heard you say you were a reporter of sorts?" Deacon pried.

Starting from the beginning, I regaled Deacon with the entire sordid tale along with my reasons for riding with Persimmon and my doubts about continuing. I realized after I described the killing of the two men in camp the night before, that I probably should not have told Deacon of it. Persimmon had not addressed the incident with the law. To my relief, Deacon let it roll off as one small part of a larger story.

When I finished, Deacon leaned forward and propped himself on the table by his forearms with both hands wrapped around his beer glass and a contemplative expression on his face.

"It amazes me how different he is today from the man I knew in Kansas... If you want to hear it, I'll tell you what it took to make a man like Persimmon Apricot but for your sake, I would suggest you never mention it to him." Deacon made his offer of gossip and I nodded my wary acceptance. There was no way I was going to knowingly broach any subject with Persimmon that might get me shot. For that matter, I was still unsure whether I would continue to ride with the madman.

"Our town started out as many before it, just a little stage stop. Once men thought to drive cattle up from Texas, after the war, we became a stop on the way to the nearest set of rails and then for about a year in '68, we became the end of the rail line until the railroad pushed on. During that time our town boomed, but with progress came blight.

"Persimmon came to town with his mother and wife not long after the first cattle. He and that horse of his broke ground on a little farm just outside of town and then he bought a building which had been built by a speculator on main street and set up a dry goods store. Selling supplies to the stage coaches and to the cattlemen in season was a lucrative business.

"Mrs. Apricot must have been the most beautiful woman to have ever stepped foot in Kansas. Persimmon adored her and did whatever he could to make her comfortable. I've known other women who, because they are beautiful, are also haughty. Mrs. Apricot was as sweet and kind as she was beautiful and I think that had to do with having a bum leg. If I recollect, someone said she had been kicked by a mule as a child but I don't know for sure. Whatever it was, it left her with a bad limp.

"Cowboys are always a rowdy bunch. Most are just letting out pent up energy from a long trail ride but some are plain bad. The second year the cattle came through the area, the herd brought with it two cowboys up to no good. They'd cause a stir in town, then head further up the trail with the herd and then come back our way and stay a while before hitting the trail back home. Occasionally one of them would wake up in a jail cell where he had slept off the night before but generally, they managed to avoid the law.

"Well, the problems started when they got their first look at Mrs. Apricot and took a fancy to her. Of course, she told them she was married but their kind don't care. They pawed at her a bit and did their best to persuade her but when she shunned them and sought help from the town marshal, the two cowboys took offense. They quit trying to win her favor and took up mocking her for being a cripple.

"Persimmon found out about it and went to the marshal. Our marshal was well intentioned and a good friend of most in the town. He tried to intervene, even spouting empty threats to lock them up if they didn't move on but the marshal wasn't a strong personality in those days and the law didn't give him what he felt was sufficient cause to arrest them.

"Back then Persimmon was a docile man, slow to anger and easy to calm. On more than one occasion he stepped between her and the two cowboys. The cowboys would bristle up at him and Persimmon would stand there, unmoved amid their insults. I think he was afraid to fight unpredictable cowboys and the cowboys were afraid of Persimmon's size and knew they would have to shoot the broad-shouldered man if they stood any hope of winning a fight. That would have sicced the law on them for sure."

Listening to Deacon's story intently, I could not imagine the timid creature he described as being the same man as the vicious brute I knew as Persimmon Apricot. However, I was certain the gorgeous woman in the photograph in Persimmon's cabin must have been his wife.

Deacon wet his throat with a swig of beer and continued. "This played out over a couple of seasons. The two cowboys drifted into town with a new scheme to win Mrs. Apricot over. I guess they were stupid enough to think the next time it might work. When she shunned them, they would still hang around, why I don't know, but they would taunt her every chance they got.

"Persimmon was wise enough not to let her stay home alone, so she usually kept to their store or at home with him. Eventually the two cowboys got bored and drifted out of town, letting the Apricots live peacefully until the next season. I think it was the third year the cowboys came when everything went to hell.

"As usual, the pair tried coming on to Mrs. Apricot but I guess they knew better than to expect something different that time and took offense right off. She stayed holed up in the store for a few days but the weather was so nice that time of year and Mrs. Apricot had had her fill of being intimidated. She went out a few mornings while the cowboys were still sleeping off the night before but one morning she had her own customers to tend to and did not get to go out until just before noon. Persimmon was on an errand himself and not there to stop her.

"A small haberdashery had opened on the second-floor above the local attorney's office. The stairs to the upper walk ran down alongside the building. Mrs. Apricot wasn't good with stairs. She had to take them each with the same leg and sideways. In fact, the townsfolk had taken up a collection to have easy risers installed on all the sidewalks around town and with a railing on each just so Mrs. Apricot could manage. That's how well liked she was.

"About the time Mrs. Apricot stepped from the haberdashery onto the upper walk, here came those two sons of the devil wobbling down the street. They saw her and started their usual catcalling and acting like they could see up her dress, and so on. After she limped a couple of steps towards the stairs, the cowboys' jeers started in on how she must have a wooden leg and how they could see it under her petticoat and that turned into vulgar claims of Mrs. Apricot having other parts made of wood to explain why she shunned them.

"I didn't witness this first hand. I regret I wasn't there to intervene. I showed up a minute or two, too late. There were other folks who witnessed it, too afraid to stop it. To be fair, they didn't know where it would lead or maybe they would have mustered the courage. I don't know why Mrs. Apricot let the likes of those cowboys get to her but I guess everyone has their limit on being taunted. With all those eyes on her, Mrs. Apricot was embarrassed to the point that she tried walking down the stairs normal like, rather than sideways like she ought to. They say she made the first step but the second time she planted her bum leg it buckled and threw her. On the way down, her head caught in the balusters and it snapped her neck... Killed her instantly."

Deacon paused again and cleared a lump in his throat before continuing at a more somber pace. Each sentence was measured as Deacon labored to maintain his composure. Out of respect I lowered my eyes to the table to save him what embarrassment I could, though Deacon need not feel ashamed. There was a lump in my throat too.

Another grunt and a sip of beer, a deep breath and a clearing of the throat, more beer and then he said, "In the commotion, the two cowboys thought it best to skedaddle. I heard the cry up the street for someone to find Persimmon and I lit out to arrive at the ghastly scene a minute before him. Persimmon came running down the middle of the street, not knowing what was wrong. When he broke through the crowd huddled around the stairs and he saw that she was dead, I'm telling you, a wail went up the likes of which I have never heard from no man. I've never seen a big man fall to pieces like Persimmon did when he scooped up her lifeless body. He staggered into the street, unable to see where he went from the tears..."

Deacon's own eyes welled up and his breath faltered. He grunted again and gulped two large swallows of his beer then breathed a long slow breath to gather his nerves. "Persimmon finally fell to his knees on the other side of the street, laid her on the sidewalk planking and collapsed over her lifeless body, sobbing something terrible. Some of the womenfolk were approaching him in a vain attempt to lend comfort but before they could, he scared the hell out of us all when he reared his head back, fists clenched in the air, and let out a screech to heaven… you'd have thought his soul was bursting from his body. Then he beat his fist into the dirt several times and fell prostrate—still, except for the bouncing of his ribs as he sobbed.

"Some of us helped him up but Persimmon shook us off and staggered down the street, pulling at his hair with both fists and belting out a howl now and then that made our skin crawl. I don't think anyone checked on him that night. We were all too afraid of what we might find. The next morning, I found the door of his store wide open where he had left it the day before. I decided to ride out to his place and found him passed out on his bedroom floor with her picture on his chest and an empty bottle beside him. In all the time we shared the same town, I had never known Persimmon to take a single drop of booze, until then.

"For the next couple of days, me and some other folks took turns checking in on him, taking him food he wouldn't eat, and so on. When he wasn't passed out, he was unresponsive. I never saw him cry again. He just sat in a stupor. I was sure he had lost his mind. We had the funeral without him—had to." Deacon looked to the ceiling in thought. "You know, when his mother passed that first year they came to Kansas, Persimmon was solemn for a day or two but he seemed to shake that off. And I was taking shelter from the storm in his store the day word came that a tornado had taken his house. Mrs. Apricot began crying over the loss but Persimmon just asked a few questions, then went to his books to place an order for more lumber to rebuild, which he did without complaint. I can remember, at the time, thinking that Persimmon was one of the strongest men I'd ever seen. I couldn't be so casual about such a loss. Could you?" Deacon asked me without looking for an answer. I shook my head even though Deacon was not paying me any mind.

"Anyway, Persimmon stayed in his house for better than a week. Then one day he ate an entire picnic basket worth of chicken that we took to him and the next morning he came to town and put his store and house up for sale. For the low price he was asking, someone snapped the store up the same day. The house sold two days later. He sold everything he had except his shotgun, repeater and that big plow horse. Afterward he didn't say much, just loaded up what he had left in his saddlebags and rode out of town. Maybe if Persimmon had had children... maybe things would have been different.

"By the time Persimmon left, the townsfolk had already begun to turn on the marshal. Then, about three weeks later, the town woke to a horrendous sight. Those two cowboys were tied to the posts beneath the stairs where Mrs. Apricot perished. I should say, what was left of them. They were bloody pulps with their teeth knocked out, their tongues cut out, their hands mangled into worthless knots. Their knees and ankles crushed. It's a wonder they were breathing.

"There were some good Christian folks in that town and despite blaming the cowboys for what happened, they choked down their revulsion at the two mangled heaps and had mercy on them, nursing them back to the closest thing to health those cowboys would ever see. The marshal and the sheriff both tried to find out for sure who had bludgeoned them but neither cowboy would tell. Of course, they couldn't speak and they couldn't write but even when they were asked directly if it had been Persimmon Apricot, neither man would confirm it. The only affirmation the law got was the extreme fear in the cowboys' eyes at the mention of Persimmon's name."

By now Deacon's beer had run dry. I splashed a little whiskey in the bottom of his mug and signaled the barkeep to bring him another beer. Deacon took a break from his story to gulp the whiskey and enjoy a couple of swallows of fresh beer. As I let him rest, I imagined the horrid scene he painted. The viciousness of the attack on the cowboys was more intense than I could fathom and try as I might, I could not put myself in a place of empathy.

The break was good for Deacon. It let him regain full composure and he began again with the vigor of a skilled raconteur.

"Without a witness to testify against Persimmon, the law let him be but the whole incident was more than some of the townsfolk could handle. Everyone felt like the marshal should have done more to prevent Mrs. Apricot's death... Truth be told, I don't know what he could have done that would have been legal... The town turned on him anyhow and rather than wait 'til the next election to oust him, some of the town fathers forced the marshal to resign.

"After that his wife left him. I think the pair was already on the outs but the embarrassment over the marshal losing his job and his increased drinking was the death knell for their marriage. You see, Persimmon wasn't the only one to be changed by all this. The marshal became a bitter man and somehow got it in his head to blame Persimmon for all his troubles. I guess he figured that Persimmon had brought it to a head by dumping those near-dead cowboys in town. A local pariah, the marshal left town, drifted out of Kansas and some way or other, finagled a job as a U.S. Marshal."

As soon as Deacon told me what became of the pitiful town marshal, I was sure I knew who he was and to verify I asked, "The marshal's name wouldn't be Edwards, would it?"

"Oh, so you've run into him too, I reckon?"

I nodded.

"Then you know he has it out for Persimmon. Edwards tried to get Persimmon convicted for shooting a man down in Yuma, Arizona about a year after he left Kansas. The court ruled in favor of Persimmon which heaped more embarrassment atop Marshal Edwards and stoked his resentment.

"As for Persimmon, now you know what ails his soul. I left Kansas after the incident too, as did a couple of other families. I think those of us who left just needed some fresh scenery. I ran into Persimmon for the first time after that trial. I didn't recognize him at first. Save for that big horse of his, there's nothing about the man that is the same as I knew him in Kansas; not the look in his eye, or the pistol under his arm, or the clothes on his back, nothing. He wears an indifference to life that makes him extremely dangerous."

This last point was one on which I felt I could contribute and I interjected with my brief but intense experience. "Yeah, I've seen him kill a number of men easily in the short time I've known him."

Deacon thought a moment then shook his head. "No, I think you misunderstand me," Deacon corrected, "I don't mean for the life of other men. I mean Persimmon has no regard for his own and a man who doesn't care if he lives or dies will wade into trouble without concern for whether he'll make it back out."

Rather abruptly, Deacon gulped the remainder of his beer, apologized for taking so much of my time, thanked me for the beer and excused himself. Of course, it was I who felt grateful. Deacon's story answered many questions that I dared not ask Persimmon. There was no way I was going to forget that terrible tale, but I took the time to scribble down a few notes before going up to my room for the night. I never asked Deacon why he decided to confide in a stranger but clearly the incident in Kansas had affected him greatly and I think he just needed to get it off his chest. On the way up to my room the wonder of it hit me. How could a man love a woman so dearly that losing her would change the very fabric of his being and torment him so for years after? I was not sure if I pitied Persimmon—or envied him.

The next morning, I woke to my eyes heavily matted from the trail dust the day before. I guess it was my punishment for pouting and trailing Persimmon at a distance. Rather than bother to check my watch, I decided that I would go downstairs to the saloon and have something to eat. Maybe Persimmon had gone on without me. Maybe he hadn't. Despite all that had happened, I could not bring myself to slip away. If someone had asked me, I would probably have said it was the writer in me who was reluctant to let go of a good story. I also did not want Persimmon to see me as a coward who slunk away.

I was taking my first bite of breakfast when Persimmon eased his throbbing head down the stairs. He saw me and slowly made his way to my table.

"That looks good," he said, spying my eggs and ham steak.

"It is," I replied and waved my hand to catch the attendant's attention.

Persimmon ordered the same but with addition of a watered-down shot of whiskey. When it arrived, he softly sucked down his analgesic and after a couple of eggs were settled in his stomach, he spoke.

"I'm headed to Richmond today. There's a ticket for you if you're coming."

Though I had known him a short time, I knew that was Persimmon's way of asking me to come along. It was nice to be wanted, but I had my concerns, though what I had learned from Deacon the night before put Persimmon's actions in a context that made them seem less irrational. I was inclined to join him and hope he could keep his promise to not kill me or let me get shot. Despite an obvious hangover, he seemed in good humor so I asked, "Do you normally kill most of a dozen men in three days?"

"It's been a busy week," Persimmon quipped in a dull monotone.

"What's in Richmond?" I inquired.

"Not sure. Some men want me to do a job, I don't know what, but they said they'd pay $400 if I came to listen to them in person. And I don't think any of Lizard Johnson's friends are going to follow us back east if that is what concerns you." Persimmon did not mention why he decided to take the meeting but $400 happened to be what he left with the reverend to help the Mexican boy and his mother.

I huffed a soft laugh. Sure, I could not help but to look over my shoulder at the thought of Lizard Johnson. His dead friends also had friends, but what worried me was the unknown. In fact, it had troubled me throughout the night. Most people, generally, can depend on a reasonable expectation of what tomorrow will bring but I forfeited that comfort when I stepped aboard the train to Richmond with Persimmon Apricot.

IX
RICHMOND

As it turned out, the telegram Persimmon sent before we headed to South Pueblo was, in part, to request a second train ticket for me and my horse. Whoever this mystery group was, they were willing to pay for Persimmon and I to have a comfortable trip. We each had a bunk in a sleeper car. We stashed our saddlebags wrapped in our bunk blankets and the rest of our gear went to the baggage car. It had been some years since I last traveled by train or steamer and all the first afternoon, I basked in being unencumbered with no horse to tend nor gear to lug about.

There was some small talk between us but I was still uneasy and weighed every word I said to Persimmon. Better to become more familiar with his moods before asking too many more questions, I thought. The first night we ate in the dining car and then repaired to a nearby coach to review the passing scenery until nightfall left us with only our reflections in the glass. I was surprised when Persimmon asked the porter for good brandy. We sipped from crystal snifters like gentlemen and talked of nothing.

The novelty of being unencumbered was soon replaced by boredom. When our idle talk dried up, it was the boredom that finally won out against my caution and I gathered the courage to ask about Richmond and what lay ahead. Before I could, a beautiful lady in a fashionable green dress passed along the aisle, herding a small child to the dining car.

Persimmon observed them until they left our car. The expression on his face darkened. He sloshed the last of his brandy against the back of his throat then pulled a flask from his coat pocket opposite his revolver and began to nurse it. With each sip he became less engaged in our conversation, preferring to stare into the blackness outside at something which I could not see. I recognized this demeanor as what I had seen amidst the rocks and again before he killed the drunk. I let him be.

The following evening began much the same way except sweatier. I had forgotten about summer humidity back east and had acclimated to the dry western air. Proper etiquette compelled me to wear my jacket to supper, but I quickly shed it in our coach. Despite barely having two dollars to rub together, I felt it was only right that I provide the brandy this time, but Persimmon paid the porter and told me to have whatever I liked because the men in Richmond were paying our expenses. All this pampering was fast eroding my angst over joining Persimmon.

After having given it careful consideration for two days, I decided to approach Persimmon with some advice.

"I don't know where you hail from originally—" I began.

"Richmond," Persimmon barked, anticipating my eventual point.

"Oh… Well then, you should know better than I do about how things are done there. I've never been to Virginia…" I was about to trail off point but I caught myself. "I don't want to get you riled at me but—"

"Didn't I tell you I wouldn't kill you? I won't. At least I won't as long as you don't shoot at me or call me a liar…" A quick thought flashed in his eyes. "You calling me a liar?" Persimmon asked from under a brow raised inquisitively and somewhat sarcastically.

"*No!*" I blurted, thrusting forward an out-turned palm in defense. "I just thought it might be good to remind you that back east is a bit more genteel and the law is less forgiving than what you have grown accustomed to these last few years. It would probably be good if you didn't shoot anyone else. Least wise, not while we are east of the Mississippi."

The tension in my chest abated when Persimmon let go a laugh and quipped, "I'll see what I can do but I make no promises."

The day we arrived in Richmond Persimmon wasted no time. After collecting our horses, we rode deep into the business district. I had forgotten how loud horseshoes could be on paved streets through canyons of brick and mortar. My mind was occupied with the passing drays and carriages and the general bustling of the town and I failed to note where we were when we stopped at a multistoried building of red brick and marble corniced windows.

I followed Persimmon to the top floor where the stairway deposited us on a large open landing. Across the room from the stairs sat a little man at a desk, shuffling through papers in a manner that seemed for our benefit. Around the right side of the room, from the railing to behind the desk, were a row of office doors adorned with gold name plates. Set in the center of the left wall was a set of double doors without labels.

The little man looked up from his alleged work and over a pair of reading glasses at us and asked, domineeringly, "May I help you?"

"I'm here to see Mr. Donovan and Mr. Connelly," Persimmon instructed without the least bit of subservience in his voice.

"Who should I tell them is calling?" the little man asked in a commanding tone which exceeded his stature and station.

"Tell them Mr. Apricot is here," Persimmon responded with equal authority.

I worried about the little man's reaction to the name, waiting for him to crack a smile or for Persimmon to put his hand on his pistol but all he gripped was his hat in his left hand. It was a good sign, but it did not ease the tension I felt.

"Mr. Donovan and Mr. Connelly are in a board meeting right now. You may take a seat over there." The little man pointed to a pew-like bench to my right, along the railing.

Persimmon's civility was beginning to slip. First, he swapped hands on his hat, swept his hair back with his left hand and chased it with his hat, placing it back on his head as I had always seen it. I saw it as a clear sign that he was done being mannerly. Then he stepped up to the desk where his cold stare would loom over the little man for greater effect.

"Listen here, I've been on a train across country at their request and—" Persimmon stopped, his attention grabbed by voices seeping from the crack between the double doors.

Turning toward the voices, Persimmon marched as if to burst through the double doors but the little man was quick as lightning. Not halfway to the double doors, he was upon Persimmon, grabbing at his elbow before he could open the door. Persimmon swung his right hand over his assailant's arm, snatching the little man by the lapel.

Before Persimmon could fling him down the stairs, which is what I imagine would have happened next, I sprung across the landing and as far between them as I could wedge myself, throwing up my left arm from under theirs and tossing my thumb back to point at Persimmon. "Do you see this face?" I asked the little man as I stared into his frightened eyes, "Does this look like the sort of man you want to test? I've personally seen him kill a dozen men this week." It was an exaggeration but not by much.

It worked. Persimmon shoved the little man aside and pushed open the double door. Inside the board room several older gentlemen stared back at us in surprise.

"I'm sorry, Mr. Connelly," apologized the little man to the pudgy gentleman standing at the far end of a table, "I told him you were in a meeting but he wouldn't hear of it."

"Who are you sir?" Mr. Connelly demanded, politely.

"Persimmon Apricot."

Mr. Connelly's face softened to what appeared to be relief and then brightened as he held out a hand to reassure the little man. "It's fine, Mr. Smith, let these gentlemen in, let them in."

The little man, Mr. Smith, looked disgusted at being countermanded and slank back to his stack of papers. The injury to his pride must have drowned common decency for he never did thank me for saving him worse injury to his person.

"Please, come in, have a seat, have a cigar or a drink. We were just discussing your imminent arrival." Mr. Connelly made gestures of hospitality while other men swept us into the room and closed the door behind.

Mr. Connelly tried to continue but Persimmon was still agitated and held up his hand. "Hold on a moment." Persimmon refused a chair and instead, rolled it under the table and stood behind it with his large hands clutching at the plush leather. "I don't mean to sound greedy but there was a matter of $400 plus expenses to be paid upon arrival."

"Yes, of course." Mr. Connelly motioned to one of the other men who nodded and left the room. "I don't want you to think we are anything less than honorable men."

The man who left the room returned and paid Persimmon. Satisfied, Persimmon stuffed the cash in his coat pocket and asked, "So, what is it that requires my traveling over half a continent to hear it told in person?"

"Mr. Donovan, would you like to explain our situation to Mr. Apricot?" Mr. Connelly asked the balding gentleman to his left. Mr. Donovan cleared his throat as Mr. Connelly took a seat.

"About a year ago—"

"Sixteen months," Mr. Connelly interjected.

"Yes," Mr. Donovan continued, "Sixteen months ago we entered into a business venture with some gentlemen to purchase lands out of speculation. Well, you see..." Mr. Donovan hesitated as he fished for a delicate way to phrase their situation.

"You got swindled," Persimmon offered as a fact, not a question.

"We got swindled," Mr. Connelly confirmed, posturing in his chair with his arms spread on the table in confirmation that the cat was now out of the bag.

The man who had fetched Persimmon's money was eying me whilst I stood in the background. I suspect he was the sort of character who becomes belligerent when embarrassed, and with his dirty laundry being aired amongst strangers, felt the need to change the subject. He forcefully interrupted, "Who is this man?" as he looked to Mr. Connelly but pointed a boney old finger at me.

"That's Pete," Persimmon said, matter-of-factly.

Mr. Connelly looked at me, then at Persimmon whose face must have indicated that he considered the question answered. I stood a couple of paces behind Persimmon. Curious but prudent, Mr. Connelly gestured in my direction while turning back to the older man to say, "That's Pete," with puzzlement in his voice. "I'm sure if he is an associate of Mr. Apricot's we can trust him with our business."

The older man was less than satisfied but he did not press the matter. I stepped a half-stride to the right to put Persimmon's bulk between me and the old man's disapproving glare. Mr. Donovan cleared his throat.

"So, yes... after several weeks without contact we began to grow concerned. Eventually we came to the conclusion previously stated and sought means of redress. That is why we called on you." Mr. Donovan seemed to have a knack for slow-walking to the point.

"You couldn't tell me that via telegram? Why didn't you contact the Pinkertons?" Persimmon prodded to get answers to the questions which interested him.

"Well, we did. We hired the Pinkerton Agency and they pursued the matter. In fact, they are still on the case but their investigation has gone down a dead end. That's where you come in." Mr. Donovan was about to stumble upon a conclusion when Persimmon interrupted again.

"How *did* you find me anyway?"

"It took a sizeable effort, I assure you," Mr. Connelly chimed back in, "The Pinkertons were more successful in that effort."

"So then, how can I be of more help than the Pinkertons and why am I here?" Persimmon's demeanor had softened since his questions were being answered.

"You're here because the matter is a delicate one and we thought it would be best to explain it in person," Mr. Connelly vaguely replied.

Mr. Donovan cleared his throat again, a habit to announce he was preparing to speak. "The Pinkertons found the man with whom we had conducted most of our business but his partners turned out to be aliases."

"Why didn't you arrest the one man they found?" Persimmon asked, still trying to steer the conversation through the order in which he was most interested.

"Because he no longer has our money. The Pinkertons did question him and per his account, his partners swindled him too. So far, his meager lifestyle has bolstered his claim. Unfortunately, he is either unable, or more likely, unwilling to reveal any information about his partners. The Pinkertons thought it might help to observe him for a time and see if he makes contact with them or leads us to some or all of the money but nothing has materialized."

"I don't understand, if he was part of stealing your money, why isn't he in jail?"

"Though we did have our attorney check the validity of the contract, it was their attorney who drew it up. We've since learned that their attorney is a scoundrel in his own right with an office in Washington. He must have been in league with the missing partners because it was he who allowed their aliases on the contracts. More importantly, he made sure the man we have under surveillance was not listed on the contract. They managed to finagle our meetings so that what he signed was not the same contract. In short, they fooled him and now we cannot prove he has any legal responsibility for the money." Mr. Donovan paused, expecting another question from Persimmon.

Persimmon obliged. "All of that is well and good but you have yet to make plain how and why you contacted me. I've never met any of you before."

"Actually, that's not altogether true..." Mr. Connelly began and then hesitated with a look of self-consternation. "I'm sorry, where are my manners? I just realized you have not been properly introduced to our other members.

This is Mr. Johnson," Mr. Connelly said, pointing with his hand palm up at the older man who was still staring suspiciously at me. "And the gentleman on the end there is Mr. Haspel. You might not remember him but he worked in the Norfolk Shipyard when you were there and knew of your background."

Mr. Haspel stood and offered a friendly hand to Persimmon who took it.

"Don't feel bad about not recognizing me after almost twenty years. The war and the Gosport Shipyard were long ago."

Mr. Haspel was gracious but Mr. Johnson sat inaccessible, trying to burn a hold through me with his squinty eyes.

"It was Mr. Haspel who first suggested that you might be of help and—"

Persimmon interrupted, "Why? Get to the point and tell me why right now or so help me—"

"Because..." Mr. Connelly squawked anxiously, then grunted and collected himself. The resignation of a cornered fugitive hung on his cheeks. He glanced at Mr. Donovan then turned back to Persimmon and in an exhausted voice he began again. "Because the man we need you to interrogate is Richard Grant."

"What in the *hell* makes you think I would want to see him again?" Persimmon boomed angrily, chiding more than asking.

Mr. Donovan answered first. "Based on your war record and more so, your relationship with Richard Grant, we thought perhaps you could ascertain information from him that others could not."

"And based on some of the stories relayed to us while hunting for you, we feel more strongly than ever that you are the man for the job," Mr. Connelly said, returning to his earlier, confident self. "I think you are probably the only man Richard Grant would be more afraid of than those he's protecting."

"Not interested," Persimmon snapped and turned for the door.

"There's $10,000 in it for you," Mr. Haspel exclaimed, throwing a hand up to indicate Persimmon should stop and reconsider.

"$10,000? Just how much did they steal from you?" Persimmon asked.

"A quarter of a million," came the embarrassed reply from the end of the table.

Persimmon grunted a laugh. "I guess it serves you right for trusting that no-account bastard... then again, I don't suppose you knew any better."

"So, you'll do it then?" Mr. Haspel asked with renewed hope. "There's $10,000 if you recoup our losses and $2000 if all we gain is justice."

"Still not interested. Besides, you wouldn't want me to find him because I would likely kill him as soon as I laid eyes on him and then what good would he be to you?" Persimmon warned, without cracking a smile.

As Persimmon stepped toward the door, old Mr. Johnson finally took interest in something other than me. He stood abruptly, slammed his palms down and leaned over the table at Persimmon.

"See here, we've gone to a great deal of effort and expense to find you and bring you here," Mr. Johnson scolded.

Persimmon spun back around and I saw his gun hand fly up but he caught himself halfway. "That is your problem," Persimmon growled.

"Then why did you come here and further waste our time and money?" Mr. Johnson argued.

"Curiosity and $400," was Persimmon's honest retort.

"Now then Mr. Johnson, as much as it might disappoint us, Mr. Apricot has no obligation to us. Finding him was our choice and his coming here without any foreknowledge as to why, was our offer. We chose to take that gamble." Mr. Connelly worked to soothe the belligerent Mr. Johnson before making one last effort to convince Persimmon. "I do wish you would reconsider, Mr. Apricot. It could very well be easy money for you."

Snatching open the double doors revealed Mr. Smith eavesdropping, drawn by the commotion. Persimmon swept the little man aside with the back of his arm and headed for the stairs. I was left to awkwardly bid the men good day but before I left the room, Mr. Connelly addressed me, nearly begging, "Please, try to get him to reconsider."

I nodded to appease Mr. Connelly, knowing full well I had no say in what Persimmon did.

With the bulk of the afternoon to kill, we rode through town in what seemed to me an aimless manner. After a bit of wondering who Richard Grant was and why Persimmon hated him so, we stopped in front of a vacant lot near the outskirts of the city. In fact, several homes were missing but vacant lots were still common sights in war ravaged southern towns. It was not until I noticed Persimmon's longing stare that I realized this particular location meant something to him. As we wound our way back to the center of town, we slowed or stopped at several other places. I desperately wanted to ask about each but I was afraid of hitting a nerve. Plus, it seemed rude to pry as one waxed nostalgic.

We did make one practical stop at a gun seller's shop where Persimmon sold the weapons he took off the corpses of the would-be assassins. If he did not want anyone to come asking questions about a familiar gun what has lost its owner, selling it a half continent away made sense. How many such transactions had Persimmon made over the years?

We arrived at Ford's Hotel in downtown Richmond around three in the afternoon. Persimmon requested two rooms from the desk clerk who handed him the keys. Persimmon took one key and motioned for the clerk to hand the other to me.

"I'll see you in the morning in the dining room," Persimmon told me without facing me.

Once he was up the first flight of stairs, I turned to the clerk and asked if Persimmon had paid for my room to which the clerk confirmed as much. I had assumed he would from the expense money given to him by the Richmond Consortium, as I came to call Mr. Connelly, Donovan, Johnson and Haspel.

Still, it was a relief because I could not have afforded a room at that hotel. The thought of it started me worrying about my finances. I knew I could not depend on Persimmon's patronage once we returned to Colorado. Following Persimmon might make for a great book, someday, but in the meantime, I had to eat. I stored my gear in my room and took a walk to ponder my options.

"Of course!" I thought, feeling like an imbecile as I passed the offices of a local paper, *The Commonwealth*. I walked right in and asked for the editor. I introduced myself as a newspaper man and author of some renown in the West. Eastern papers looked down their noses at most of their western counterparts so I doubted the exaggeration of my credentials would ever come back to haunt me.

I explained my current project and gave examples of the storyline and when I left the editor's office it was with a written agreement for a serial based on the exploits of Persimmon Apricot. I had not abandoned the idea of a book, but in the interim, I could be earning a living with a serial and then later combine my short stories into a novel. My agreement was to mail in regular stories with instructions as to where to wire my payment. The editor could also offer the serial for syndication but only along the eastern seaboard states per our agreement.

The latter restriction was a precautionary one. I figured I could tell the entire story as I experienced it, even the shooting of the two men in the rocks, as long as the information did not get back to the authorities in Colorado. As an added measure, I decided to change Persimmon's name for the stories. I would decide on a name later.

I began writing the first installment that evening in my hotel room and would finish it up on the train. Things were looking up, although the deal I had struck meant I was bound to Persimmon if I wanted it to pay off. Oh, and of course it required that I did not get killed either.

X
BACK TO COLORADO

Mornings seemed to favor Persimmon's mood, at least when he was not being ambushed. He found me in the dining room of Ford's Hotel where I had coffee waiting. I've never seen a man for whom a mild hangover suited him but it tended to mellow Persimmon. Despite that, I had poor expectations for our first day back on the train due to the stirring of sentiment by his visit to Richmond.

On the other hand, I was far chipper with a contract in my pocket guaranteeing me my first steady income in years and already a month's worth of material to write about. At one installment per week, I was sure Persimmon would resupply me with material before I ran dry. The one point which continued to nag me was whether I should wrap the story in anonymity? Unlike what the reader finds in these pages, I decided that for the casual newspaper reader, the character names and a few details could be fudged and the readership would be just as happy and none the wiser.

On the train, I excused myself for the afternoon to write my first installment. I took the first hour to decide on the similar sounding name Pete Simmons for Persimmon's serial alias. By 4 o'clock I handed the porter an envelope containing my first installment to be mailed to the paper in Richmond. With that accomplished I sought out Persimmon, who I found asleep on a bench. I sat contently across from him, satisfied with myself more than I had been in ages.

When Persimmon woke, we went to the dining car, talking of nothing important. Afterwards, we adjourned to our bench seats with our now customary snifter of brandy. Persimmon's mood had not soured, so, after a few minutes of internal debate, I decided to carefully choose my wording and asked, "Would it be improper for me to inquire who Richard Grant is?"

The hair on my nape bristled from the cold stare Persimmon gave me. The pursed lips and scrunched brow were uncomfortably reminiscent of the scene in the rocks. I threw up my hands in submission and swore, "I won't mention it again."

Persimmon turned to the window and a few moments later let out a long sigh. His expression softened and I do believe he was remorseful for having reacted so to me a second time. Though he did not say as much, his apology was in his tone when he said, "I will be glad to discuss almost anything else you like."

Not wanting to lose the invitation, I smiled to buy a moment's thought and raced through my list of questions which had been growing. I chose one I thought might be a good primer and hoped it was not too personal.

"That Mr...." I stumbled. I should have brought the man's name to mind before speaking. "Mr. Haspel, was it? He said he knew you at the shipyard? Will you tell me about your time there? It sounded as though you had an interesting war career."

"I don't remember that old man but I did work at the Norfolk Shipyard. It was still known as Gosport back then." Persimmon breathed deeply and let out another sigh to reset the story. "I was sixteen when the war started. I was the head of the house but *the cause* was calling away my friends and I wanted to join them. My mother and I fought about it for a bit, but my mother had a friend who had a relative, high up at the shipyard and could put me to work. It was a compromise which I had intended to be short-lived.

"As it turned out, I arrived at the yard while the *CSS Virginia* was taking shape. They had her raised from where the Yankees scuttled her. I know some folks never stopped calling her the *Merrimac*, but the *Merrimac* was just the burned hull we started with. She was a completely different boat when she took the name *Virginia*."

It was the first time I had heard what pride sounded like in Persimmon's voice. Not prideful arrogance but pride of accomplishment. I never expected where this story would lead.

"I turned out to be an office boy at the yard. I thought I was going to build ships and maybe set sail on one but instead I ran errands. She never admitted to it but I think it was my mother's doing. As it turned out, it was fortuitous. There was a fella' at the yard whose seniority put him above suspicion, and due to my lowly position, he never paid me any mind. I don't know that I would have paid him any mind either, except that I started noticing him in places I didn't think he should have been. I thought he must have been put on the *CSS Virginia* build but when the topic came up, I was told that this fella' had nothing to do with that project.

"Thinking back on it, I don't remember what made me so suspicious, but I started spying on him and eventually found him to be taking documents and drawings and giving them to a man he met late at night outside of town. The short of it is, I caught a spy. Word went up the chain of command and someone got the idea I would make a good spy hunter, because no one would expect a boy to do the job. They quietly moved me from job to job wherever they thought something might be compromised. It wasn't long before my age caught up with me and not being a soldier was going to seem more suspicious than any spy so I was ordered to feign a clubfoot. Wore the instep of a boot out that way, dragging it around.

"By then, several of my friends were dead. One was missing a leg. What I was doing seemed a lot safer and then again, more dangerous at the same time, and I got to sleep in clean sheets. Only one other time did I get on the trail of another spy but he got nervous and fled up north."

Persimmon's story was lackluster but interesting, though I could not help but to feel he was leaving something out. What, I don't know, but Persimmon had made it very clear that what he shared with me was his prerogative. One thing of which I was fairly sure, whatever the reason for the Richmond Consortium to seek out Persimmon, it had more to do with his relationship with Richard Grant than his spy catching days.

Our conversation on the return trip was always pleasant, though I never felt I had an invitation to pry into personal topics. Despite this, I did learn valuable lessons for if I ever got into a shootout. For instance, never holster your gun after you shoot the fella' shooting at you. Watch the crowd because he might have a friend waiting to shoot you in the back. Keep your eyes on the crowd and back your way out. It was advice I had witnessed firsthand with Persimmon but hoped I'd never use it personally.

This was followed by a darker suggestion to be careful when granting mercy. "Most folks who would offend you in the first place do not have the sense to discern mercy from weakness," were the words of Persimmon. He also gave the same advice from the opposite point of view. "Careful you don't confuse mercy and weakness; it's a deadly mistake. Mercy stems from power and if you offend the one with that power, there is no guarantee you'll get another chance."

There was no fault in what Persimmon said but it struck me that his mention of, "another chance," conflicted with the portrait of him, painted by Deacon, of a man who disregarded his own life. At least I thought so before he added, "Avoid a fight if you can, because once the bullets start flying, the outcome is never certain."

"But I have seen you trudge headlong into a fight that wasn't yours or wasn't necessary," I said, vigorously challenging his wisdom with his own actions.

"Yep," was Persimmon's chilling reply.

Not having been shot at for several days was spoiling me. That and my newly found financial security had me in a relaxed state. It was not until we had ridden half-way up the valley from South Pueblo that I noticed the tension creeping back into my chest. Persimmon said he wanted to, "check on things," by which I assumed he meant the boy and his mother. If Persimmon ever planned more than one day in advance, I could not tell it, hence the tightening of my ribcage. Somehow, I felt like if I could plan on being shot at I could prepare myself. What I did know was that Lizard Johnson still had friends who were alive and hunting revenge. By now, those same men were also missing their buddies whom Persimmon killed in the rocks, not to mention the one he shot in the street and the others he cut down in the Bansheen saloon. Our return to the contentious little town was good for my stories but bad for my nerves, if not my health.

We entered town between the saloons where I had first met Persimmon. I looked to my left at the Bansheen Saloon and prayed a silent prayer of thanksgiving that it seemed quiet for now. For a moment, I thought Persimmon might pass on by without stopping for refreshments but that was wishful thinking. My nervous gaze searched the town as we dismounted. Finding no threats amongst its quaint store fronts, I followed Persimmon by ear as I stared anxiously over my shoulder at the Bansheen across the street. For my fearful investigation, the only danger I discovered was gravity when the toe of my boot hung on the lip of the porch, nearly pitching me headlong.

We had barely broken into the gloom of the no name saloon when the heartening cry of McLaglen hit my ears. "Welcome back, my friends!"

Persimmon held up a greeting hand. McLaglen marched across the room to meet us, wiping his hands on a filthy bar towel along the way. At the last step he whipped the towel over his left shoulder and took Persimmon by the hand, shaking it vigorously.

"How are things around here?" Persimmon asked.

McLaglen understood the question was not just casual banter. "Restless," the saloon keeper answered, the cheerfulness draining from his voice. "Rumor has it a couple of Lizard's friends went looking for you and no one's seen them since."

"Is that so?" was Persimmon's neutral response.

"Everyone thinks you ran off and hid. Everyone but that US Marshal. He's still trying to trap them Jensen boys but said he had some questions for you when you were man enough to turn up again. How he figured you would come back, I don't know." Being a bartender, and by extension a meddler, McLaglen had told what he knew, setting up the topic he wanted to know more about and now he was ready to listen.

Persimmon did not take the bait. His business was his alone. Instead, Persimmon asked, "Have you seen the reverend?"

McLaglen held up a finger indicating Persimmon should wait a moment, then walked to the door leading to the back room. He stuck his head in and yelled out as if calling someone from deep in a cave. When the young man emerged, McLaglen ordered, "Go fetch the reverend." As the boy headed across the empty saloon, McLaglen added, "And keep Mr. Apricot's being here to yourself."

McLaglen had time enough to pour two beers before the young man, who I gathered to be his son, returned with the reverend in tow.

"He was already on his way up here," the young man announced as he burst in, tossing his thumb up over his shoulder to point at the reverend.

"I thought I recognized that horse," the reverend declared in a voice which seemed genuinely happy to see Persimmon.

The two swapped pleasantries briefly before Persimmon asked how the boy was doing.

"Fine, considering. Doc has his eye bandaged up. He said we won't know for a week or two if the boy will be able to see out of it or not. Whatever amount of vision returns, it might be some time before we know just how much." The reverend was even tempered, knowing it was the best to be made of a bad situation.

"It was completely uncalled for," Persimmon snapped, his increasing irritation resonating across the room. "If I could kill him twice, I gladly would."

I could see the reverend was taken aback by Persimmon's hateful words but being unsure how Persimmon would respond, he chose not to address them. Nevertheless, as the reverend continued, I realized he understood Persimmon's hate was driven by concern for the boy. It was loathing for the evils in the world.

"The money you left us made the payment. The bank didn't give me any trouble but Mrs. Sanchez still owes the bank almost $12,000." The reverend did not verbally declare her situation hopeless but doubt filled his voice. "I've been talking to Mr. Fortson, the mine owner, again. I've been trying to convince him to invest in a small herd of cattle. Unfortunately, like everyone else, he seems to see Mrs. Sanchez as simply a widow woman with a huge debt, no collateral and an extra mouth to feed."

"Well... maybe that's the way of it," Persimmon said, snidely.

Persimmon was no optimist but his calloused remark surprised me. The reverend's brow rose in disappointment. I got the impression he was up to something and Persimmon's was not the response for which he had hoped. Undaunted, the reverend was prepared to advance his plan.

"Maybe it is, but it doesn't have to be. If she had a partner who could manage the herd, someone who her investors could see as competent to run the place, I'm sure it would make all the difference."

"I don't know anything about raising cattle," Persimmon rebutted, anticipating that the reverend intended to corner him.

Prepared to meet resistance, the reverend paused to regroup his thoughts then said, "You told me you believed in God but had not seen Him come to town in a while. What if He sent you to town, to this town?"

"I hardly think He sent me. The only place He's ever sent me was to hell," Persimmon growled.

A solemnness struck me as Persimmon's resentment toward God reminded me of the story Deacon had conveyed. I carried my beer over to a table and sat down, feeling the weight of wonder as to the point of life. A series of choices, that is life for most people. There are the bad choices, the ones you know are accompanied by bad consequences and are not surprised when that is what happens. Then there are all the other choices. The bad choices seem to be the only ones with guarantees as to their outcomes. The ones that seem like good choices only come with probabilities of a good outcome; nothing is certain. Then you have the neutral choices—the majority which fall somewhere between good and bad. The only way to see their outcomes is through hindsight but hindsight often leaves you with regrets and speculating on what-ifs.

I knew what the reverend would say, that God gives us guidelines so that we live the happy lives he desires for us, but I could not help thinking of Persimmon's choices and wondering where he could have gone wrong to deserve, well...

I might have asked the reverend about it but, realizing he was not going to make headway with Persimmon through the guilt of spiritual duties, the reverend had turned to arguing the financial virtues of his plan to Persimmon.

Frustrated, I stopped listening to the reverend or my melancholy inner voice. Instead, I wished loudly in my head for a distraction. It came in the form of the Mexican boy's mother, Mrs. Sanchez. She blew through the open door and strode across the empty saloon. Persimmon turned, startled at the commotion she made.

"Mr. Apricot, I am so happy you have returned. I am sorry I was not gracious before. I thought you might be some of Jenkins' men. Please, please come with me... You too," Mrs. Sanchez begged, looking to me and motioning for me to join.

Her English was good and her accent delightful in the ear. I felt a bit silly when I realized how wide my grin had stretched. As I approached the group, I caught her glance at the reverend and the sheepish expression on his face. Had the reverend set this up? Were the pair of them in cahoots?

"Come, I will cook for you. Please let me, it is all I know to do to thank you."

Not having yet received my first payment from the Richmond paper and no longer being patriated by the Richmond Consortium, I was unsure where my next meal lay. Mrs. Sanchez's gracious offer was a small blessing in my opinion. I watched Persimmon's eyes, unsure of how he would react to a beautiful woman tugging at his hand. When finally, Persimmon gave in, I was happy to tag along.

Mrs. Sanchez had a one-horse shay that she drove into town and I guessed she would have sold it if not for the long walk it would have left her. We followed her out of town a few miles, then down into the valley where her modest ranch house sat. The house was in good order, but barren and a bit stuffy inside. A few chickens pecked about the yard and a milk cow crowded the corner of a pen intended for a dozen more. Beyond that nothing moved and inside the home, the main room was stark except for one plush, high-backed rocker and a small dining table with four uncomfortable, straight-backed chairs.

Mrs. Sanchez insisted that Persimmon take the rocker. I pulled one of the dining chairs near the front window and sat in its fresh air. It was late afternoon and I watched as the mountain shadows stretched ever closer to the river below. Mrs. Sanchez disappeared into the kitchen and Persimmon had fallen asleep with his head propped in the wing of the rocker. The dining chair was stiff and writhing around in it only made it creak disturbingly but did not make it softer. My rear end was a bit saddle sore anyway, and I decided to go outside and wash myself in the soft, early evening breeze.

It was a nice ranch. I did not know how many acres but it was as pleasant a setting as ever one sat. I was thinking it was a good place for a boy to grow up, when it dawned on me that I had not seen the Sanchez boy. Soon, I could see through the window that Mrs. Sanchez was setting the small table. I offered to help but she would not hear of it. Instead, I went back inside and nudged Persimmon to wake him. When he cracked his eyes open, I gave a sideways nod toward the table. He looked, saw the dishes and sat up, rubbing his eyes. When Mrs. Sanchez emerged from the kitchen again, I asked her about her son.

"He will be here soon. Mr. Freeman gave him light duty at his store. He has Sancho sweep the clean floor and then pays him far more than the job is worth. Mr. Freeman thinks he is fooling us but I know better. I am thankful to have such good friends as him and his wife and the reverend and his wife too. Now I also have you two as my new friends. I..." Mrs. Sanchez choked up unexpectedly and said nothing more while she fetched the food from the kitchen.

When she returned, her voice had settled but her mood was more solemn. "Was the reverend trying to convince you to help me with the ranch?" Mrs. Sanchez asked, rhetorically. She knew the answer and continued without waiting for a response. "I told him not to. He, and his wife, they mean well. I think they would like to play matchmaker but do not worry, I have told them that such things aren't theirs to meddle in. You are just a stranger who has shown us kindness and I do not wish to burden you further."

I could not gauge what response she wanted, but no response is what Persimmon gave her. He remained silent, either uncertain about what he should say or lost in thought about his late wife. We ate quietly. I felt awkward about interjecting into a conversation which was Persimmon's, especially since he was not participating.

When I could stand the silence no longer, I asked, "How did you come to have the ranch?"

"My husband, Juan, his family has a little money. Not very rich but enough to help him buy this ranch. We were drawn north by the cattle boom in Wyoming but on the way, we found out about this valley and prices were good. It's a good place... a good town. It's a small town but filled with good people. At least it was before Jenkins came with his men. He lives near Leadville and that town suits him. Very violent there. His men manage the land he has stolen throughout the valley and they hang out here and blacken our town.

"We have a few prospectors and a few ranchers but it is the Fortson mine that keeps the town alive. If it dries up, the town will dry up with it. Then we will be caught between South Pueblo and Leadville. It doesn't matter though, because me and Sancho, we must leave here soon. I only feel bad for all the money we have wasted from the pockets of others. I wish I could sell the ranch to Jenkins for what we have paid into it but he has no reason to pay me when he can foreclose on us soon."

I knew I was prying into her business but unlike Persimmon, I didn't think she would shoot me, so I asked, "Where is your husband?"

Her elbows were on the table and her forehead propped on the heels of her hands. She shook her head slowly, pitifully and whimpered, "I don't know."

The crunch of wagon wheels on the rock-strewn road grew louder. Persimmon sat up at the ready and we both stared apprehensively into the twilight. Spotting the diminutive figure of the boy perched in the front seat let me catch my breath but Persimmon's shoulders returned to the slump of a man who knew no enemies.

I've always been accused of eating too fast and I was done, so I carried my chair back to the window, then opened the front door to let the boy inside. Sancho stopped, not knowing me at first but Mr. Freeman saw me and waved without hesitation. I assume he knew who I was, probably something to the effect of, "that bookish fella' who's ridin' with Mr. Apricot." At least that is the way I suspect most people referred to me. I waved back and our friendly exchange set Sancho at ease and he breezed past me to his mother. Mr. Freeman made no motion to intrude. He turned his wagon around, waved again over his shoulder and headed back from whence he came.

Inside, I sat near the window and pulled a small pipe from my pocket. It was a vice which I partook only occasionally, when the weather was right. This night, the air was soft with the breeze breaking warm then cool as it varied in direction and speed. I held up my small tobacco pouch to Persimmon who shook his head. I realized I had never seen Persimmon smoke. As far as I could tell, except for drinking, carousing saloons and killing folks, Persimmon did not have any vices.

The boy ran to his mother and she hugged him and then introduced us, explaining who Persimmon was and what he had done for them. Then she told him to sit in her chair while she went to the kitchen to fix him a plate. Instead, the boy stood next to the chair, staring at Persimmon with his one good eye. His left eye had a patch over it and a bandage which wrapped diagonally around his head. Persimmon stared back at the poor child. I was behind him and could not see his face but I saw Persimmon put his fist to his right eye and rub it. Had a tear welled up? The boy immediately stepped up beside Persimmon, paused a moment, then wrapped his arms around the big man and the stiff chair back.

Persimmon froze for a moment then spun his chair half around and rested his hand on the boy's head, letting it slide down to his shoulder. I could see a notion flash in Persimmon's eyes before stuffing his thumb and index finger into his vest pocket. From it, he drew the folded telegram from the Richmond Consortium and glared at it while he rubbed it between his fingers. I knew then, we were about to travel.

XI
SHORT ON SLEEP

The reverend showed up not long after the boy got home. A couple of Jenkins' men had gotten wind that we were back in the area. The men had left town suspiciously early in the evening and the reverend was concerned they might lay in wait, hoping to ambush us along the road. It was the reverend's suggestion that Persimmon and I stay over at the Sanchez ranch.

Being once a working ranch, there was a small bunkhouse. The reverend and I cleared the cobwebs and shook the dust off the bunk mattresses. Mindful of proprieties, the reverend bunked with us. Mrs. Sanchez did not appear to give the matter a bit of thought but the reverend was concerned for her reputation. I thought it was quaint until I found out how ferociously the reverend snored.

As Persimmon and I lay tossing and turning in our bunks, trying to find a position that would plug both ears, I remembered hearing tell of John Wesley Hardin shooting a man for snoring. It was a cowardly act with which I had never thought I could sympathize, but I was wrong. Persimmon was a far more dangerous man than Hardin, but honorable. That was good news for the reverend and bad news for our slumber.

The only saving grace was that the reverend was a very early riser. I finally fell sound asleep just before dawn and slept until late morning. When I woke, I found Persimmon in the main house and soon after, the reverend returned from where he had gone to town. He handed Persimmon a telegram as I stood on the porch with a cup of coffee and my shirt tail hanging out. Persimmon read it and then scribbled a reply on the back, sending the reverend back to town.

The reverend had volunteered to be Persimmon's runner to the telegraph office, desiring Persimmon to remain safe at the ranch. He was good intentioned but I am not sure how the reverend expected the rift between Persimmon and Jenkins' men to be resolved other than gunplay.

I caught a glimpse of the telegram and what Persimmon scratched on the back of it. He was negotiating with the Richmond Consortium to do the job for significantly more money. Persimmon offered to find Richard Grant's partners for $20,000. The Richmond Consortium had countered with $15,000. Persimmon gave them a final offer of $15,000 if all they received was justice but the full $20,000 if they recouped most of their money.

While we waited for the reply, a wagon approached. My stomach knotted up until the wagon came close enough to recognize the driver was Deputy Jim. He shook my hand and called me Pete. I was surprised he remembered my name, even if it was the wrong name. The deputy removed his hat as Mrs. Sanchez welcomed him inside.

"I was passing through and heard you were here," Jim said while shaking Persimmon's hand. "I wanted to thank you for saving my hide. You were right, we shouldn't've tried taking the Jensen boys, just the two of us."

"You thought it was your duty. Just remember to mix in a little common sense with it and you'll be fine. Duty might trump common sense when lives are on the line but getting yourself killed so Edwards can collect his bounty is foolish. How's the shoulder?" Persimmon nodded toward Jim's left side.

"Sore. Probably be awhile before I can mount a horse. In the meantime, I am stuck in a wagon which is easier on my shoulder but harder on my butt. They tried to get me to layup but I can't do it. I might not be of much use but I'm outside. Speaking of Marshal Edwards, I saw him in town, that's how I knew you were here. What does he have against you anyway? He has it in his mind that you know the whereabouts of a couple of missing fellas that work for Jenkins." Deputy Jim was one lawman who was on Persimmon's side and I was glad to see it.

Persimmon shook his head, "I'm not worried about Edwards."

"Well, watch yourself just the same. He strikes me as a bit touched," Deputy Jim warned. "I guess I best be going. I've got to make a delivery and finish my route. Best of luck to you."

The deputy shook hands with us again and left. About an hour later, the reverend returned with another telegram. The Richmond Consortium had consented to Persimmon's offer but wanted a guarantee that he would see the job through to the end. Persimmon huffed a short laugh, "Guess they think we just want to live off their money."

The last comment was pleasant to hear as I was happy to know Persimmon had included my expenses in the deal. What guarantee he could give them I did not know and maybe he didn't either, because his reply was simply, "I will."

Mrs. Sanchez fed all of us and then the reverend left again to send the message. Persimmon was sitting in the rocker when Mrs. Sanchez asked him, "Is it dangerous what you are going to do?"

"Maybe," Persimmon responded.

Mrs. Sanchez softly walked behind the rocking chair, reached over the back of it and cupped Persimmon's cheek in her hand. "Then don't go. Stay and let us work the ranch, or leave it behind, I do not care. But don't risk your life."

Persimmon's eyes softened and he reached up to clasp her hand in his. "You don't know me or the things I've done."

"I have heard many stories since that day you stood up for Sancho. Not one of them ever said you harmed an innocent man. We all need to find peace. If you will stay, I will help you find it." Mrs. Sanchez's words were sincere.

I am certain she had no idea what Persimmon was bound to do or why. As far as I knew, the reverend had not been told either. All I knew was that the men in Richmond hired Persimmon to find a man that he once knew and who had cheated them. Why that might be dangerous compared to any other day with Persimmon was speculative.

The sound of hooves drew Persimmon's attention away from Mrs. Sanchez. It was too soon to expect the reverend's return, had he forgotten something? I poked my head through the window to look around the corner of the house. It was Marshal Edwards and two other men.

Persimmon stood slowly, adjusted his holster under his arm, walked to the door and leaned nonchalantly against its frame. He faced the open valley ahead but his eyes cut to the right to follow Edwards' every move. Marshal Edwards rode front and center with what looked to be a couple of Jenkins' men tagging close behind. I could not tell if the Jenkins men were present to attest to Persimmon's guilt or if the marshal had deputized them, as none of the three sported badges.

The marshal waited until he was square with the front of the house before addressing Persimmon. When he did, pleasantries were skipped as he dove directly into a line of interrogation. "There are two men missing. What do you know about it?"

"What makes you think I know anything about it?" Persimmon answered with some semblance of calm.

"They left here on your trail and a couple of days later their horses came home without them in the saddle. It doesn't take much to put the facts together." The marshal's tone was stern and accusatory and I knew it would not be long before it wore thin with Persimmon.

I did not know if Persimmon would confess to killing them in self-defense and tell Edwards where to find their bodies amongst the rocks or if he would stubbornly persist in saying he knew nothing about it, but either way, I was willing to back him. Edwards was mean hearted and dare I say, crooked and a disgrace to his badge.

"Two men go to hunt me down and instead, they come up missing. What exactly are you driving at, Marshal?" Persimmon's calm was evaporating.

"You killed them, didn't you?" accused Edwards.

"Had two men tried to ambush me, you're damned right I would have killed them and I would have been justified in doing so..." Persimmon was riled but he paused and took a deep breath to cool his anger. "But I don't know anything of the men you are talking about."

Persimmon turned back into the house, indicating to Marshal Edwards that he considered the interrogation over. Being inside also forced the three men to have to funnel through the narrow doorway to get to Persimmon, and the contrast of the dark room to the daylight outside gave Persimmon further advantage. Persimmon looked at me, raised his brow and nodded sideways in the direction of Mrs. Sanchez.

Nodding that I understood, I put an arm behind Mrs. Sanchez and swept her from the room. It was then I realized I had not seen the boy all morning and was relieved to learn that, while I was asleep, Mr. Freeman had picked Sancho up for work at the store. The kitchen had a door leading out back of the house. When I was satisfied it was safe, I told Mrs. Sanchez to make her way to the root cellar a few yards away.

By this time, Marshal Edwards had dismounted and was on the porch, approaching the open front door. Persimmon had sat back in the rocker with a pillow in his lap. I tucked myself behind the kitchen door where I could witness the scene through the crack between the hinges.

"Where's that fella that's been riding with you? Get him out here so I can find out what he has to say about it." Marshal Edwards was demanding to see me but I had no intention of volunteering.

"What, you expect him to tell you something different? Sounds to me, Edwards, like you are calling me a liar." Persimmon was irritated and with his short fuse it would not be long before he was mad enough to kill.

About then I heard boots along the kitchen wall, outside. Looking at the back door, I noticed I had left it unlocked. Moving in haste but as quietly as I could, I managed to get to the kitchen door and lock it, then I sat down in front of it to be sure the Jenkins men could not out flank Persimmon. I heard the latch clatter lightly above my head when one of them tried to open the door. Then I thought I heard fast approaching hooves.

"Where is he?"

"Edwards, you've been out to get me for years and I'm tired of it," Persimmon growled.

The two men at the back door were distracted by the rider and retreated to their horses, much to my relief. However, the situation in the other room was quickly deteriorating and I had no idea who else had arrived.

"I said, where is he?" Marshal Edwards demanded.

The marshal's behavior was what I considered utmost dangerous. I do not know if he was fearless or simply mad. Would presenting myself alleviate the tension? I thought better of it. At best, the marshal would likely turn his anger to me and at worst, the men outside would then know where I was and that my attention was engaged.

"That's it. You want to go heels with me so badly, let's go!" Persimmon shot up from the rocker, flinging the pillow aside, exposing his gun hand already bearing his Schofield but still pointing it to the floor.

I scrambled across the kitchen floor so I could see both men. The marshal had flinched but was smart enough not to try to outdraw an opponent with gun in hand. From beyond the front door I heard someone yelling, "Stop! Stop!" followed by a scuffle of boots on the porch and, "Get out of the way," as someone shoved past another. The reverend rushed through the door and between Persimmon and the marshal.

"Stop it this instant! What good do you expect to come from this for either of you?" the reverend scolded. I was impressed with his courage to wade into such an unstable situation.

"You threatened a United States Marshal with a firearm. You're under arrest," the marshal boldly declared, assuming he was safe in the presence of the reverend.

"I never pointed my gun at you," Persimmon rebutted.

"I have a witness," the marshal replied, backhanding a thumb toward the reverend.

"No, you don't," the reverend snapped, "I could see Persimmon from the time he jumped up out of the chair. He never once pointed it at you. That's the truth and that's what I will tell the court. It's no wonder why he would have his pistol out with the likes of these men you have in tow." The reverend tipped his head back in the direction of the two men who worked for Jenkins.

"It'll be your word against mine," the marshal said snidely.

"A marshal's word vs that of a preacher's? That would be an interesting day in court." The reverend was out of ideas and he knew if he could not alleviate the matter here and now, either someone was going to get shot immediately or if Persimmon was arrested, it was likely someone would kill him while he was awaiting trial.

It was not my preference to do anything to get myself on the bad side of the marshal but I felt compelled to show myself. Stepping into the room cautiously, my open hands held out forward and spread, I was still moving when the reverend and marshal locked eyes on me.

"You, tell me what you saw here," the marshal demanded of me.

"I saw just what the reverend described." I am sure my delivery was unconvincing but on this matter, I was telling the truth.

"What were you doing back there anyway? Did you have me at gunpoint?" the marshal asked. Perhaps, from his point of view, it was not a paranoid question.

"I don't have a gun on me or in the kitchen. I was at the back door when you came inside and I was afraid that if I walked in and made myself known, I might startle you and you might mistake me for an adversary and shoot me." This statement could have been true had things played out differently. It was believable.

"You are all in cahoots. We can let the court decide and you can still sit in jail while we wait." The marshal was flustered and sought reprisal.

The reverend saw an opportunity in the marshal's voice and pounced. "It will only be an embarrassment for you if you do. It's also inappropriate for you to have brought those men here and you know it. If you arrest Persimmon, I am writing a letter to the governor and to your superiors."

Marshal Edwards cursed us for being in cahoots, threatened that it did not matter anyway because he would still see Persimmon at the end of a rope before long and then he shuffled outside, angry and humiliated. It was difficult to reconcile the belligerent US Marshal Edwards in front of me with the timid, town marshal Edwards of Deacon's story, but I believe it was the latter which bubbled up and broke the standoff.

The two Jenkins men who were on the porch protested loudly and vehemently when the marshal told them to saddle up. I stayed in the house and waited for the commotion to move up the road. When they were gone, the reverend spun out a dining chair and sat in it.

"You know you need to control that temper of yours," the reverend admonished Persimmon. "If you live on the edge of fury all the time, being too quick to anger will one day lead to your doing something you will regret the rest of your days."

Persimmon did not answer him. I could not tell if he knew the reverend was right or if he was irritated and hoped that by holding his tongue, the reverend would quiet down on the subject. Either way, the reverend had sense enough to let it go and move on.

"I passed the marshal up the road a piece and figured I had better turn around and come back. I did not make it to the telegraph office with your last message. Why don't the two of you follow the river down to South Pueblo before there is more trouble? I will add to your message to send the reply to the South Pueblo office. It will be there waiting on you when you arrive." The reverend waited for a response which came in the form of a nod from Persimmon. "I know what it is you are up to. I still say the Lord sent you to town. Don't worry, I will take Mrs. Sanchez to stay with my wife and me for a few days, until things settle down."

Mrs. Sanchez tried again to talk Persimmon out of going, but we were on the trail within the hour. All day I kept spinning around in my saddle, watching the horizon behind me for Jenkins' men or even Marshal Edwards. Despite poor sleep the night before, we rode late into the evening and when we made camp, our fire was kept small and left to smolder rather than flame up.

It was a new moon and the extra darkness made me feel more secure, even though it meant the light from our puny fire could potentially be seen from a greater distance. Before the sun rose, Persimmon was toeing me with his boot to get moving, but it did not startle me because I was not asleep. I slept very little and I think Persimmon slept none at all. We could sleep on the train.

Anxiety waned a bit the second day, but I still checked behind me often. Somewhere along the ride it dawned on me that I had not seen Persimmon with a bottle the previous two evenings. I would have thought being around Mrs. Sanchez would have sparked painful memories. Anything I might say about it further would be pure speculation but something was different. However, I did not expect Persimmon to curtail his drinking permanently. Drinking was too fine a compliment to his other vices of carousing and killing folks. I humored myself but at my own peril. I was barely able to stay in the saddle due to sleep deprivation and any laughter could dislodge me.

Not having bodies to bury, we began our day earlier than last trip and made it to South Pueblo before the telegraph office closed. Persimmon retrieved the telegram, read it, then made a face of annoyance.

"What's the problem?" I asked.

"We have to meet a Pinkerton agent in New Orleans."

XII
MR. SMITH

Our train tickets took us from South Pueblo, Colorado to St. Louis. The ride was uneventful and I took the confinement to get ahead on my serial. Before we arrived, I gave a letter containing my next two installments to the porter to mail for me.

We had been given vague instructions in the last telegram to meet a Pinkerton man named Smith. Meeting him was less involved than I had expected because by the time we collected our horses and gear, Mr. Smith had found us.

"Are you Persimmon Apricot?" came a voice, indifferently.

We both turned to see a short, stocky man in a western suit and grey hat with a wide flat brim.

"I'm Mr. Smith," he introduced himself coldly, without the offer of a friendly hand. "I was told to meet you and see that you get to New Orleans... Frankly, I don't care for the idea of having to play nursemaid to the two of you."

"I suggest you watch your tone with me or you'll be needing a nurse," threatened Persimmon. Never have I known a man whose words struck as forcefully as Persimmon's when he was angry.

"I don't mean to rile you, mister. It ain't your fault that—"

"We don't need a keeper. Just give us our tickets and any other information you have and let us be on our way," Persimmon commanded. If Mr. Smith thought he was in charge, he had best drop such pretenses in a hurry.

"Well, that sounds right satisfactory to me. I have enough to do as it is. Here's your tickets. Boat leaves this evening around seven," Mr. Smith said, thrusting the tickets at me rather than Persimmon.

"Boat? Why not a train?" Persimmon challenged.

"I guess they didn't figure the time difference between a train and a boat headed down river was enough to squabble over and maybe you'd like the comfort of the boat... and then again, maybe they just wanted to save the difference in fare." Mr. Smith's mood had brightened without the burden of watching over us. "But that doesn't much make sense though, a quarter million at stake and they want to squabble over a couple of dollars? Whatever the reason, consider yourself lucky. You'll be on a Thornton packet called the *Miss Emily*... named after one of his daughters, so she's one of the finest boats on the river."

The news was welcomed by me. I, for one, was glad to leave behind the jostling about on hard seats which was the hallmark of rail travel. A smooth ride and spacious living would be a pleasant change.

"When you get to New Orleans, go to this address and meet Mr. Zimmer." Smith handed Persimmon a card with an address scrawled on it. "He's a Pinkerton man and he'll fill you in on what you need to know... Like I said, I don't mean to rile you, but I don't see what you are going to get out of Richard Grant that Pinkerton agents couldn't. You strike me as a man who draws trouble easily, but what help is that?"

Persimmon stopped tying his bags to his saddle and turned to stare menacingly at Mr. Smith. Smith stared back a moment, then glanced to me, then back to Persimmon. His smile shrunk under the weight of Persimmon's glare. Aware his welcome had worn thin, Mr. Smith threw up a farewell hand and said, "Have a good trip." Then he turned abruptly and left.

We had time to comfortably load our horses aboard the boat but not enough time to peruse the streets of St. Louis. My horse had never stepped off of terra firma and was reluctant crossing the stage until she cleared the gap between the boat and wharf and even then, she remained skittish, her ears twitching in a show of her angst. Whereas Samson, Persimmon's horse, climbed aboard like he was eager to ride the river.

Persimmon and I had separate cabins, which led me to believe that perhaps the Richmond Consortium really was concerned with our comfort, but why did they feel the need to sweeten the deal for Persimmon? And why had Mr. Smith thought he was going to be tending to us?

The mighty wheels began to back-paddle, slapping the water at first, then churning it into a froth. Gradually, the *Miss Emily* pulled away from the landing as the sky burst red with the setting sun. We were upriver of the Eads bridge and it was quite the sight to watch a locomotive pass overhead as we threaded an archway beneath.

Again, unencumbered by my horse, tack and baggage, I felt as though I was on vacation, even part of genteel society, because my every need was met without my lifting a finger. We dined graciously and afterward strolled the main deck, weaving our way around cargo. We stopped to watch the roustabouts, denim clad and the youngest barefoot, gathered amongst the crates, taking turns dancing while one picked a small guitar.

"I think it is about time for a brandy, don't you think?" I asked Persimmon. It was a new vice Persimmon had ingrained into my evening constitutional while traveling on the railroad.

The saloon was well adorned and cozy and our first evening passed pleasantly. The only negative was the occasional bursting of the silence by an inebriated drummer. A fellow, at a table next to us, made a crude comment about how he wished someone would stuff the drummer's samples case down his throat to shut him up. Persimmon nodded in agreement but kept quiet. He knew the drummer was harmless.

By the next afternoon I must admit, I was feeling a bit confined. A stop at a fair-sized landing lent me a much-needed distraction. It had been years since I had seen the workings of a busy landing and the grace by which so much heavy lifting is accomplished.

The second evening mirrored the first until we entered the saloon. The drummer was already boozed and occupying a table along our path to the bar. Cackling about something he found far funnier than anyone around him, the drummer was a loud but happy drunk with a toothy grin from ear to ear. All was well until he grabbed Persimmon's coat tail as we passed.

"Hey stranger, what's your name?" the drummer slurred through a choking laugh for which I don't think even he knew the origin.

Persimmon stopped fast and snapped his head around to glare down upon the drummer. Annoyance shown on Persimmon's face but his expression lacked the hatred I had seen during other confrontations. The drummer still clung to Persimmon's coat, chuckling, staring up at Persimmon but oblivious to his captive's displeasure.

Persimmon's right shoulder dipped forward and at first, I thought that he was going to take a step and pull free from the drunk's grip. Instead, he whipped his arm into view, brandishing his Schofield. Pressing the muzzle into the drummer's eye socket, against the bridge of his nose, Persimmon held it there in silence to let the drummer steep in fear. The wind caught in the drummer's chest in two quick snuffs of panic.

"My name's Persimmon Apricot," Persimmon introduced himself as cordially as if he were shaking hands.

"Pleased to make your acquaintance," came the drummer's articulate response from a mind sobered by terror.

Persimmon held the muzzle in place another moment while the room held its breath, frozen in anticipation.

"Likewise," Persimmon reciprocated in the most affable voice I had yet to hear him use. Then he withdrew his pistol and holstered it, gave the drummer a friendly pat on the shoulder then proceeded to an empty table.

Persimmon habitually scanned the room for threats. Everyone who had been apprehensively staring at Persimmon, instantly went back to what they were doing before his gaze passed over them, afraid they might lock eyes with the devil.

We sat and ordered brandy, and as we sipped it, I remembered the first time I laid eyes on Persimmon and how he had uncovered his revolver threateningly before he introduced himself to the sheriff's deputy. It was his name, and his pride for it, that was the catalyst in both situations. Though I had never heard anyone fun him over his name, I could imagine it would be the last thing they ever did. How about the likes of loose tongued drunkards like this drummer? After considering what could have been, I realized that Persimmon's display was meant to save a life. One might question whether his reasons were selfish or humanitarian but based on my experience with him, I know it was the latter.

"Well, you're one intimidating son of a gun, I grant you that," jested a bold voice from above.

Persimmon and I looked up to find the voice's owner striding up to our table, it was Mr. Smith. Without asking, the Pinkerton agent spun a chair around backwards to the table and sat in it, propping himself on his arms atop the chair back.

"Maybe you can scare some information out of Grant... maybe... if you are as, persuasive, as you seem to be. Fewer limitations..." Smith leaned in, looked about the room to be sure no one was watching and said softly, "Us Pinkertons have to work within the law you know."

"Sure you do," I droned sarcastically.

"I told you at the train station that we don't need a nursemaid," Persimmon growled.

"Relax, I'm not here because of you. I have other business aboard," Mr. Smith reassured Persimmon.

"Like what?" I asked, only slightly less sarcastically than before. My not being much of a drinker meant it took little brandy to loosen my tongue but a flicker of good sense told me I had better rein it in.

Smith gave me a hard look but let my impertinence pass. I think he was bored, perhaps lonely, and he wanted to answer my question whether I had asked it or not. He stood and spun the chair back around and sat in it, proper like. This afforded him more room to lean in closer.

"I suppose you two are sort of in the same line of work as me so I don't suppose there's any harm in telling you. There've been a number of thefts on Thornton boats and the company has hired us to solve it. Thornton has two packets that ply the river between St. Louis and New Orleans. The thefts have always occurred on south bound boats and always against property loaded in St. Louis," Smith explained.

"Why don't you just bait them?" I asked, as though it was an original thought.

"We have, with no luck, but then we figured out that property stolen was always insured. So, then we looked at the clerks in the insurance office and thought we had our man after we witnessed what seemed like a clandestine meeting between him and another man. In fact, we almost took him into custody but thankfully we didn't because, after surveilling the second man, we learned he had nothing to do with it. We need to catch the thief in the act so we have baited him again but this time with insured goods... jewels..."

Mr. Smith was animated with excitement which was not the personality I expected from him after our first meeting at the train depot. I think Persimmon would have happily shot him at the depot and was slow to warm up to Mr. Smith even now. As for myself, I was enjoying it immensely. Not only did I get to feel like I was on vacation but, if Mr. Smith's ploy to catch the thief panned out, it could be great fodder for my writing. Maybe it would also distract me from the monotony of slowly plowing along the Mississippi.

While in hopes that it would play in my favor, the thought crossed my mind, "Shouldn't you be minding the bait?"

Mr. Smith nodded and said, "I have a man on it. The boat's clerk is tending to it right now but I don't expect anyone to make a move until we have a stop around mid-evening. That way the thief would feel comfortable that my cabin would be unoccupied and that he can disembark soon after before I would notice the valuables missing."

"When do you expect such timing to occur?" Persimmon pressed. If he was going to be subject to Smith's presence, he might as well have his own questions answered.

"Two evenings from now would be the most likely time. We shall see." Smith stood to leave and bade us good evening.

Funny how riverboats and trains seem to shrink in proportion to the distance traveled. By the third day I was anxious to set foot on dry land and stretch my soul. All the relaxation was taking its toll and we were a mere half way through the trip.

We spent our third day the same as the two days prior. On the way to supper, we made the acquaintance of the drummer but sober this time. He tipped his hat and apologized for his imbibed behavior but Persimmon assured him that he need not worry, that he had not done anything wrong, at least not yet. This left the drummer more confused.

Afterwards, as our routine dictated, we strolled the deck. We were near the bow, inspecting the cargo that had been added at the last landing, when we heard someone cry out, "Stop that man!"

Footsteps raced toward us, pounding along the main deck, the runner about to burst into our view when a shot was fired. The bullet splintered a support post two feet in front of Persimmon. Persimmon reached for his pistol but before he could clear leather, the runner turned the corner around a stack of nail kegs and, not expecting an obstacle, plowed right into Persimmon. The pair of them bowled over across the forward deck. The pursued man was quick to his feet but Persimmon grabbed his coat sleeve.

I thought to lunge and tackle the man but someone ran up behind me and took me by surprise, it was Mr. Smith. Before he could get past me for a clear shot, the fleeing man had wriggled free of his coat. The suspect dove over the gunnel as Mr. Smith brought his revolver to bear. A moment passed of dumbfounded silence from Persimmon and I, and of spitting curses by Mr. Smith before a realization struck all of us, "The paddlewheel!"

Smith raced to the starboard side and along its length to the stern, with me two steps behind. We scoured the river behind us for any solid lump that might be a paddle bludgeoned corpse and then watched the churning wake of the paddlewheel for a minute to see if a dead man washed up but there was nothing. The darkness thickened a few yards out from the boat. There was no hope to see a man swimming to shore or hear his flailing over the fwap, fwap, fwap of the paddles.

Persimmon strolled up nonchalantly with the suspect's coat in hand. Snatching the coat, Mr. Smith rifled through its pockets and in vain according to the long expression on his face.

Being caught up in the drama, I was startled when a strong voice behind me said, "I hear there's been a bit of mischief about my boat." I turned to find a man comparable in stature to Persimmon, with a wide, evenly brimmed grey hat and dark suit. It was the striking figure of a southern planter.

Except for the hat, I expected the stranger to be introduced as the boat's captain but I had quite the surprise in store for me.

"Yes sir, I'm afraid our thief jumped ship. Worse than that, I believe he got away with the jewels," Mr. Smith said with an apologetic tone.

"Don't worry, those jewels were fake. They are expensive costume jewelry at best, no loss. Who are your friends?" the stranger asked.

"Oh, Mr. Thornton, this big fella here is Persimmon Apricot and this here is Pete... I'm sorry, I never got your last name." Smith looked to me to offer it.

Before I could, Mr. Thornton stepped forward and held out his hand. "Persimmon Apricot. Persimmon Apricot..."

My gut wrenched, if this man had any notion of the dangerous ground he tread, if he made light of that name, he would hold his tongue.

"Mr. Thornton is the owner of Thornton Transportation and wanted to oversee our capture of the thief personally," offered Mr. Smith in conclusion of introductions.

"I know you, Mr. Apricot. I thought you looked familiar as soon as I laid eyes on you but surely there is no other man with the name Persimmon Apricot." Mr. Thornton stirred the mystery.

The two men were still shaking hands, perhaps the only reason Persimmon had yet to reach for his gun. The knot in my gut tightened.

"You have me at a loss. I think I would recall knowing a man such as yourself," Persimmon replied, his cordial manner reassuring to my nerves.

"Well, I wasn't the owner at the time. The company was started by my father before the war. When you met me, I was a scared boy tending bar in a saloon in Arizona City. You should remember, you came to my rescue." Mr. Thornton turned back to Mr. Smith and I and continued, "This man saved me from being robbed and very likely from being killed... In fact," Mr. Thornton pulled the left breast of his coat open to expose the Smith & Wesson under his arm, "he's the reason I wear this. His was the first shoulder holster I ever saw and I have found, over the years, that it works very well in my line of work."

"Huh, I remember that. I had no idea I was saving aristocracy," laughed Persimmon. "I see you came out of your shell."

"What you know about me at that time is just a drop in the bucket but yes, Arizona City was a turning point in my life for several reasons and I'll always be very grateful to you. Anything you need from me, you let me know. In fact, please dine with me the remainder of our trip. I want to hear more about you and what brings you on my boat."

Mr. Smith leaned in timidly, "Sir, I don't wish to interrupt your reunion but what are we going to do about the thief? If he did make it to shore, he is sure to send word back to St. Louis and we are going to miss capturing him or his accomplice in the insurance office."

"Don't worry, the few lights you see on land are just farms. He'll have to make his way to the nearest town to send a telegram. I'll order the captain to bring us into the next landing that has a town and you can head up to the telegraph office and arrange it with your partners to seize any messages and their recipients." Mr. Thornton shook our hands and asked us to meet him in the saloon later, the brandy was on the house.

Courteously, I waited until he was out of ear shot before turning to Mr. Smith. "I thought you said the thief would wait until tomorrow night?"

"One of the stewards was telling me of a passenger he recognized from a previous trip but by a different name. I made the mistake of discussing it outside the man's cabin and the suspect came around the corner and saw us talking. I thought I had played off the incident well enough but it must have spooked him. I guess the alleged value of the jewelry must have been more than he could resist."

With the thief having leapt overboard the excitement was over, but I still had the potential for some good stories for my notes. Who knows, maybe Mr.

Thornton's tale was one worth printing and perhaps he would do me the honor of writing it?

Later that night the boat made an unscheduled stop and Mr. Smith left us to take a train back to St. Louis. As I had hoped, the monotony was now eased by Mr. Thornton's stories, all of which I scribbled down in detail. He seemed to take a liking to me, and Persimmon's mood was buoyed by the friendly company.

We said goodbye in Vicksburg where Mr. Thornton disembarked. By the time we made New Orleans, Persimmon and I had our fill of boats. Even our horses were a bit wobbly legged at first. All the rest and relaxation had worn me out and I was ready to find a hotel midafternoon but this was not my journey. Persimmon had a mind to find Mr. Zimmer's residence right away and retrieve from him our next set of directions.

Mr. Zimmer's home was in the French Quarter, a two-story Spanish stucco in peach, ornate with a wrought iron gallery along its front.

"Pinkerton's must fair pretty well," I commented.

"I suppose so," Persimmon agreed as he climbed the steps to the front door.

Three firm raps of the bull's head door knocker were sufficient to conjure the sound of feet shuffling inside. A moment later the door cracked open with a snap and the red, puffy face of a woman poked through. "Can I help you?"

"We're here to see Mr. Zimmer," Persimmon answered.

"He's not here," the wild haired woman sniffed and went to shut the door.

Persimmon slapped his hand against the door to hold it open. I knew he was already perturbed and felt I should move the conversation to the point of our visit.

"Ma'am, we were told to meet him at this address. This is Mr. Apricot and my name is Pete—"

"I said he isn't here. You'll have to come back later." This time the woman threw her weight into the door and slammed it shut.

Persimmon commenced to beating on the door with his fist, rattling the huge slab of oak in its jam.

"What do you want?" the lady cried from within, but before Persimmon could spew obscenities at her there came the sound of two voices, the agitated voice of the puffy-faced woman and another, softer voice.

Footsteps belonging to the softer voice approached the door. Persimmon held his tongue, knowing a calmer, and hopefully more cooperative hand, had grasped the door handle on the other side. There were a few more appeals to hush the puffy-faced woman from the person near the door. Then it opened and a woman in nurse's garb stepped outside, pulling the door closed behind her.

She spoke in better English than we did but wrapped in a French accent. "I am sorry, gentlemen. If you are looking for Mr. Zimmer, he will be back tomorrow. Please call again around two." She glanced back at the door as if she was seeking permission to continue. "Mrs. Zimmer will be sleeping."

Persimmon thanked her cordially but, as the nurse slipped back inside, he added. "I don't blame him for not being home."

We left to find a hotel. That evening as we dined, we were surprised when a gentleman approached our table. "Mr. Apricot?"

"Yes."

"I am Mr. Zimmer. May I join you?"

"I thought you were not expected back until tomorrow," Persimmon asked, ungraciously.

"How did you find us?" I added.

"Gentlemen, I apologize for my wife, she has been ill for some time now. Doctors disagree as to what is wrong with her, which means they don't know. I'm very sorry. Yes, I was supposed to be back tomorrow morning, but I received word that your boat was to land today so I cut my trip short. As for finding you, I figured since you were not footing the bill you would be in one of the best hotels. I just went from desk to desk until I found where you were registered; took three tries."

"Well, I do appreciate you seeking us out and saving me the trouble. Now if you will just tell us where to find Richard Grant, I can take care of matters and be on my way." Persimmon coldly stated. Since Mr. Zimmer seemed a pleasant soul, I assumed Persimmon's abrupt manner was due to his eagerness to be done with his business with Grant.

"Did they not tell you?" Mr. Zimmer paused and Persimmon stared at him with eyebrows raised. "Grant boarded a boat to Cuba by way of Key West."

Persimmon wiped his mouth and threw the wadded napkin onto the table with a thud. "When was that?"

"Almost a month ago," Mr. Zimmer said sheepishly.

"Those bastards in Richmond knew this, didn't they?" Persimmon asked, annoyed at the answer before receiving one.

"Yes. I reported it when he left. Before anyone asked, I told my superiors that I was not going to chase after him with my wife in the shape she's in and besides, Grant doesn't have the money. Whether he knows who does or not, I couldn't say for sure, but if he does he isn't going to tell. Someone put the fear of the devil in him," Mr. Zimmer explained.

"He doesn't know the devil, not yet," Persimmon snapped. "That's why they kept pressing me as to whether or not I would see this job through, because they knew he was way the hell off down in the Caribbean somewhere… Did he get off in Key West or did he go to Cuba?"

"I don't know. The ship on which he sailed has not yet returned." Mr. Zimmer's soft eyes told me he felt bad about the situation. Because of it he offered, "I will be glad to find you the finest cabin aboard ship between here and Key West and Cuba."

"What about a train?" asked Persimmon, anxiously. "I've had enough of boats."

Mindful of proprieties, Mr. Zimmer choked down a laugh. "I'm afraid there are some places where trains still don't go. And even if you decided to ride a horse through all of Florida, you'd need a boat to get to Key West. It's an island. The fastest route is across the gulf."

Persimmon groaned a few times and blew heavy breaths between. He drummed his fingers on the table, wiped his mouth again and shifted in his chair. Was he irritated or nervous?

"Do you not like traveling by ship?" Mr. Zimmer asked.

"I don't know, I have never been on one," was the surprising answer from Persimmon.

"But you told me you worked in a shipyard," I exclaimed without thinking.

"I didn't sail them…" Persimmon replied, indignantly. Then he turned to Mr. Zimmer, "Get us a big boat."

XIII
UNEXPECTED

We waited three days for the next ship heading to Key West. It was scheduled to round Florida and follow the gulf stream to New York but Mr. Zimmer reassured us that if we failed to uncover Richard Grant in Key West, catching a boat to Havana would be a simple matter. Before leaving we boarded our horses in New Orleans. It was Mr. Zimmer's suggestion that we would likely not need horses in either port so why subject them to a confined trip over big water?

Our paddle steamer departed New Orleans under clear skies, but by late afternoon a series of moderate storms crossed our path. Persimmon's face grew longer than usual before taking on a greenish hue. He retreated to his cabin and I saw nothing of him for the rest of our voyage. Alone, I dined and after supper I kept up our ritual of a snifter of brandy. Though the conversation was thin amongst strangers, I'm ashamed to say that I reveled in Persimmon's absence. It is a petty thing, I know, but to weather rough seas with a sound stomach was thus far the only circumstance where I could truly claim superiority over Persimmon. Rising in the morning before Persimmon was hit or miss and no real feat. Of course, I would never brag to him about having an iron stomach and likely he would think it inconsequential. Nevertheless, he knew it and that was satisfaction enough for me.

Persimmon emerged from his cabin during our approach to the Key West dock. Over his shoulder were slung his saddlebags which he handed to me, the first words out of his mouth in days being, "Tote these for me, will ya'?"

I obliged and stuffed them into a dark-green carpet bag I had purchased cheaply from the steward. Its handles made it easier to lug about and I figured it would draw less attention than would saddlebags without a horse. As soon as the plank dropped to the dock, Persimmon wobbled off the ship. Following the directions of one of the roustabouts on shore, we ambled to a nearby grocery with a bakery. From the look on his face, I thought Persimmon might vomit before we cleared the smell of the neighboring fishing boats but if he had, I doubt it would have been productive. According to the porter aboard ship, Persimmon had eaten nary a thing since we left New Orleans. I had asked the porter to look in on him, too afraid of Persimmon's ill temper to do so myself. A little water and a pinch of hardtack was all the porter could get into Persimmon.

After some bread and water, Persimmon worked up to coffee. His color was better but his expression weak. Mr. Zimmer had made note of the ship aboard which Richard Grant had sailed. I volunteered to go see the harbormaster and inquire about anyone who disembarked that ship. Meanwhile, Persimmon would sit in the shade of some large flowering bush I failed to recognize, and regain his strength.

The harbormaster referred me to a clerk who confirmed Richard Grant did, in fact, disembark with no record of his having left Key West since. I returned to find Persimmon still sitting in the shade, his forehead beaded with sweat but in a chipper mood. I reported my findings to him.

Persimmon's refreshed countenance soured at the mention of Richard Grant. After a minute of aimless staring down the street, he let out a big sigh of resignation and said, "I guess we best be getting on with it then."

We began our search with the owner of the grocery. He had not heard of the man we sought but he was helpful in giving us an idea of the layout of town, including a hand-drawn map, in pencil, of the main streets. It was much the same story at the dry goods store down the street but we did get directions to another bodega where I convinced Persimmon to put something more substantial in his stomach. The hand-drawn map was invaluable as most of the buildings were painted white and streets began to run together in the eye of the sojourner.

Alas, on the edge of a predominantly Cuban neighborhood, we stumbled upon a bodega whose clerk knew a man fitting Richard Grant's description. The man's first name was right. The shop owner did not know about the last name. The friendly Cuban pointed us up a street through an adjacent neighborhood.

Each block was clad in fine homes, most of them wooden, most of them painted white, but following an alley into the interior exposed tiny hovels. Some were well maintained shacks, others, kindling awaiting a flame.

Between buildings, and sometimes inside them, were cisterns. For the entire island, fresh water came from the sky or not at all.

I dipped my hand into an open cistern and took a drink, then, removed my hat and wiped my brow. A felt hat worked well in the dry, often cold climate of the West and was tolerable in the Eastern states, but it was unsuited for this subtropical sun. In comparing our clothing with that of the local Cuban population, which was light in both color and weight, I realized we were sorely overdressed.

Allow me to digress a moment and say that if you, the reader, find it unexpected that our search would lead us to this island clinging to the edge of the U.S. map, might I suggest you experience it firsthand. Only then will you truly know my surprise and displeasure at the sweltering summer sun and biting gnats. If our heavier clothing was of any use to us, it was in defense of the latter. However, if not for these impediments to paradise, it would be a pleasant and relaxed town with a curious draw about it.

Persimmon asked everyone we met if they knew Richard Grant. Gradually, the directions became more specific until we were standing before a one-room shanty with missing shingles, white of course. Rather, it was mostly white with specks of grey on the shady side and mostly grey with splinters of white on the sun-beaten areas. It rested on blocks of coral, not too high but enough to keep the floor off wet ground and afford shelter to rats.

Persimmon climbed the six-inch stoop and knocked on the door. I kept my distance behind Persimmon where I could see the door. I could not see Persimmon's face but the way he ground his balled fingers together gave me the impression he was nervous.

A voice with an American accent called out from inside, "Who's there?"

"Open the damn door!" Persimmon barked.

The single front window was covered by a shutter that tipped out from the bottom and through its slats I caught a glimpse of a face peeking at Persimmon. Then I heard the dull clatter of a door lock before the door slowly swung open. An old man with sleepy eyes appeared, dressed in white linen from head to toe. He stood, staring at Persimmon through a visage of astonishment.

"You?" the old man exclaimed.

Persimmon said nothing. The old man was mildly startled to notice me and peered around Persimmon for an estimation of me. When he was satisfied he did not recognize me, he glanced up and down the alley, then turned back into the shack.

"Sit yourself down," I heard him say.

I trailed after Persimmon. Inside, there was a small weathered table with two chairs, each faintly colored with flecks of light green. Atop the table sat a nondescript jug of booze, a checkerboard and a box of dominoes, instruments to while away the time. The rear wall held a matching window, allowing the faint breeze of the island's interior to pass through. The only other seat was a stool shoved under the table so I drug it clear and perched atop it with a good view of the scene.

"You've changed a fair bit since I saw you last. You have a rough look about you but then I suppose you have to look the part, else the west will eat you alive," Richard Grant commented.

Persimmon sat in the chair nearest the door, still silent. His eyes were expressionless but his mouth was drawn in annoyance and his jaw muscles clenched and unclenched repeatedly.

"I wasn't surprised at the knock on my door but I never expected it to be you. How did you find me? Why did you find me?" Richard Grant spoke like a man in control of his situation.

I was shocked that he could know Persimmon and not cower in fear. Just as oddly, Persimmon had yet to say anything and, after a few empty moments, I was uncomfortable and answered the questions myself.

"We were sent by some men in Richmond who say you absconded with investment money. As for how we found you, Pinkerton agents directed us," I answered, somewhat coyly.

It did not feel like my place to be our spokesman but Persimmon seemed dazed. It was much the same impression he gave when he would drift off in thought after a few drinks. I fiddled with a red checker to soothe my angst.

"A Pinkerton is who I expected to be knocking on my door. I figured that agent in New Orleans would have followed me here." Richard Grant pulled the cork from the jug. "Rum?"

"No, thank you. Why did you come to Key West, anyway?" I asked. "And why didn't you use an alias on the boat, then?" The question had been nagging me.

"No point. The Pinkerton man watched me board. He warned me that someone would be watching. I could have gone to Cuba and still further but those Pinkerton fellows will find you if they have a mind to," he said, then took a slug of rum.

"Why didn't you keep going?" I prodded.

Richard Grant wiped his mouth with his sleeve then answered, "'Cause Key West is a good place to disappear without having to know Spanish... although it wouldn't hurt to know it with all the Cuban revolutionaries here abouts. You tell me something, why did those men in Richmond send you after me... although I suppose I know why... they thought you could work on my sympathies, didn't they? Well, you can forget it. I didn't tell the Pinkerton agents and I ain't telling you. If the fellows that double crossed me were to find out where I am, they would kill me. I don't have the money or anything to gain from testifying and I'm not going to." He took another drink of rum.

"You're gonna tell me everything I need to know," Persimmon growled. His lip quivered and his eyes squinted menacingly at Richard Grant. Persimmon's balled fist rested on the table, knuckles white.

"It wasn't worth my life to tell those agents. I'm sure as hell not going to tell you, boy." Grant started to lift the jug to his lips.

Explosively, Persimmon lashed out with his leg from beneath the table, hurling Grant's chair over and against the wall. Grant's head bounced off the cheap plaster and before he hit the floor, Persimmon flipped the table into the corner, lunged forward and punched Grant in the nose.

"Stop! Stop! What are you doing to me?" Grant screamed, blinded by a broken nose and flailing his hands out in front of him in a pathetic defense.

Checkers were still clinking in the corner as Persimmon bellowed, "Your life ain't worth spit to me! You're gonna tell me what I want to know or I'm gonna beat you to death."

"Wait! Wait a minute..." Grant rubbed his eyes with his left hand, regaining some of his vision. With both palms turned outward, he squinted through the tears. "I know you're angry with me, son, but take pity on me. That just wasn't the life for... When I heard about your mother, I felt the loss too. I—"

Persimmon slapped Grant's arms away and a huge right hand wrenched chokingly on Grant's collar while the left seized a hunk of hair and snatched Grant's head in place with two quick jerks. "Look here you no account bastard, abandonment isn't loss. You don't get to feel anything about my mother... All the time we were in Kansas, she never stopped hoping you'd return. Why the hell couldn't you have joined the army, like you made out, and been killed? At least we could have celebrated a dead hero like other families, instead of the shame of everyone knowing you fled... I'm not fifteen years old anymore. What happens to you doesn't mean a damn thing to me."

With that, Persimmon commenced to wailing on Grant's left eye with his fist while still clenching him by the hair. After the third punch, Grant cried, "OK, OK," but it did not stop the fourth punch from being delivered.

"You gonna talk?" Persimmon snarled, through gritted teeth.

Grant's head hung bleeding from Persimmon's hand, his neck and shoulders limp. His eyes were closed with the left one swelling fast. He could not nod. Instead, he waved weakly with the back of his hand, "I'll talk."

Persimmon released Grant's head with a toss, slamming it into the base of the wall. Then he stepped outside for fresh air, while Grant lay bleeding.

Stunned by it all, I said nothing, but out of nervous tension I stood and hoisted the table back into place. I left the jug and game pieces on the floor, all save the one checker I fiddled with.

Grant was struggling to his feet so I grabbed his elbow and the chair and helped him back into it. The blood streaming from his nose stained his white shirt down the front and around the collar. After a good review of the pitiful little man, I decided the jug might do him some good. I picked it up, and spying a cup on the windowsill, I poured Grant a gracious amount of rum and took a large swig myself. I thought Persimmon might like one too but, on second thought, whiskey always seemed to make him more dangerous and rum likely would do the same. I was not sure if that was possible in this case but, for safety, I tucked the jug under my stool.

Persimmon came back inside and sat down at the table as before. The manufactured calm in his voice was a welcome surprise. "Now tell me everything you know about these partners of yours. I want the whole story."

A couple of minutes felt like ten as they passed in silence. I expected Persimmon to lash out impatiently but his composure held. Richard Grant took a few shaky sips with the cup clasped in both hands. A tear rolled down his cheek from his good eye. He blinked hard and a second chased after the first.

"You're right," Richard Grant said in a broken voice, "you're not as I remember you."

Persimmon held his tongue. Worried that further delay in the conversation might spark his temper again, I tried to act as mediator.

"Why don't you start from the beginning so we can understand what exactly the situation is and what happened?" I said in as comforting a voice as I could muster.

With the empty gaze of his open eye fixed on the table, Richard Grant began a slow recitation of the events which led to him sitting here, dripping blood into his rum.

"Two men approached me in a back-alley saloon. Said they had been watching me and that I had two qualities they needed; I knew one of the men you met in Richmond and I was flat broke. They said they'd cut me in on the deal if I could introduce them to Donovan and Connelly. I only knew them second hand, but it was enough for an introduction."

Richard Grant was still speaking when Persimmon, bored with the backstory, twirled his index finger in the air to indicate to the old man to get to the point.

"Well then, I guess you know about the shyster they had for an attorney. He put the contract in the name of their land company but no one ever put me on the company roll. I guess you also know that their company was a sham and their names were aliases?" Richard Grant asked, watching as Persimmon twirled his finger again.

"I'm sure that shyster knew more than he let on but he convinced the Pinkerton men that he didn't. That left me as the only connection they had."

"So why didn't you tell the Pinkertons what you knew? If you didn't have the real names, why do the Pinkerton's think you're lying to them?" I asked.

"'Cause I left town with the two men and the Pinkerton's later caught up with me in St. Louis. I was being chased by a killer and wasn't about to tell them what I knew," Richard Grant answered.

Impatient, Persimmon twirled his finger more vigorously.

"When we got the money, I insisted on following the two men west. They were reluctant, but they obliged me as I would not let them out of my sight. We ended up in a house on the outskirts of Denver where we met two other partners I had not known about. I had a funny feeling about how they were acting, then the four of them sat at a table with no chair left for me and no invitation to fetch one either. So, I moved off into the next room and sat in a wingback chair where I could hear what went on. I was out of sight but I could see them if I wanted to. At first they were friendly, telling each other what they planned to do with their share of the loot. The one who had told me his name was Pearson said he actually planned to buy land ahead of a rail line that was set to be laid not far from where we were."

Richard Grant was giving us the details which I was soaking up, trying to keep mental notes on it all so I could write it down later. The intrigue was lost on Persimmon who cared only for the information pertinent to catching the thief and collecting the reward. Again, he twirled his finger in the air.

Richard Grant took a swallow of rum and continued. "Well, the gist of it is, they had set out in pairs to swindle big money and then return by a certain date to divvy it between them. But the other pair had only managed twenty thousand. It was big money but not compared to two hundred and fifty thousand. I guess they didn't trust the fellows I came with so they started pressing them as to when they were going to divide it up. Then Pearson said something about dividing it proportionately which didn't set right with one of the other fellows. He asked Pearson what he meant by proportionately and he commented that twenty thousand was a far cry from two hundred and fifty thousand. Then the other one said that Pearson just got lucky, but that they had all put in the same effort. Some more was said that I didn't catch so I peeked around the chair to see the other fellow stand and pull a knife and stick it in the middle of the table and that's when he said, 'Look here, Jenkins, you ain't about to get cheap on us are you?' Then Pearson said, 'I told you never to use my real name.' Then the fellow with the knife leaned over the table and said, 'What are you gonna' do about it?'"

My brow went up at the mention of the name Jenkins. I looked to Persimmon and his attention had also been stirred. Was this the same Jenkins who held a lean against Mrs. Sanchez's ranch? What were the odds that two scoundrels with the name Jenkins were buying up land ahead of a railroad somewhere in Colorado?

"I could see Pearson had his hand in his lap under..." Richard Grant began to say but his voice hung in his throat so he cleared it and lubricated it with more rum, "...in his lap, under the table. I saw the glint of steel as he pulled his hand from under the table. Shot the man in the face. The bullet broke the back of his skull out, his head whipped back and then he collapsed dead on the table. The other man I didn't know threw his hands up and yelled not to shoot him too. Pearson told him that he didn't need any witnesses with big ideas about double crossing him. When the man told him he didn't have to worry about that, Pearson told him that if he wanted to keep breathing he had to take care of their other problem and nodded in my direction. I had already pulled a single shot derringer from my vest pocket but getting out the door meant crossing their line of fire. I know, I should have been more prepared among thieves. Since I couldn't shoot my way out, I darted to the window on the back wall and flung it open."

I was on the edge of my seat when Richard Grant had to take another swig of rum and a breath as his own heart raced with the quickening pace of the story.

"The window clapped open and I heard boots and chairs scuffling. I was half out the window when the third man, the dead man's partner, came charging through the house, about to take aim on me. I had one leg out the window but managed to point and shoot that little derringer before he could shoot me. I aimed square in his middle but at eight feet away the bullet had already drifted several inches. I think I lucked out and hit him in the heart because he fell like a sack of flour. The other two were right behind him but slower, I guess because they thought he'd get me and not the other way around. I just fell on out the window and scrambled up into a run along the house, rounding the corner just ahead of a bullet. It was dark so they couldn't find me in the rocks. Pearson hollered out that if they found me, I was dead and that he had other men that would strip my hide if I ever thought of stepping into a courtroom."

Throwing back the remainder of his rum, Richard Grant put the empty cup in front of me to fill it, which I did. Persimmon gave me a hard look when I pulled the jug from under my stool but he did not ask for it. I thought the story was finished but not quite.

"After hiding for a couple of weeks, I headed to St. Louis and after a long while I thought I was free and clear but Pearson's partner found me. I thought I gave him the slip and was ready to board a boat when he found me again and took a shot at me. He missed and there came the whistle of a policeman, so he ran. The police took me in for questioning. I pled ignorance to the whole matter. When they let me go, I headed down river but when I got off in Memphis, that's when a Pinkerton man nabbed me. They tried to play like that shyster lawyer had told them something and that I had better cooperate but they couldn't fool me. I knew they had nothing on me so why risk it?

They've been watching my every move since. A couple of others grabbed me thinking they could get something out of me the others didn't, but all they could do was slap me around a bit. I knew no matter how much they let on they wouldn't kill me. If not for the law's sake, then because they need to know what they think I know."

Persimmon, who was slumped as much as the straight-backed chair would afford, sat up and arched his back before speaking. "So, that man Jenkins, do you think he might be outside of Leadville?"

Richard Grant nodded. "Could be."

"Describe him in detail," Persimmon commanded Grant, then he turned to me and said, "You're a writer, jot this down."

I took down the descriptions of Jenkins and the man who shot at him in St. Louis. Richard Grant said the man who shot at him called himself Mr. Heeley, certainly an alias. Heeley's description garnered no distinction from that of a million other men but Jenkins's had two traits that, in combination, should prove his identity. He was towheaded, his hair practically white. Secondly, he had two moles on his cheek, side by side with one smaller than the other. This was a combination of traits not easily hidden.

Persimmon got up and stood in the doorway, looking up at what I assumed to be the breeze blowing in the tops of the palms. Maybe it was the palm tree itself, as I am not sure either of us had ever seen one in person. Stuffing my notebook and pencil in my pocket, I stood to follow and noticed my innards were jittery. Desperately, I wanted to discuss either shocking revelation with someone, the potential correlation of two villains named Jenkins and the fact that Richard Grant was Persimmon's father.

For the sake of proprieties, I did hold myself together. I could not speak to Richard Grant on either point and I would have to find the right moment to discuss him with Persimmon. I would take it slow and maybe Persimmon would broach the subject if I did not. Despite Persimmon's promise to me, his father was clearly a sore subject and one which might get me shot. I pushed my chair back but before I could start toward the door, Richard Grant was up and halfway there.

"I don't know why you care about this matter but I told you everything I know about it and at the risk of my life, if one of them finds me. Promise me they won't find me." Richard Grant was looking meekly at Persimmon who had his back to him.

When Persimmon did not answer, I spoke up and reassured Richard Grant that there was no reason they would find him. After the beating he took from Persimmon, I was amazed at his next request.

"Son... I know you hate me but could you find it in you to leave me a few dollars?"

Persimmon turned partway around and said before leaving, "I left you alive... that's mercy enough."

By the time I got to the doorway, Richard Grant was standing in it, leaning against the jam. As I squeezed past him, he spun his head far around to see me through his good eye and said morosely, "I wonder if it was?"

XIV
ACCLIMATING

We headed back to the western side of the island, nearer the water, where the gulf breeze would cool us and blow away the bugs. I had no idea where we were headed. Neither of us had spoken a word since leaving Richard Grant's hovel.

We strolled down Simonton Street, dodging about from shade to shade as much as we could. When we turned on Front Street, I could see smoke rising between the tops of two masts. Watching the smoke drift past what I suspected was the forward mast, I almost missed the saloon as we passed it. I was surprised Persimmon did not smell it through its open door but he said nothing. After what I had just witnessed, I could not believe he did not want a drink because I sure did.

"How about I buy you a drink?" I asked. It was nice to have a bit of money again and be able to make that offer.

Persimmon turned to find me pointing at the open saloon door, gave me the sideways nod of uncontested surrender and followed me inside the Weatherford Saloon. At the bar, I took the liberty of ordering and asked the barkeep what he recommended which turned out to be Cuban rum.

Persimmon took a shot of rum and while the barkeep was refilling his glass, Persimmon said, "I knew I should have brought my horse. I guess we'll buy horses and ride home. I don't want any more to do with ocean-going boats."

Overhearing this, the barkeep chimed in, "You know you are on an island, don't you?"

"Yeah, but aren't we very close to the tip of the mainland?" Persimmon asked.

"Not really. It is a pretty far piece, especially if you want dry land," the barkeep answered.

"What do you mean, dry land? What other sort is there?" The comment had piqued my interest.

"Oh, well a vast swath of South Florida is marsh. Some Indians live in there but you don't want to trudge through it. If the gators didn't eat you, the mosquitos would. No, if you were going to find the nearest town, I would say that is probably Tampa. It's a frontier mudhole from what I hear but it has a road. Just a few hundred people, mostly logging I think. Last I heard, the railroad had yet to reach it but a stage line would take you up to the rail line. But if you have taken a ship from here to Tampa, you've gone better than halfway to the northern gulf coast. Besides that, far fewer ships leave here headed for Tampa."

Figuring we would be waiting for a ship, I inquired, "By the way, is there a place we can get a room?"

"The Russell House is on Duval, a couple of blocks over. It's billed as a resort so it is a pretty nice place."

I thanked the barkeep for the information and took our bottle to a table in the middle of the room. Out of the sun and with both doors open on either side of the room, the gulf breeze was quite refreshing. Persimmon removed his hat and let the salty air blow through his damp hair. Something was different about him. The meeting with his father had changed him somehow. What a meeting it had been. Before we came to Key West, I thought I understood Persimmon Apricot. I thought his personality was the product of losing his beloved wife but maybe her death was the match that lit the powder keg.

Though I wanted to talk to him about Richard Grant, I thought it wise to let it lie a while. That left me to satisfy my questions through assumptions, therefore, I assumed Persimmon's whaling on the father who abandoned him and his mother relieved some pent-up anger. That, coupled with his worry of being sick on another ship, accounted for his odd mood.

Persimmon seemed to be enjoying the breeze on his face, deep in thought. I know it is odd, but I felt sympathetic, almost motherly, to Persimmon. Sure, he was violent towards his father but didn't his father deserve it? Though I had no personal reference in which to empathize, I was confident I would feel much the same anger as Persimmon.

Anyway, that was my thinking, and because of it, I suggested that Persimmon stay and enjoy the breeze. The wharf was three or four blocks away and I would head over to inquire about ships and perhaps stop in and reserve us rooms at the Russell House and be back for supper.

To the west, the sky was darkening. Having read tales about hurricanes, I said a little prayer that this was merely a squall similar to those we sailed through to get here. There were a number of shops along my path. I purchased a handful of cigars and debated on a linen suit. Finally, I told the clerk that if I found myself in town for a few days, I would be back for a cooler wardrobe. He and I conversed for several minutes. He was curious about a stranger from the continent and excited to tell me about his town. I learned there were several trades in Key West. It had been built by the wrecking industry and navy power. Most of its continued sustenance came from cigar factories and fishing. Its latest industry, that of Cuban revolution, threatened the town because the government of Spain was none too happy about it.

At the wharf, I found the shipping agent and asked about packets headed to New Orleans.

"I expect the *Belle of the Gulf* to be here in the next few days. Should be four days from now if the weather doesn't interfere. She should be headed to New Orleans or Mobile, sometimes Galveston," the agent informed me.

"Any of those ports would be fine. I don't suppose you have a boat to Tampa?" I knew Persimmon might ask about Tampa and I wanted to be ready.

"Tampa?" the agent exclaimed more than asked. "No. Every once in a while we do. For that matter, we could get a ship in unexpectedly that's headed north. How can I reach you if we do?"

"I plan to get a room at the Russell House. Please leave a message for me there, unless I inform you otherwise." I gave him my name while staring out through the large open door, admiring the double masted steamer. "Where is she headed?" I asked, of the ship.

"Oh, she's headed up the east coast from here," he said, taking down my information.

"Is she going to Virginia?" I eagerly asked.

The odd excitement in my voice drew a raised brow from the shipping agent. The agent looked outside, pointed and said, "I believe she is. That man there is the captain if you'd like to speak to him. Should I keep you down for passage on the *Belle*?"

Confirming that I wished to go to the northern gulf coast, I thanked the agent and walked briskly to the captain who was walking the length of the wharf, smoking a pipe and inspecting his ship and the dark cloud behind it. Perhaps I could mail back the latest installment of my story aboard his ship. If I could get it written in time, that is. I was anxious to fictionalize today's happenings.

"Excuse me, captain," I called out. "Will you be going to Virginia?"

The captain removed his pipe from his lips and answered, "I will."

"Might I inquire, how long until you expect to arrive?" I am not sure why I asked this question, for what other options did I have that would be faster delivery?

"Well, I have a stop to make in Savannah, that will take an extra day. I don't expect to stop in Charleston, unless I take on cargo in Savannah bound for Charleston. Either way, I should be in Virginia within the week." The captain pointed at the long, dark cloud with his pipe. "At least as long as this blow doesn't turn back on us. I hear there is a hurricane south of Cuba. Likely, it will keep tracking west but those monsters have a mind of their own."

Upon hearing the word hurricane, I interrogated the captain further as to why he pointed at the cloud I could see if the hurricane was south of Cuba.

"That's a squall line and later on there'll be another behind it. Hurricanes shed them. It will put up a fuss for a few minutes and then be gone," the captain reassured me. "Why did you want to know where I was headed?"

Having nearly forgotten why I was there, I grunted a quick laugh over my cowardice at the mention of hurricanes, then asked, "I was wondering if I could press upon you to take a letter and mail it when you get to Virginia?"

The captain was happy to oblige and held his hand out to receive it but I explained that I did not have it with me and asked when he would be leaving?

"I think I made a mistake in letting my crew have shore leave. I intend to leave tomorrow afternoon but the departure time will be dependent on when I have all of my land-loving crew back aboard. I'll let them straggle in and sleep it off a few hours. Slight delay but better here than Havana. There, I might be days waiting for a full crew and still not get them all back. When you return with your letter, give it to the ship's purser. I will mention it to him when I see him."

I thanked the captain and headed back the way I came. First, I returned to the shop and bought the linen suit. I was tired of baking in the dark clothing I wore. Next, I took a small detour up Duval Street to the Russell House, an imposing structure, a three-story clapboard hotel in the style of the island, with galleries for both upper floors running its full width. There were plenty of rooms. The desk clerk informed me that it was the off season. Apparently, the affluent would sail to Key West in the winter to escape colder climes. I could not fault them for wanting to escape the cold but more so, for not coming to Key West in the summer.

The clerk gave me rooms next door to each other on the second floor. A bath was available, but I did not want Persimmon to be jealous to find me clean and refreshed. I also did not want to get into my clean island garb covered in grime. Instead, I locked the carpet bag and my linen suit in my room and headed back to the saloon with plans for a bath later that evening.

The wind picked up as I walked in, sweeping me and a bit of the dusty street, inside. Across the room some men were pushing a table aside while two others were settling in with a guitar and what looked like a smaller, teardrop shaped guitar. I noticed the barkeep had picked up my empty glass so I went to the bar for another and found myself waiting with a man of Cuban descent.

The bartender returned from the back room with an unopened bottle of rum and handed it to the man and asked jovially, "Aren't you supposed to be out fishing?"

The Cuban man placed his index finger in front of a guilty grin. "Don't tell my wife." The two men laughed and then the Cuban man answered more seriously, "The weather chased us back in."

With a new glass, I returned to the table with Persimmon. I was afraid, by now, I would find him glassy eyed but the level in the bottle was his witness that he had been sipping the rum slowly. After filling him in on all that I knew about ships and our hotel accommodations and what the store clerk told me of the island, I offered him a cigar. Then I told him about my new suit and said I would have purchased him one but I did not know his size. It was excuse enough.

Persimmon shrugged and pulled back his coat to remind me that he wanted to remain clothed sufficiently to conceal his pistol. When he flapped his coat closed, he caught a whiff of his own stench and recoiled his nose as far as his neck would allow. "Maybe I will see that store clerk about some clean shirts."

The musicians began playing and several other men took turns dancing in pairs as the mood struck them. We ate conch and bread. Since Persimmon was drumming his fingers on the table with the music, I did not bother him with my questions. The bottom dropped out of the cloud. Rather than drown out the instruments, the musicians played all the louder and the roar of the rain became part of the music. As if it knew, the rain stopped with the end of the song too. Out of the window, I watched the clouds flashing as they drifted away, the rumble of thunder fading.

The Cuban gentleman I had stood with at the bar was the most prolific dancer. Around the time their bottle of rum was empty, the Cuban man lost his balance but recovered it against our table. "My apologies, señores. The music makes me excited. My name is Julio. What are your names?"

"Pete," I said, maintaining my alias.

My gut tightened a little. I assumed Persimmon would pull his Schofield before he answered and trouble on an island was not what we needed. To my surprise, Persimmon made no threatening gestures. He simply said, "Persimmon Apricot."

"Per... Perseemon you say?" the Cuban man asked, dragging the name through a more pronounced accent than I had noticed before. "This name is new to me."

As he spoke, another of their group, an American, came close enough to hear. Being nosey he asked, "What's new to you?"

"Perseemon."

"Persimmon? You mean the fruit?" the American asked in a southern accent.

"It is a fruit?" Julio asked, surprised.

"Yeah, it's a small, mushy fruit. If you catch one when it is really ripe they're sweet but if it is, the least bit green it will dry your mouth out like a bale of cotton. You have to pick them off the ground before the ants get them if you want one worth eating. Why are you discussing persimmons?"

"That is his name, Perseemon." Julio pointed toward Persimmon.

The American smiled wide and said, "Persimmon, that's an odd name."

I was watching Persimmon and I have no idea what possessed me to do such a dangerous thing but when Persimmon's right hand went for his pistol, I reached out and lightly caught the crook of his elbow with the tips of my fingers and held on. Persimmon rolled his head around on his shoulder and glared at me. I could feel my life slipping away but I held on to his elbow while the American kept babbling.

The transplanted southerner was tattered but clean. His shirt was white but there was a stain on one suspender strap and the denim which hung from them had a few small holes in the thighs and knees. His speech was educated but not the least bit haughty. What I knew about the island was enough to make me undecided if the American was slightly down on his luck or only well assimilated into the local populace. I also did not know, in the next few moments, if he was going to live or die.

"You know, I like it. It's unusual, but it is a strong name. My name is Tom." The American held out his hand to Persimmon with the jolly look in his eye of a rum soaked good heart.

When Persimmon took Tom's hand, I breathed a sigh of relief. Once my chest quit pounding, and all seemed well in the room, I wondered, had Persimmon mellowed?

His expression relaxed and then he said, "Why don't we go clean up? Take me to see that shop clerk."

We stood to leave and Julio saw us, dancing over to our table where he almost strained his neck looking up at Persimmon.

"Are you leaving us my friends? We have much more to come," he declared.

Persimmon glanced over at the cheery party of fishermen and replied, "We're going to clean up. We'll be back later."

Julio let out a, "Hey, hey," with the music. "We will be waiting for you with a fresh bottle of rum."

Never had a bath felt so good. I would have soaked longer, but I was anxious to get started writing the next installment of my serial while Persimmon steeped in his bathwater. I wanted to get these most recent developments on paper before my memory faded and if I missed sending it on the ship heading to Virginia, it would likely be a month before this installment would reach the editor at the newspaper.

Of course, I changed Richard Grant's name in the story, making it Robert Grant instead. It was enough to claim it was someone else and I did not want to change the names so much that I had to think on it to remember who the character was when I tried to reassemble the pieces into a novel. One thing I did waffle on was whether or not to leave Robert Grant as Persimmon's father, because anyone who had not known Persimmon personally might take him to be a savage the way he attacked his own kin. In the end, I decided to reduce the severity of the confrontation for the serial instead.

I managed half of the story before there was a knock on my door. Opening it I found Persimmon, resplendent in his new white suit. Where I had opted for a shirt and pants, Persimmon added a loosely fitting jacket which concealed his Schofield well. We ate in the hotel dining room. The conch we had earlier had not stuck with us.

As promised, we returned to the saloon to join the fishermen in drinking rum if not dancing. Julio welcomed us, complimenting our outfits through slurred bilingual speech. I told him we felt far cooler in them.

"I'll drink to that!" was Julio's response, a phrase he repeated often once the rum took a firm hold.

We sat at a table closer to the revelry and still in the cross breeze between the open doors. I let Persimmon get a drink in him and then I asked, "So, what now?"

"I suppose I need to go back to Colorado and put a bullet in Mr. Jenkins," answered Persimmon.

"What about Mrs. Sanchez?" I asked.

By his answer, I was unsure if Persimmon did not grasp my intended meaning or if he was ignoring it. "If he's dead, she'll keep her ranch."

I waited a moment before continuing. Sensitive conversations with someone as enigmatic as Persimmon require listening with more than one's ears.

"That's not what I meant." I paused again and Persimmon turned to look at me. "I mean... I sort of thought that you and Mrs. Sanchez had an understanding, so to speak."

Persimmon turned away. "You sure do make assumptions easily... Mrs. Sanchez is a fine lady. She doesn't need the likes of me."

"She's a beautiful woman and desperately in need of the likes of you," I exclaimed a little too vigorously.

Persimmon huffed a laugh, I think at my excitement. "I have my own burdens and she doesn't need them put on her shoulders."

"I have no doubt that she would reduce those burdens immensely," I retorted.

Persimmon shook his head lightly at my suggestion and frankly, it irked me that someone would have such an opportunity and throw it away over nonsense.

I snapped, "Damnit man, I know you like the woman. Don't you think it is her choice too? Would you deny her happiness because of your fear?"

Persimmon's face puckered into a scowl and his eyes bored into mine. I knew I had better tug the reins.

"Now remember, you promised not to shoot me. I don't mean to sound insolent. The thing is, it frustrates me to see you throw away that chance for happiness, not only for you but for her as well. I'm speaking as a friend. We are friends, aren't we? I figure if a man nearly kills you and you're still riding along with him, you must be friends." My philosophical words surprised me. Funny how I had never thought of them before.

Persimmon found them funny too. He laughed and replied with an affirming, "Maybe."

"Well then, if you are going to give it a try, and you should, then killing Jenkins isn't going to work. Even if you prove him to be the same Jenkins who stole the money, the law considers shooting him down to be murder. You'll be on the run and giving Marshal Edwards reason to pursue you. Better to let the Pinkertons handle it." Having never been a confidant before, I was impressed by the good sense I made.

Persimmon countered, "I don't trust them not to take credit for it and cheat us out of the reward money. If Jenkins is convicted, we might not have to buy the note from the bank, but even if we don't have to settle with the bank, that reward money is a new herd of cattle and cattle punchers to oversee it."

My ears hung on the word, "us." Did he mean the two of us or he and Mrs. Sanchez, or the lot?

"Maybe we should send a telegram to the men in Richmond and tell them what is going on first?" It was my suggestion, but I was not confident about it.

"I don't trust them either. But it makes no never mind, unless they can get to Jenkins' private papers and find proof, how are they going to prove he's the scoundrel?"

Persimmon made a good point. We were acting on our own assumption that this was the same Jenkins. Odds were good that it was the same man but if it was, Jenkins did not sound like the sort of fool who would incriminate himself easily. He would know we had no proof. Richard Grant mentioned a partner but that partner could be standing right beside Jenkins and we would not know him. Only Richard Grant could identify both men. The answer was clear, but I hated to say it.

Racking my brain for a couple more minutes, I could not come up with another guaranteed means of proving it was Jenkins. With all the other options I could muster discredited, I finally broke down and mentioned the one I did not want to consider. "We can take Richard Grant back with us to testify."

"I'd just as soon shoot him," came Persimmon's prompt response.

"But shooting Jenkins without proof is definitely going to get you brought up on a murder charge," I replied, irritated that Persimmon was resisting reason.

"I wasn't talking about Jenkins," Persimmon quipped.

"Oh. I see that you are not fond of Grant but his testimony is the best evidence," I contended.

"I never sought out my father because I knew if I ever found him, I'd kill him."

"But see there, you dealt with him today and you didn't kill him. I know you are angry with him but you don't want to shoot him." What little did I know?

Persimmon threw back the last gulp of rum in his glass and turned to me, his entire person exuding a deadly seriousness. "My dear father put the family deep in debt and then abandoned me and my momma to try to scrape by. We didn't go to Kansas because we wanted to. We sold the farm to pay some of the debt and ran away from the rest. My mother died of a broken heart in a place that she never considered home. Today, it took everything I had in me not to unload my pistol into the bastard."

Pouring Persimmon more rum gave me a few moments to think. "I will volunteer to talk to him. I'll get him aboard ship and keep him away from you on the train."

Persimmon mulled it over a few moments and nodded. "If you go talk to him, he's going to wait until you are gone and then hide out until he can find a boat to Cuba. Then we'll never see him again."

"I'll wait until the day we are going to board a ship. I won't leave his side," I explained, a glimmer of hope lifting my voice.

"I know it needs to be done. I will be grateful if you would do that. I know you have been tiptoeing around me all day. It really wasn't necessary but I appreciate the thought anyway." This was the first time I had witnessed Persimmon express gratitude.

"Well, to be honest, there was a selfish side to my treatment of you today. I know you promised not to shoot me but I figured I shouldn't press my luck," I offered, with a smile.

Persimmon laughed, "I appreciate it just the same." Then he stood abruptly and looked down upon me. "By the way, let me correct you on one thing... I promised I wouldn't kill you. I never said I wouldn't shoot you."

With that, Persimmon strolled over to the two-piece band. He threw his right leg over the corner of a table, sat back on the same haunch and began tapping his toe with the rhythm. Julio approached him and said, "I'll drink to that," took a sip from a bottle and handed it to Persimmon.

A little while later, a big, burly woman stomped in through the other door and yelled, "Julio!" Julio nearly jumped from his skin. The woman marched up to him and grabbed Julio by the elbow. "You best be getting home."

"Come on Ella, let the little guy have some fun," begged the tattered American.

Ella slapped the poor southern gentleman, "Good for nothing!" Then she slapped Julio hard followed by two other Cuban men whom she left with her handprint on their cheeks. When she turned toward Persimmon and saw the bottle in his hand, she reared back to slap him as well. Persimmon tucked his chin down, glared at her from under his brow and said with a low, menacing voice, "You'd best not."

The big woman dropped her hand and jerked Julio out the door.

The barkeep joined the rest of the room in a big laugh and then one of the fishermen exclaimed jovially, "That's why I never married!"

Julio was a small man who made for a good joke but without Julio to drive the fun, the party soon disbanded. Persimmon and I returned to the Russell House and though my eyes felt crossed with all the rum I imbibed, I finished the serial installment, tucked it into an envelope and then myself into bed. Thus, concluded our introduction to Key West.

XV
EVENTFUL SOJOURN

I was up an hour after daybreak, though I strongly wished I was not. My head was still swimming in rum but I did not want to miss mailing my letter. Assuming Persimmon would sleep a couple more hours, I went downstairs, chugged a glass of water then enjoyed half a pot of coffee with a side of eggs and ham. Afterward, I made my way to the wharf. I lucked upon two sailors returning to their ship. I asked the one acting as a crutch for the other if he would fetch the ship's purser for me which he obliged. The purser assured me my letter would be mailed once they reached Virginia.

I thanked him, asked him to thank the captain again for me and sought out the shipping agent to request a third ticket on the *Belle of the...* something or other, I couldn't remember. The agent wrote it down and said he expected her to arrive tomorrow or the next day. I thanked him and since the ham and eggs had absorbed some of last night's latent rum, I decided I should run one more errand before returning to the hotel.

It was less than a mile to Richard Grant's shack. Rather than wait until I was ready to confront him, I thought it might be best to go check to be sure we had not spooked him and sent him packing. The streets were bustling, not like those of St. Louis or New Orleans but there were horse carts and the odd carriage. In the distance rang a hammer. My ears latched onto the sort of squeak my shoes made on the gritty street. The earth below me was made from a mixture of pulverized shell, sand, bits of coral and the odd dark speck of decomposed matter. I could have walked along the raised sidewalk but the clop of my own feet on the boards annoyed my rum-soaked senses. Instead, I traced its length, circling around the ramps protruding into the street from the walk and the occasional mounting block or small boat.

It was a pleasant observation that I gathered far fewer spectators in my new outfit. I do not think I blended perfectly into the populace but it was sufficient for anyone with their own business to mind. When I came to the alley which I was sure was Richard Grant's, I approached cautiously. Slipping up to the back of the one-room shanty, I peeked through the dirty window to see Richard Grant playing dominoes with a Cuban man.

They were talking and I eavesdropped for as long as I dared but enough to make the assumption that Persimmon's father was working with a group of Cuban revolutionaries. I gathered they had him doing simple tasks for which a Cuban might seem suspicious. The man playing dominoes with him was complaining that Richard Grant could not be used to spy on passengers disembarking an upcoming ship from Cuba if Grant's eye did not heal quickly.

It was no concern of mine if Richard Grant made a meager living spying on ships for revolutionaries. The good news was Richard Grant appeared to have no plans for escape. With that, I left. I did not want to risk being discovered.

Back in the hotel lobby I spied Persimmon in the dining room. He started to interrogate me as to my absence but before he could ask his questions, I answered them, telling him that I had gone to check on Richard Grant and what I had overheard.

"He always was one to prefer stretching an easy dollar than to work for ten. I still say I'll likely kill him before we get him back to Colorado," Persimmon commented.

I made no effort to reply. I was going to tell him that I would send a telegram to the men in Richmond, requesting someone official to meet us in South Pueblo to arrest our suspect once Richard Grant agreed to accompany us, but Persimmon did not need to know that so why rouse him further. Another band of storms was bearing down on the island and would arrive within the hour so we prolonged breakfast. I ordered a second round, my appetite aroused by my walk.

In the late morning we sat on the front porch, close to the wall where the gallery above could shade us, and enjoyed the island breeze. Around dinnertime the sun was high but obscured by another band of storms. The dining room served fish. That afternoon, we strolled the western side of the island while puffing on locally rolled cigars. My white shirt and pants made the sun far more bearable but so did the overcast skies.

After supper, we found our way back to the saloon. Persimmon did not say so but I think he hoped the group of fishermen would return, which they did.

Julio welcomed us as if we were lifelong friends. I had not intended to drink heavily this night but Julio forced the rum onto us and after three gracious pours, my resistance was drowned.

Early in the evening Julio's burley wife, Ella, marched in and tried to drag him home but all the fishermen put up a fuss and Julio pulled away and hid himself behind the band. Never have I heard such words come from a woman's mouth. No wonder she was comfortable entering a saloon. Once Julio promised to be home by ten, she capitulated and stomped off in a huff. Persimmon and I discussed it and could not come up with a reason why that happy little man had a wife like that, short of her hogtying him.

My plan for the evening to be near teetotal was foiled by prodigious drinking. When the party broke up, Persimmon and I staggered out the door, unsure which of us was holding up the other. We wobbled and swayed our way down the street, past dark alleys between warehouses. In our new island garb I am sure we resembled vulnerable drunken tourists, if not tame drunken locals. From out of one of the dark alleys ahead of us stepped a disheveled man with a long fillet knife.

"Give me your valuables," he demanded firmly, as he slashed the air with the blade to make his point.

To the thief's great consternation, I glanced at Persimmon and Persimmon at me, and the pair of us burst into laughter. Persimmon careened into the building next to us, hands on the wall, struggling for a breath amidst convulsive laughing. Seeing him gasping only seasoned the situation for me. Involuntarily, I let out a howling cackle before launching into the same breathless laughter. Doubling over with my hands on my knees, spinning on one heel, then stumbling a few steps in the crouched position, I struggled to keep my feet under me.

I gathered myself a little and reeled over to where Persimmon was recovering while our would-be robber chastised us.

"You drunken fools! Do as I say or I will cut you," the thief threatened, presenting the blade with a slow twisting motion so it could catch the lamplight.

"He's gonna cut us," I mocked to Persimmon, barely getting the words out before I choked on the hilarity of it.

Persimmon squealed back into drowning laughter and leaned into the same wall with his right shoulder.

"What is wrong with you?" asked the would-be thief, contemptuously.

His befuddled irritation swept my legs from under me and I fell to one knee on the sidewalk, grabbing at Persimmon as I went down. The limit of the thief's patience was met and viewing Persimmon and I as nearly incapacitated, he started towards us from eight feet away. Before he could plant his second step, Persimmon bounced himself off the wall and jerked his pistol from under his coat.

"Ay!" The thief's eyes gaped and he turned and dashed into the darkness.

The alley was three steps behind the thief, normally plenty of time for Persimmon to shoot him down. In this case, it would have been a feat, given Persimmon's condition. Yet, when I saw the comical shock on the thief's face, I dropped to both knees. One hand was on the ground while I swung from Persimmon's sleeve by the other, drooling like a madman, my eyes sloppy with tears of the absurd. My weight dragged Persimmon off balance and he stumbled around me, pivoting on my grip.

We laughed our way into the middle of the street and took deep breaths trying to regain our composure so we could stagger a straighter line to the hotel. We giggled the entire way, gathering shushes from the desk clerk as we fumbled through the lobby. If only the clerk knew I wasn't much of a drinker...

The following morning, we both slept late. With no place to be, I aimed to stay tucked under a single sheet until the room stopped spinning. Around noon, the aroma wafting upstairs from the kitchen drug me, reluctantly, from bed. Persimmon and I ate, filling up on coffee, water and juice. Then we adjourned to the porch chairs, coffee in hand, to take on the day by our terms.

Another storm rolled through but the frequency of the storm bands was less like clockwork and their structure more ragged. I mentioned my observation to the clerk who told me the barometer was rising. By his explanation, that was a good sign. It meant the hurricane that had been reported south of Cuba was not looping back through the gulf in our direction.

It was welcomed news but the threat of the approaching storms intrigued me and when the next one bore down on the island in the late afternoon, I urged Persimmon to take a walk, assuming we could duck into shelter somewhere for the brevity of the storm. We strolled slowly down Whitehead Street toward the south side of the island to see something new. I think we both felt weak inside. I know I did and Persimmon never outpaced me.

The sweet smell of tobacco flooded my nostrils and I looked up to find we were passing a cigar factory. A monotone Spanish voice, tarnished by echo, resonated from the open door. Persimmon took the opportunity to buy another double-handful cheap but neither of us felt like a smoke at the moment. While he paid for them, I poked my head inside to discover a man on stool perched still higher on a platform. In his hand was a book and he was reading loudly to all the cigar rollers below him. The Cubans in the factory made me think of the revolutionaries which brought my mind back to Richard Grant and whether or not I could get him to go with us. As we continued our easy stroll, I thought on my plan of how to approach him.

As if he read my mind, Persimmon said, "I'll be glad to conclude this business."

I agreed and mentioned my plan to deliver a written message to the telegraph office to be sent to the Richmond men, notifying them to meet us in South Pueblo to arrest Jenkins.

"Don't tell them who we are after. I don't trust them or the Pinkertons," he instructed. Then in what seemed to me to be a rare qualification of his words, Persimmon said, "I don't know that any of these men are untrustworthy but those Richmond men will owe us a large sum if we catch Jenkins and the Pinkertons have been embarrassed by the ordeal. Both sides have a reason to take it from us if they were inclined to, so don't give them reason for temptation."

His logic made sense. Now if we could just get a ship home before Richard Grant vanished. I was still devising my plan when Persimmon mentioned going back to the saloon again later that evening.

"I haven't fully recovered from last night. Besides, the agent told me to expect our ship in port as early as tomorrow. The island is growing on me but I don't think we need to miss that boat."

My reasons were valid but Persimmon did not care. He cajoled me all the way to the ocean with promises of not drinking and explanations of how he felt the same way but would like to say goodbye to our new friends.

What was I to say? Persimmon was not the sort of man to beg, or explain himself, or to give a damn if anyone followed along with him or not. To be the object of that exception felt good and outweighed the queasiness in my innards.

That evening at the saloon Persimmon requested rye whiskey, saying he would drink it far slower than the sweet rum. Our fishermen buddies showed again but a little later than expected. I think they had actually gone fishing and caught something to boot.

About nine o'clock, Ella stormed into the saloon. There is no way for me to know if Julio caroused to get away from her meanness or if Ella was cantankerous because Julio was out carousing every night but the two issues fed off each other. This evening, Ella was boiling. She slammed a chair under a table where two gentlemen were quietly playing cards. Then she marched up to Julio and jabbed a finger into the soft part of his shoulder, ranting loudly in Spanish all the while.

Julio's brow crumpled and his demeanor turned serious. He barked something in reply, also in Spanish. Ella jabbed him again. Julio must have cursed her in response because Ella walloped him upside his jaw. It was an open hand slap, but she sent the little man spinning and laid him out in the floor.

"Ella…" the American said, disapprovingly.

Ella's response was to slap him too. She reared back to take a swipe at one of the other Cuban fishermen but he cowered. Hunting another target in her fervor, she swung before she looked and left a red handprint across Persimmon's cheek.

Instinctively, Persimmon whipped his forearm out and punched Ella square on the chin. Her head buckled to her bosom and she flopped back into a sprawl on the floor.

"See here now! No matter how she has behaved, she's no man to be struck," scolded one of the tourists playing cards.

"She was man enough," replied Persimmon.

From the floor behind the American came the familiar, if muffled, voice of Julio, "I'll drink to that."

I shook my head. We really needed to get off of this island before serious trouble discovered us, I thought. To my left, the barkeep ambled across the room with a pitcher in hand.

"What do we owe you?" I called to him. We might be stuck on the island but we could leave the saloon.

"It's on the house," the barkeep replied with a smile. "I should pay you for the entertainment your friend gave us. That woman would pick a fight with a fence post."

Persimmon saw that I was trying to leave and did not make me beg him. We hurriedly told our fishermen friends goodbye and that we were leaving Key West soon. They promised to relay our message to Julio when he came around. Before we were out the door, the barkeep dumped a splash of water from the pitcher onto Ella's brow. Curious to know if Persimmon or the floor had hit her too hard, we paused until we saw her flailing to get up, then we made our escape.

One good thing to come from all this, I went to bed at a decent time and in a room whose walls stayed where I left them when I laid down. I told myself I would not even partake in my evening brandy before I reached Colorado, but I knew that vow was made to be broken.

The next morning, I awoke to a knock on my door. It was a bellboy. He delivered a card from the shipping agent; the *Belle of the Gulf* had arrived and she intended to sail before dark. I rushed to dress myself and wake Persimmon. Taking time from breakfast gave me a chance to scratch out a telegram to Richmond. It also gave me time to develop some doubts. I was going to be heading down an alley inhabited by some questionable people, to see a man Persimmon had beaten, who also worked with revolutionaries that might not take kindly to my taking their informant. I went back to my room and stuffed the Smith & Wesson Model Three Persimmon had loaned me into my waistband— just in case.

XVI
EXTRA BAGGAGE

Slipping up to Richard Grant's shack as I had before, I peered through the back window but no one was inside. A bit of panic grabbed me. What if Richard Grant had fled after all? Without knowing where else to look for him, I stood there by his shack, looking about me, worried that someone would see me and grow suspicious. What felt like twenty minutes was probably only five before I heard voices coming down the alley.

Carefully, I peeked around the corner to see Richard Grant approaching with the Cuban man I had seen him with two days prior. They were talking about a passenger who had disembarked the ship that morning. I assumed from what little I heard, that the man was from Spain and there was conflict currently underway in Cuba. What it all meant, I did not know, but I did not plan to stick around and find out. The Cuban man thanked him and before he left, he gave Richard Grant a handful of coins. Silver, I estimated, by the flat sound of their clanking.

I watched through the window as Richard Grant tucked the coins under a floorboard, then I took a deep breath, went to the front and knocked on the door.

"Forget something, Guillermo?" Richard Grant was saying as he opened the door. "Oh, you, you're the man who was with Persimmon." He grew nervous at his own mention of Persimmon's name and glanced around me to see where Persimmon was.

"I'm alone. Can we talk?" I asked.

Richard Grant left the door open and retreated back into the shack. I took it as an invitation and entered, closing the door behind me.

"Your eye is looking better," I said in a friendly, encouraging voice, trying to build a rapport.

"What do you want?" he snapped. Clearly, Richard Grant did not see me as a threat.

Deciding it was best to get straight to the point, I made my intentions plain. "We need you to come to Colorado with us to identify Jenkins."

"Are you crazy? I'm not safe there. This shack isn't much but I'm saving for something better."

"I know," I replied with a smirk and tapped the floorboard with my heel. That drew his ire but was nothing to convince him to come with me. In an attempt to stir his sympathy, I explained, "There is a Spanish woman with a small child for whom Persimmon is going to all this trouble. Finding the money for the men in Richmond means saving that woman's ranch, which we think is also being threatened by the same Jenkins."

Richard Grant sat dribbling a small stack of dominoes on the table. "Lord knows I've not done the best by Persimmon and I owe him something, despite the beating he gave me, but if I go back there Jenkins or Heeley or some of their men will kill me. I'm sure with that kind of money they have plenty of hired men to do their dirty work now."

I nodded. Then I let my smile fade, crumpled my brow and tried to project a voice like Persimmon, deep and deliberate. "If you won't do it for your son, you had best do it for your life because Persimmon *will* kill you. Forget about Jenkins or Heeley, I've seen Persimmon kill around a dozen men in the few weeks I've known him. He doesn't bat an eye, doesn't worry the least about consequences, he just kills them. What's more, I've never seen anyone rile his blood like you. I'm here without him because he was sure he would kill you if he had to deal with you any further. Life has not been kind to him and you were one of the main instruments of his torture. I am certain that if I tell him you refused, he will scour this island until he finds you and he'll kill anyone that gets in his way."

"Aren't you afraid to be tagging along with him if he's so terrible?" Grant asked, sarcastically.

I thought about it for a moment and responded with a resounding, "Yes, yes I am. He's nearly killed me twice. I guess why I stayed on isn't your business but I will say, it was only after he gave me his word not to kill me. In my experience, no one has to fear him unless they wrong him... that means you have everything to be afraid of."

"I can always go to Cuba," Grant snipped in a contemptuous tone which struck me wrong.

Perhaps I had failed to portray a believable threat. Maybe I overplayed my deliberate voice or scrunched brow? Whatever the reason, I did not feel I was being taken seriously.

Aggravation, no, disgust welled up inside me unlike I had ever experienced. Sure, I had seen worthless people before but I had never had to deal with someone so selfish firsthand and maybe it was my concern for Persimmon which stirred the pot but, in that moment, I wished Persimmon would burst through the door and shoot Grant down. The thought crossed my mind to do it myself. It was the first time I had ever felt what it was like to metaphorically wash my hands of a situation. This mood was dark but liberating and I stood slowly, gravely.

"Fine. You make your bed. I don't have the patience to haggle with you and whether you live doesn't concern me either. I'll go back to tell Persimmon how you've acted."

Whether he believed me now or simply felt he had pushed me too far, I do not know. His tune changed abruptly, "No, no, you're right, I should do this for Persimmon." Richard Grant became quiet for a minute and I could see in his good eye that he was racking his brain for an alternative. His options were limited and he knew it. Finally, he whimpered, "What day are we leaving?"

"Today," I answered.

"Today?" he blurted. "Well then... I tell you what, I'll meet you at the ship in two hours. You can tell Persimmon he can count on me."

Grant's eye told me that what I could count on was him to beg his Cuban contacts to hide him away. "No. You're coming with me."

With grit and decisiveness I never thought I possessed, I squatted down and pulled the floorboard up and nabbed his cache of money. The flour sack held a tidy assortment of coins and paper money and I knew it was all he had to his name. Grant picked up his rum jug with the intention to attack me but I jerked the Model Three from my waistband and held it pointing at his feet.

"I'm holding onto this until you follow through. I don't want you getting any ideas to part ways with us too soon." I motioned with the muzzle, "Get your things together, let's go."

The walk out of that alley was the longest. I forced Richard Grant to go ahead of me a few feet and I managed to stuff half his money in one pants pocket and the other half and flour sack into my other pocket as well as hide my pistol in my waistband as before. Unfortunately, it was all I could do to keep my pants from falling off, especially in the heat. I sweated all the more profusely with the fear that someone who knew Richard Grant would see us walking away and find it suspicious.

Oh, was I glad when the hotel came into view. Inside, I left Persimmon to guard Grant while I retrieved the carpetbag and my things. Most of Grant's money and the pistol, I stuffed into the bag. It was a pleasant relief to again not have to hold my pants up as I walked. As far as I know, neither Grant nor Persimmon said a word to each other in my absence, but at least no one got shot.

On the way to the ship we passed the telegraph office. I dug the previously written message from my pocket. Grant saw it and started complaining.

"Look, I'll go with you but only on the condition that you don't tell anyone I'm coming. If word gets out, I'm dead." Grant sounded sincere this time.

"What does it matter? You didn't even use an alias on the ship down here. The Pinkertons know where you are and you're still alive." My manner was belittling and forceful. I think it impressed Persimmon, though that was not my intention.

"If they hear I am on my way back with you, they'll assume it is for good reason. They might get the idea to play me off against that lawyer again. I don't trust him and neither do the Pinkertons. If they think he'll talk to save his own hide, they'll use me as leverage but if he finds out I am coming, then who else might find out?" Richard Grant was insistent and his point was sensible.

I took a pencil from the clerk and scratched out the line about our bringing Grant with us. Then I handed the paper to the clerk and paid him with some of Richard Grant's money.

When I met the agent to retrieve our tickets, he informed me that the ship was bound for Galveston, Texas rather than New Orleans. Under normal circumstances, I would have celebrated. I had never been to Galveston, but I knew of it. It was the Jewel of Texas with the largest population of any city in the state. However, the longer passage by ship did not bode well for Persimmon. It also meant a longer train ride because there were still no railroads across West Texas. The shortest route meant heading northeast to St. Louis before taking another train west but our horses were boarded at the livery in New Orleans. To retrieve them meant we would be adding that much more distance and all the while with Richard Grant in tow.

For his sake, I withheld the change of destination from Persimmon. Since our ship was not ready to depart, I gave the carpetbag to Persimmon for safe keeping and put Richard Grant in his cabin with instructions to stay put. Without telling either man, I slipped away and ran back to the telegraph office. I sent a telegram to the owner of the livery in New Orleans explaining our problem and telling him that if he would send someone with our horses and tack to meet us in Galveston, we would pay him twice for his trouble. After all, it was the Richmond Consortium who would be footing the bill. I gave our ship's name and an approximate date of arrival and asked that he send word if he could not accomplish this.

The Gulf of Mexico was much calmer this voyage and Persimmon fared better. Richard Grant stayed in his cabin most of the time. I checked in on him occasionally and made sure he was comfortable. For that, I believe I earned his trust but what good is the trust of a thief, I wondered.

Before we arrived in port, Persimmon and I changed back into our western attire, which I had asked the porter to have cleaned. I suppose vanity was to blame, neither of us wanted to look out of place though the white linen would have been more comfortable. South Texas is not exactly a frigid destination. When port turned out to be Galveston, Persimmon was surprised. Since he had been seasick for the trip to Key West, the longer trip to Galveston did not seem any longer to him.

First, he began to complain about the extended train ride and then Persimmon fussed about having to go to New Orleans to fetch our horses but I stopped him. There was nothing I could do about the longer train ride but I told him what I had done about the horses and that I was hopeful we would find them waiting. We did.

A young man stood on the wharf holding a sign with my name on it. We met him and he took us to the local stable where we collected our horses in good order. The young man timidly gave me the bill, ashamed of the price written on it by the livery owner in New Orleans. It was high, triple rather than double the cost by my estimation but I paid it out of Richard Grant's money and even tipped the young man on top of it. He left grinning ear to ear and Persimmon was very pleased at my management of the situation. The only person not tickled over the deal was Richard Grant but I assured him I would replace the funds once we were reimbursed.

On the train, Richard Grant was more personable. He rode in another car and had to sleep on a hard bench using a board to make it a bed but to his credit, he did not complain. Occasionally, I would visit with him. We talked of various subjects. I never pressed him on anything particular but as he became more comfortable with me, he offered nuggets of information voluntarily.

"You might not believe me but I thought Jenkins and Heeley were legitimate when I first met them. They both looked the part of eastern tycoons, with their dark bushy beards and beaver hats. Of course, it didn't matter to me either way but I have to say I liked the feeling best when I thought I was legitimate too." Whether Richard Grant was lamenting his decision or only telling his story, only he knew.

He told me he wanted immunity for his part and when I told him I would speak on his behalf but that I could not control what was done, he said I had to get a written paper stating he was not at fault before he would testify. I told him I would do what I could. I figured it was not a point worth arguing on the train and Persimmon could press him if need be.

One evening he had a few drinks and began talking of Persimmon and the old days. "Persimmon's mother thought she could hold me down, and saddle me with responsibility. I don't know what she ever saw in me but she was beautiful so I didn't care. As always, I put my happiness first and when the war came along, I saw my opportunity to escape the mundane life of a farmer. I admit that. The further I walked, the freer I felt. I never did make it to the office to join up, I just kept on walking. After the war, I figured Persimmon was grown so why did they need me? He's a lot like his mother's side. The Apricots were responsible, hardworking people. They warned her not to marry me."

Ah, one of my long-standing questions was answered and it should have been obvious. I once asked myself what sort of father would give his son such a name? The somber truth was that a teenage boy felt so betrayed by his father that he would rather take his mother's maiden name, even if that meant enduring the ridicule certain to accompany the name, Persimmon Apricot.

Later that evening, Persimmon walked in with a bottle in one hand and three snifters laced between the fingers of the other. He sat down next to me, handed Richard Grant and I both a glass and filled them with brandy. I was astonished and my chest tightened as it always did when I did not know what to expect next from Persimmon. Persimmon, Grant, alcohol, all in the same room? It was a powder keg waiting for a match. My mind teetered between the reasons behind Persimmon's olive branch and worrying that Richard Grant would say something to light that keg.

Richard Grant had been telling of his work with the Cubans when Persimmon entered. Slowly, he resumed his story followed by more of the same. Persimmon never said a word and when his glass was empty, he stood and left the car, leaving the bottle of brandy on the bench.

The next morning, we arrived in St. Louis. We had to switch trains and there was some question as to whether we needed to collect our horses or if rail staff would transfer them to the other train. Persimmon took our receipts for the horses and left the train ahead of me, to check on the matter. I went to the other car to fetch Richard Grant. He and I exited his car. He stepped down first with a small duffle over his shoulder. I followed with the carpet bag. Far ahead, I saw Persimmon moving away from us. My attention had turned to a beautiful woman across the platform and I was soaking in how flattering she was to her dress. Richard Grant and I had walked the length of the car when I heard him utter his last words, "Oh hell, it's Heeley."

XVII
FOR NAUGHT

Richard Grant's exclamation jerked my attention from the girl in time to see the blast from Heeley's muzzle. Despite the sharp echo, I heard the ghastly thud of the bullet burying itself deep inside Richard Grant's chest. He grabbed my arm and wheezed as he sank to the floor.

The shooter had passed Persimmon without knowing him but I was not as lucky. I was prey by association. From a railcar's length away, it took little for our attacker to bring the pistol to bear on me. I dove between two cars as our assailant fired. The bullet clanged through the railing of the railcar's stairway. Struggling over the coupler, my britches hung, and then the carpet bag. The screams of people running for cover stoked the panic in me. There was no doubt in my mind that my attacker would, at any moment, turn the corner and shoot me at point blank range. Snatching the bag free, I heard a shot. I spun myself around the corner of the car, expecting a bullet to chase me but when I cleared the gap between the cars, I saw my attacker leap from the other end of the car.

Assuming it was an attempt to outwit me, I spun back into the gap for cover before I realized the shooter was running away. Stepping into the clear I saw Persimmon sail from between two cars, one gap further down the train. The last shot had been his. What good I thought I would be, I don't know. The Model Three I carried was somewhere in the bottom of the bag but with Persimmon between me and the assassin I felt protected and ran after him. Trying to unlatch the bag and then rifle through it blindly while stumbling over tracks and timbers was a joke I did not find funny. We wove between trains on various tracks. The attacker managed to repeatedly duck from Persimmon's aim but Persimmon held his fire, waiting for an opportunity.

Persimmon was squatting to look under a car for legs on the other side but before I caught up with him, he rolled under the car and popped up into a run on the opposite side. As I broke free from the rail yard, I had yet to find the pistol in the bag. Persimmon was rounding the corner of a building in the distance so I gave up on fumbling for the revolver and lit out in a sprint.

After making half the distance, the sharp echo of a gunshot rattled from between the buildings. I kept running but closing upon the turn the thought struck me, what if Persimmon had been shot? My boots clattered to a halt near the brick facade of the building. Creeping along it to peek around the corner, my ears burned with the fear of fast approaching steps behind me. If the assassin was alive, he could round the building and catch me with my back turned or I could poke my head from behind this corner to find him waiting for me. Either way, I could get shot!

Hat in hand, I slipped my right eye beyond the brickwork to discover Persimmon casually walking away from me toward the stilled body of the assassin who lay face down near the far intersection. I jogged to and then past Persimmon, wanting a better look at the dead man. Persimmon had plugged him in the back.

St. Louis is definitely a part of the civilized East because, before I could speak to Persimmon, two uniformed police officers came running up, guns drawn. Knowing the officers would be high on alert and low on information, I did not want them mistaking either of us for trouble so, stretching my arm in a most exaggerated fashion, I dabbed my forefinger at the corpse and cried out, "That's the bad guy!"

"Who are you, then?" one of the officers asked me in an Irish accent.

Breathlessly, I told him how we were traveling with a witness to a crime and how the man on the ground before them had assassinated our witness.

"Well, we better go down to the station and let you tell it to the sergeant," the officer instructed in a tone of voice which reassured us that, though we were in his custody, he was not casting judgment upon us.

Persimmon surrendered his Schofield to the policeman speaking to us. The second officer flipped my coat open but finding no pistol on my person, asked nothing further so I did not volunteer the Model Three. It would have meant wasted time digging for it and I had no intentions of shooting anyone.

The same officer took the gun from the dead assassin's hand and waited with the body. The other marched Persimmon and I through the rail yard, around the front of our train, and back to the scene of the crime. A crowd of people stood at a distance, chattering under their breath to each other. Many of the women either stood with their hands over their agape mouths or trying unsuccessfully to shield the eyes of their children. None of them could pull themselves from the spectacle.

The body of Richard Grant was encircled by more policemen. The officer escorting us broke through the ring of uniforms, turned to view the body and then asked us, "So, this is the man you said was with you?"

Persimmon and I approached and I nodded to the officer as I stared down at the body. Richard Grant lay crumpled, half on his side, his eyes open, the corner of his mouth encrusted with dry bloody foam, and an expression of pain on his face.

Persimmon glanced briefly, then turned and walked several feet away.

"Hey, big fella, don't you go wandering off," the Irish officer called out.

I held out my hand and gently waved him off, "Our witness was also his father."

"Oh, I'm sorry," the office apologized. "We don't need to be here, let's get you two down to the station and tell the sergeant all about it."

"We have horses on this train," I blurted, surprised I remembered them amidst the chaos.

Taking the receipts from Persimmon, I gave them to the officer who delegated the collection of our horses to another, his junior. Then the Irish officer tagged another policeman to come along and the pair led us to a police station on Clark Avenue where I regaled the sergeant with our story.

"If you are Pinkerton agents, you should have identified yourself to my officers," the sergeant commented, having misunderstood me.

"We aren't agents, we are just assisting on a case," I corrected him.

Looking at the paper on his desk, the sergeant nodded in acknowledgment. "Do you have any identification?"

Shrugging my shoulders, I replied that we did not. I looked to Persimmon to see if he had anything to add that I had forgotten but he was staring aloof at the wall behind the sergeant. I doubt he would have admitted it but I think the death of his father disturbed him.

"McInny," the sergeant called out.

"Sir?" answered the officer who had escorted us to the station.

"Go fetch the Pinkerton man who's been working the wharf," the sergeant ordered.

"Yes, sir," McInny bellowed before heading out of the station.

"Maybe he can shed some light on this," the sergeant mumbled to himself. Then he turned to face Persimmon and I. "You two can have a seat over there," he told us, pointing with his eyes to a bench along the wall.

When McInny returned, I was relieved to find our luck had turned for the better. The "Pinkerton man" the sergeant had requested was Mr. Smith.

"You two again, eh?" Mr. Smith blustered with facetious accusation, obviously glad to see us.

"You know these men, then?" the sergeant asked Mr. Smith.

Mr. Smith confirmed our story. Satisfied, the sergeant released us with what could be translated as an obligatory warning.

"I'd recommend you men head on to wherever it was you were going. St. Louis is a respectable town. We don't need the likes of gunfighters mucking things up."

"I'm not a gunfighter," Persimmon barked. This was the first full response he had uttered through the entire ordeal, other than to nod or maybe answer in the affirmative when asked a question.

Given what I knew of Persimmon, I was glad the sergeant had not yet given Persimmon back his Schofield. The sergeant was a big fellow himself, a little pudgy in the middle and grey in his mustache, but a strong-willed man who spoke his mind.

"I've seen your kind. You have death dripping off of you. You say you're not a gunfighter, how many men have you killed?" the sergeant challenged Persimmon.

Persimmon said nothing at first, I don't think he knew the answer. Maybe Persimmon was reflecting on the sergeant's point, maybe not, but the sergeant took Persimmon's hesitation as such.

"See what I mean?" the sergeant snapped in assumption.

"I never killed a man that didn't have it coming and I never worked as a gunman for money," Persimmon explained to justify his past.

"You're not working this case for money?" the sergeant sarcastically asked.

There was a pause in the volley of conversation before Persimmon ambivalently responded, "Not exactly."

"Well, I don't know what that means but nevertheless, remember what I said. You're free to go. One of the officers has your horses outside. Here is your Schofield back... try not to use it anymore while you're in St. Louis."

Persimmon holstered his pistol without further comment and we left the police station with Mr. Smith. As one might imagine, we found our way to a nearby saloon.

"Did you catch your insurance thief?" I asked Mr. Smith as we walked.

"We did. I see your trip had been successful...until you got here. I assume then that Grant was going to testify?" Mr. Smith asked me as we entered the saloon.

Persimmon took my horse with his to the hitching post, leaving Mr. Smith and I to enter the saloon and hunt up a table.

"Yes, he was going to help us identify the culprit and testify against him," I answered, seating myself at a corner table.

"Your friend seems pretty upset about it. I guess I would be too if it looked like I was going to miss out on the kind of reward money I heard you two agreed upon with those Richmond fellows," Mr. Smith jested, despite the circumstances. A dead confidence man was nothing to be upset about.

"I think you had better know, Richard Grant was Persimmon's father." My revealing comment was meant to caution the free speaking Mr. Smith.

Mr. Smith's eyes widened with surprise. "Oh," he nearly gasped, taken aback. "I wasn't expecting that. Now I see why they thought he could handle Grant."

Persimmon strode in solemnly and sat down. Without revealing why, Mr. Smith bought him a drink and was gracious enough not to leave me out.

"So, did you find out who the thief is, then?" inquired Mr. Smith in an artificially optimistic tone.

"We think so," I replied, trying to mimic the buoyance of Smith's voice. "The man's real name is Jenkins and based on some other information, we think we know where this Jenkins is. We needed Richard Grant to identify him to be sure."

"Not necessarily. If you have sufficient information to give us cause to investigate the man, we have ways to identify him." Mr. Smith's words offered renewed hope. "Who then, was the assassin?"

"That was Heeley, one of the partners. I suspect you know him by that name because that is an alias. I don't know his real name. Richard Grant said there were four partners. Two were already dead. Persimmon's killing Heeley leaves only Jenkins left." I tried to keep my explanation short as my experience with lawmen had prescribed. Mr. Smith could ask if he wanted more details. "What I don't understand is how Heeley knew where we would be. We sent word ahead for some of your men to meet us in Pueblo, Colorado but…"

"St. Louis is a railroad hub. Heeley has probably been watching every train arriving from south or east of here, hunting." Mr. Smith's explanation made sense but something still bothered me about it.

"If he knew we were coming and what for, why didn't he wait for us in Pueblo? That seems simpler."

"If he knew you were heading to Pueblo, then my guess is that he figured Pueblo was too close to home. Also, St. Louis is a big town. Maybe he thought he could disappear more easily. What amazes me is his gall, to shoot a man down in the train depot like that. Maybe he thought the crowd would offer him cover. If he could get a block away, pass through a building to another street, disappear and leave town, that would probably have been the last we saw of him." Again, Mr. Smith's analysis was rational. Likely it was the best we could do unless we could eventually get Jenkins to confess.

"What do you recommend now?" I asked Mr. Smith.

"I'll accompany you to Pueblo to meet whichever agents or lawmen are awaiting you. Do you have a description of this Jenkins character?" Mr. Smith asked.

I nodded.

"Well, maybe we can still flush this rat out."

XVIII
SECOND CHANCE

The summer sun in St. Louis did not have the wilting effect it did in Key West but it was hot on our shoulders as we stood in a semi-circle around the grave of Richard Grant.

"He wasn't there for my mother's funeral or my wife's. I don't see why anyone needs to be there for his," was Persimmon's reaction when asked about burying his father. Despite this, I made arrangements for Richard Grant's funeral and paid for it out of what money was left in his flour sack. Persimmon didn't balk or threaten to leave me behind. Like the time I buried those two men in the rocks, he was accommodating and quietly contributive, supplying me with Richard Grant's date of birth, hometown and so on, for the tombstone. I got the sense that Persimmon appreciated what I was doing, in his reserved way.

Mr. Smith graciously offered to take care of rescheduling our train tickets for after the funeral. He turned out to be a bright spot amid the gloom, certainly not what I would have predicted upon our first meeting.

Persimmon remained aloof. Maybe it was the death of his father. Maybe it was the realization that he had no more family, maybe I do not know what I am talking about. Persimmon was, after all, difficult to read more often than not. I did worry that his silence was much like that of a volcano's, seemingly harmless until it explodes with little or no warning. I was glad when we boarded the train for Pueblo, hoping that a change of venue would be therapeutic.

Two Pinkerton men met our train in South Pueblo. Mr. Smith introduced us to Agent Heinz, a greying gentleman with the confidence of experience in his eyes, and Agent Thompson who was about my age, well dressed and eager. The Victoria Hotel's saloon was quieter than others, so after a visit to the livery, we adjourned to conduct our business there.

The proprietor served us a round of drinks as we scooted our chairs and shuffled about to get comfortable at the table. Mr. Heinz removed his bowler hat and placed it on the table. Mr. Thompson took his cue from the senior agent and did likewise.

"So, what information do you have?" Agent Heinz asked, glancing between Persimmon and I.

Pulling my notes from my coat pocket was unnecessary as I remembered what little information they contained, but I retrieved my notebook and placed it open on the table anyway, for effect. I described Jenkins' extremely light hair and the two moles on his cheek and topped that with how he planned to buy up land ahead of a railroad near Denver.

Mr. Heinz was quiet. He raised his brow and brought his head down to meet his hand to scratch above one eye. "It's a shame what happened to Richard Grant. His testimony would probably have garnered a conviction in court. I'm amazed that you got him to cooperate in the first place. Wouldn't have hurt our case either, if you had only winged the assassin," Mr. Heinz cast his eyes toward Persimmon but prudently cut his admonishing glare short.

The apprehensive tone he used and the fact that Mr. Heinz had yet to comment on the information I gave him, led me to prompt him, "Isn't what we have enough?"

"Maybe," Mr. Heinz began indecisively. "We still need a witness or some documentation that can prove without a doubt that he is our man. If we could tie the assassin in St. Louis to Jenkins, that would be great but so far, we've found nothing. Well, other than his hotel room but even there we found no identifying documents. I don't know who he was, but he was smart enough to leave no trace. You say this Jenkins character has a place outside of Leadville?"

I nodded.

"Have you met him?"

I shook my head.

"What we will do is head up there and find the local sheriff and see what he knows about Jenkins. Then, with his help, we'll pay Jenkins a visit and unless he turns out to be three feet tall or confesses, we'll get a photographer to take a photo of him... probably get a handwriting sample too. We'll mail that and a photo of the assassin to our agent back east to see what the men in Richmond think and the attorney in Washington," Mr. Heinz explained.

The plan seemed reasonable but slow. It would take better than a week to get a photo back east from Leadville. Richard Grant had been shot over this and I did not want to join him, so I beseeched Mr. Heinz, "Will you please keep Persimmon and I anonymous?"

Up until then Persimmon had appeared distant, staring blankly at the table, but he looked up at Mr. Heinz and seconded my request. I guess he was listening.

Mr. Heinz agreed, "I don't see why not, at least until we need you in court. Do the two of you plan to stay here and wait?"

Mr. Heinz looked at me and I looked to Persimmon, who nodded. It was during this conversation that I realized I was not the neutral observer I set out to be as a writer. I had become an integral player and had been for some time, though I was not sure where on the timeline to demark that change. Did the dangers of the case make my participation compulsory or was I drawn in by an honest friendship with Persimmon? The answer would probably always elude me. Persimmon was still an enigma.

"Fine," Mr. Heinz said with happy resolve, "we will take the stage into Leadville and locate the sheriff. There's no sense in mailing the photographs from Leadville, so we'll bring them back with us. I might even send them east with Agent Thompson, here." Mr. Heinz dipped his head slightly in Thompson's direction. "We'll work those details out when we return."

"Unless you need me," Mr. Smith interjected, "I am going to be heading back to St. Louis." Mr. Smith boarded the train the next morning after leaving instructions that we were to look him up the next time we were in St. Louis.

As for the plan hatched by Mr. Heinz, I was wrong, it would be at least two weeks before we had an answer. More than a week passed before these men returned from Leadville. Until then, there was little for Persimmon or I to do but wait. We took rooms with weekly rates and wandered, first the streets of South Pueblo, and then those of Pueblo. Our sojourn felt a good deal like our stay in Key West, without the palm trees, and gnats, and torrid sun, and white suits, and ocean breeze, and good cheap cigars. However, we still had a cache of the latter.

I swear, I had forgotten why I was in South Pueblo by the time the Pinkerton agents returned with news from Richmond. One afternoon, Persimmon and I were having lunch in the hotel when Mr. Heinz appeared.

"Ah... there you are. I am glad I found you so easily, but then again, I am a detective." Mr. Heinz wore a big smile but his attempt at humor merely drew a patronizing grin from me and nothing from Persimmon.

He sat down, his girth filling the gap between the chair and table. The attentive waiter had only one other table to tend and was upon the agent in an instant, so Mr. Heinz left us in suspense while he ordered his lunch.

"We missed you when you came through town before," I said, intending to make him feel he had slighted us and thereby, prod him along.

"Yes, I am sorry about that. The stage had trouble and we arrived with barely enough time to catch the train. I sent Mr. Thompson east, but I needed to go to Denver this week on another matter. However, Mr. Thompson has just sent word from back east and I am afraid it is not what we wanted to hear. It seems the Richmond fellows can only give us a maybe on the dead man and are pretty sure that the photo of Jenkins is not our man." Mr. Heinz's report was disappointing to say the least.

"You saw him. Did Jenkins match the description I gave you?" I asked, growing dissatisfaction prompting my interrogation.

"He does but the Richmond men said that the man they met was dark haired. As for the dead man, the alias we included did match. Even if they could agree without a doubt, that Heeley was one of the partners who swindled them, it does us no good because we don't know who Heeley really was. We also had Jenkins sign his name as Jenkins but also as Pearson. Our men compared the signatures with those on the contracts and they didn't match," Mr. Heinz reluctantly explained.

"Couldn't he fool you with the signatures?" Persimmon queried.

"It's possible. We checked the signatures he gave us with other documents he had and with documents at the local bank and they match but if he thought ahead to purposely change the way he wrote the signatures on the contracts back east, well, that could explain it. Still, we need a means to prove it." Mr. Heinz seemed nearly as frustrated as we were but there were limits to what he could do.

Persimmon followed quickly with, "What about the attorney in Washington?"

"He emphatically denies it is them. I don't buy it but I have no proof. Maybe he is a crook or maybe he's just an unscrupulous lawyer with shady clients whom he doesn't want to scrutinize too closely because he might very well turn up a problem that would cost him a dollar—a matter of what he doesn't know, he doesn't have to deny." It was clear Mr. Heinz had been thinking the issue through.

All this gnawed at me and I felt as though I could solve this case if I could gain firsthand knowledge of it. I had yet to lay eyes on Jenkins, so I asked, "Do you have a copy of the photograph made of Jenkins?"

"I do. I believe it is in my luggage in my room. If you think it will help, I'll be more than glad to fetch it."

I looked to Mr. Heinz and shrugged, "I don't know if it will or not but I can't help but to think we're missing something."

For an older, stout fellow, Mr. Heinz was spry and he hopped up from the table. "If the waiter returns before I do, tell him I will be right back."

Persimmon was staring at the table again, with a gloomy expression which was different from any other I had seen him make. He needed some distraction, but I did not know what to say so I tried to drag him into my attempt at detective work.

"I don't see how the descriptions given by Grant and by the men in Richmond can be so different," I lamented, hoping to solicit a response from Persimmon.

Taking a drink was all Persimmon did at first. I rambled on a bit more about how blind Donovan and Connelly and the rest of the Richmond Consortium must be, and how crooked the attorney was to let that deal go through. I paused in thought and was about to continue my rant when Persimmon spoke.

"You know... you had gotten me thinking that maybe I could be happy here."

"With Mrs. Sanchez?" I asked softly, my desire to rant broken.

Persimmon nodded. "It was a fool notion anyhow."

"No, it isn't, and no matter how this Jenkins mess turns out, Mrs. Sanchez would welcome you with open arms. I know you haven't known each other long, but she's a broken woman and broken people need help mending." I did not mention how broken Persimmon was. He knew and my point was made without drawing his ire. "Besides, there is still a chance to solve this. I'm willing to pay that shyster a visit if you are." I looked to Persimmon to see if any glimmer of hope stared back.

Before Persimmon answered me, Mr. Heinz returned, slapping a photograph on the table in front of me. It was the bust portrait of a blonde man. He was clean shaven and to my disappointment, he did not appear dastardly at all. However, two moles, one smaller than the other, were prominent on his cheek just as Richard Grant had described.

"He is a perfect match for the description Richard Grant gave." I examined the photograph as I combed through everything Richard Grant had told me. I remembered him saying that he believed the two men to be legitimate at first. Then it hit me. "Wait!" I belted, "I remember Richard Grant told me that he believed these men to be legitimate business men because of how much they looked the part. He distinctly said the men had dark beards. They must have been in disguise. He said Jenkins was a towhead in one description but had a dark beard in another. He must have had a false beard and wig or dyed his hair… something."

Persimmon's attention perked.

Mr. Heinz nodded, bored. "For the caper they pulled, it makes sense that they would have thought that far ahead. Still, without a witness, trying to prosecute Jenkins is a waste of time. If the victims themselves cannot point the finger at him, who else would?"

"The attorney," I asserted confidently, pushing back in my chair.

"I've done all I can do with him for now. I have no reason to harass him further. If the two of you can persuade him like you persuaded Grant, we might have something," Mr. Heinz said through a devilish grin.

The waiter arrived and served Mr. Heinz his lunch. Mr. Heinz tucked the corner of his napkin into his collar and spread the remainder of it across his belly. When the waiter left, Mr. Heinz picked up his fork and knife to cut his pork chop but paused, looking up at me from under his brow. "Do keep in mind, however, the court will frown upon a witness with a black eye."

Though I continued to run the matter through my head repeatedly, I remained quiet while Mr. Heinz ate, but not for his sake. I thought it might be best to let Persimmon's thoughts settle. His face was not as long as it had been and in his eyes was a glimmer of what I took as hope. My time with Persimmon was teaching me to be more suspicious. Whatever we decided our plans to be, perhaps Mr. Heinz did not need to know about them.

Once the portly Pinkerton agent had eaten, Persimmon and I adjourned for a walk and to enjoy one of our Key West souvenirs, cigars. The dirt street was wide and unusually peaceful and the scene felt like someone had set the town down in the wrong place. Persimmon propped himself on a post, staring at the mountains, and puffed on his stogy as if he were in control of tomorrow. So, I asked him, "What's our plan now?"

Persimmon drew long on his cigar, then with his index finger wrapped around it, rested his hand on the opposite elbow and blew a large smoke ring. "Like you said, I guess I need to pay that lawyer a visit, although, Jenkins is closer."

"Yeah, but you need this to play out in the court. Jenkins isn't going to confess but I am betting that an unscrupulous attorney will follow whichever path promises to save his hide," I added, trying to sound encouraging and help guide Persimmon down a path of his own choosing that would not lead to destruction.

"We'll get that attorney's information from Mr. Heinz tonight but before we go back east, I think it would be a good idea to check in with the reverend and Mrs. Sanchez, since we're so close," Persimmon recommended.

More than likely, Persimmon wanted an excuse to see Mrs. Sanchez again but checking in with them felt like the responsible thing to do. The next morning, we set out up the valley.

Our ride was uneventful, except that my horse had not been ridden since I boarded her in New Orleans and she wasn't taking to the idea of going back to work. She twitched and danced a bit at first, not liking the extra one hundred fifty pounds on her back. After the first mile, she stopped arguing and after the second she felt like her old self but Persimmon's horse, Samson, was glad to have his friend back. Persimmon rubbed the horse's neck and Samson would turn his head into the rub as if trying to give Persimmon a hug.

Traveling by road was faster than across the valley floor like when we left. We entered the south side of town, between McLaglen's place and the Bansheen Saloon, early on the second day. Of course, Persimmon was not one to pass a saloon upon arrival, so the two of us entered McLaglen's place. McLaglen was not behind the bar but his son served us and we sat at a table where we could watch out the window.

"Looks like there are a number of new men in town," I commented, after watching several unfamiliar faces enter the Bansheen. "All Jenkins men, I would bet."

"Most likely," Persimmon replied.

I was about to speculate on how many might have been friends of the late Lizard Johnson when McLaglen entered the back door. When he saw us, he immediately ran up to our table.

"I'm glad y'all are back. I hate to rush you with news when you've just hit town but I saw the reverend yesterday and he told me that if the two of you showed up, to tell you to come find him quick like," McLaglen informed us and then, anticipating our question, he added, "He didn't say why but it seemed urgent."

"I see there are more men in town since we left," I repeated my earlier comment to McLaglen, expecting a revealing reply.

"Yep, all Jenkins men as far as I know. Oh, and that marshal...Marshal Edwards, he's still in town too. I thought you'd want to know, seeing's as how you don't get on with him too well." Barkeeps are always founts of good information.

"What's he still hanging around for?" Persimmon grumbled. I doubt he expected an answer.

"He's still after those Jensen brothers but they are long gone. No way they are coming around here until they know he's gone, but that's his excuse anyway. He took a room for let, up the street. He doesn't talk to me. He spends his drinking time in the Bansheen but I get the feeling he's waiting around for you to return and see if he can catch you mixed up in something."

"You're an insightful man," Persimmon told McLaglen.

We thanked him, and headed to find the reverend, stopping by his modest home first. The reverend's wife opened the door.

"Is the reverend home?" Persimmon asked.

"No, he and Mr. Freeman, the gentleman who owns the hardware store, they both went up to the Sanchez ranch," the reverend's wife answered.

"Excuse me, ma'am, but do you know what he wanted to see us about?" I asked. I did not want the mystery to trouble me all the way to the ranch.

"Mr. Jenkins called the loan," she whispered, as if the trees had ears.

Persimmon swung himself onto Samson with haste, then tipped his hat and thanked her before launching into a gallop. I thanked her as well, then lumbered onto my horse, having to set out into a brisk run to catch up.

At the ranch, the reverend and Mr. Freeman piled out of the house door armed with shotguns at the sound of fast approaching hooves but when the reverend saw it was us, he leapt off the porch and ran to meet us.

"Am I glad to see the two of you! Although, I don't know what you can do. Jenkins called her loan," the reverend gasped in excitement.

"Have you been to the bank?" I foolishly asked, as if these good men were sitting around on their hands.

"We have, but we got no satisfaction," Mr. Freeman called out from the porch.

"I want you to take me back there tomorrow," Persimmon commanded, as he climbed down from his mount.

As he was approaching the front porch, the boy ran out and latched onto his right leg and Mrs. Sanchez rushed him, clamping Persimmon's face in her hands while saying something in Spanish, then taking him by the arm, she swept him inside.

I sat in the rocking chair as the other men took positions around the table. Mrs. Sanchez entered the kitchen and then returned with coffee for Persimmon and I. Persimmon was fired up and taking control of the conversation.

"Why did he call the loan?" he asked.

"We don't know," began the reverend, "but two days ago he suddenly decided to call it."

"Sounds like this is all connected." Everyone heard me but only Persimmon understood my meaning. "I bet he got the word that the Pinkerton's investigation was a bust and that caused him to act."

"Maybe, but what does the one have to do with the other that he would act like that?" Persimmon questioned.

I threw up an open hand and shrugged. Of course, my comments sparked inquiry from the others and Persimmon and I spent the next hour regaling the group with an abridgment of our exploits.

The reverend and Mr. Freeman were mulling over what we might have missed as I had done with Mr. Heinz, when another set of hooves thundered to a stop outside. Being closest to the door, I was first out onto the porch where I found three riders, Jenkins men all.

One rider slipped down off his horse, pulled from his saddlebag what looked like pitch-covered cloth wrapped around a stick. There was the unmistakable rasp of a match being struck. Persimmon was alongside me in time to see the man with the torch hoist the cloth end of it up to the rider with the match. It burst into flames.

XIX
FATE STEPS IN

"What the *hell* do you think you are doing?" Persimmon roared.

"Mr. Jenkins owns this property now," the man with the match authoritatively answered, flicking the match across the yard. "He wants to make sure no one has any ideas to the contrary."

The man with the torch approached the house.

"You touch that blaze to this house, or anything else on this property, and I'll blow a hole through you!" Persimmon had not yet reached for his pistol, he didn't have to. These men knew who he was and that he meant what he said.

The man with the torch stopped just out of reach of the eave of the roof and glanced back at the man with the match to see what the other two riders were going to do about Persimmon.

"You have no right to interfere with us. All of you need to clear out. You're trespassing." The man who had struck the match enjoyed what he thought was a position of authority.

"I beg to differ. The matter of this land isn't settled yet. Until it is, I expect this house and all else to be left alone... and so it shall." Persimmon's cavalier attitude rivaled the man's arrogance for control. My money was on Persimmon.

"You expect?" the man with the match huffed contemptuously. "You can't stop us unless you shoot us but what good would that do you? There's better than twenty of us in town."

"I bet I can. I can because if this house catches fire, I'm going to kill *you*. I don't care if you burn it or one of your crew does, I'm gonna kill *you*. If the prairie catches fire from a lightning strike, you had best come stomp it out because no matter how this house burns, I'm going to hunt you down and kill *you*. The same goes for any other damage to it. Now, tell me you don't believe it."

The third rider remained in the saddle, the furthest man from the house. When he spun his horse halfway around to the right, it appeared as if he were going to leave. Instead, he spun back to face us, brandishing his revolver in his right hand and testing Persimmon's dare by announcing, "I don't believe it."

The rider's horse raised up and before he could lift his arm to clear the horse's head with the muzzle, Persimmon snatched me behind him with his left hand while jerking his Schofield with his right. Unable to see any more of his target for the horse, Persimmon shot the rider in the face.

I think the bullet struck him in the left cheekbone near his nose but it all happened so quickly I cannot be sure. The rider's head whipped back from the impact and he toppled over the right haunch of the animal, his left boot heel raking up the ribs of the horse holding the man with the match. The dead man's horse bolted, tearing off across the valley with the dead man bouncing along from the right stirrup.

The man with the match struggled to regain control of his own mount, while the man with the torch danced about to avoid being trampled by the animal. When the man with the match got the animal's head pointed toward the road, he dug his spurs into her flanks and lit out at a gallop, leaving the torchbearer alone in the yard with Persimmon's muzzle trained on him.

"Don't shoot! I was just doing as I was told. I, I, I'm going, I'm going," the torchbearer stuttered.

"Your horse ran off." Persimmon pointed behind us with his thumb. "Put that torch out in the sand yonder, drop your gun belt and head back the way you came."

The man did as he was told, twisting the torch into the sandy spot Persimmon had indicated. Then he slipped his gun belt from around him and laid it carefully on a pile of grass and began walking.

"Hey," Persimmon called after him, "Why are you with this bunch?"

Surprised at the question, the man hesitated a moment then answered, "No good reason, I guess."

"I'll make a deal with you if you like. You can have your gun back if you promise to leave Colorado," offered Persimmon from behind his own six-shooter.

"Sure... sure, I will," came the uncertain reply.

"Before you do, you need to know there's a catch," Persimmon warned. "If I see you in Colorado again, I will kill you. I don't care if you are shaking hands with the sheriff when I do it either."

The man began an accelerating nod. "Sure. I'll go." He started toward his gun belt when Persimmon stopped him.

"Hold it," Persimmon commanded, then he called on me. "Pete, would you please get all of his bullets?"

I walked out to the gun belt and squatted to the side of Persimmon's line of fire, just in case. I emptied the revolver first, followed by stripping a dozen or more .45 Colt rounds from the loops on his belt. Then I picked the belt up and handed it to the man.

The man nodded to me, then raised a thankful hand to Persimmon and said, "As soon as my horse wanders back to the stable, I will leave."

As he set out on his hike back to town in boots made for riding, I turned to Persimmon, befuddled. "Why did you do that?"

"Did you see how he took care to lay his gun belt in that patch of grass so it wouldn't be scratched or get dirty? A man that will care for something like that ought not to have to part with it. Of course, had he given me the least bit of trouble he would have parted with far more than his gun belt."

Shaking my head in disbelief, I went into the house with a double handful of bullets. Maybe there was no limit on how many times Persimmon would surprise me. That was not all. I had not doubted his sincerity about keeping me from getting shot but I never expected he would have really put himself in front of me as a shield. I would not say I was choked up but there was a rather intense feeling in my upper chest that was not altogether unpleasant. It was, however, a bit embarrassing and after I dumped the pile of bullets on the table, I crossed the room and stretched my arms out in a deep breath.

The bizarreness of it all struck me funny and I cracked a smile where no one could see. It was not that a man was killed that was funny. It was that a dead man went bouncing across the prairie behind his horse and such things had begun to seem normal to me. I had paid it no mind until my thoughts backtracked to it while trying to comprehend Persimmon's motives for giving the gun belt back to the other fellow. I had not been in the war to know firsthand but veterans had told me how a man can get used to anything. I had never understood what they meant, but I was beginning to.

Mrs. Sanchez had gone to the kitchen when I came inside and by the time I was stretching she returned with a small cup of whiskey for my nerves. The other men came in but did not sit.

"What now?" Mr. Freeman asked. "I don't want to give into these men but I don't want to get shot either."

Mr. Freeman's sentiments rang familiar. Persimmon approached me and looked into my cup then took it from me, smelled of it, then drank the remainder of my whiskey in one gulp.

Leaving me dry, Persimmon reloaded his Schofield with a full complement of six rounds. No longer adrift in thought, he was confident and his tone exuded it. "Let's go to the bank and see what they have to say. I don't think anyone is going to come back out here today but to be safe, Reverend, will you keep the woman and boy at your home for now?"

The reverend took Mrs. Sanchez and her son by wagon, dropping them off at his home as we entered town. His wife met him at the door and ushered the boy and his mother inside while the reverend rejoined us. To be clear, the town was not so much a town as it was a support center for the nearby mine and the bank had begun as an assayer's office and became a bank, mostly to manage payroll for the mine. It was the only brick building in the area but unimposing, as a tall man could stand in the center of it and nearly touch two walls at once.

"I'm here to pay this month's payment on the Sanchez ranch," Persimmon announced to the bank manager as the rest of us followed him inside, besieging the tiny room.

The manager was alphabetizing a six-volume set of file boxes atop a table. "I'm afraid there's nothing to be done with that." The manager's words were to the point but empathetic.

Persimmon was not moved by the manager's sympathetic tone and demanded to know, "Why not?"

After sliding the entire set of files less than a half inch to the left, the manager stepped back to gauge if they were centered on the table, then slid his chair to center it on the desk before he sat down. "The Sanchez loan was a demand loan. Mr. Jenkins bought the loan from the bank. The bank acts more like a broker now. He can call in that loan at any time without notice and I know that Mr. Jenkins wants the land, not your payment."

"Then why in tarnation didn't he take the land when he bought the note instead of having her paying on it every month?" Mr. Freeman challenged calmly but with an aggravated lilt.

"Because that was all the more money he could pocket," the reverend answered, contemptuously.

"Well, doesn't he have to at least pay her the difference between what is owed on the land and what it is worth?" I added.

The bank manager bounced slightly in his chair to alleviate his weight as he twisted it about, dissatisfied with its position relative to the desk. "He should, but then who is to say how much the land is worth?" Giving up on the chair, he stood and spoke softly as if someone were eavesdropping. "I shouldn't say this but Mr. Jenkins knows that Mrs. Sanchez doesn't have the money to sue him. She'll never see a dime out of that ranch."

Everyone in our party continued to grumble. The stale air of the little room didn't help our demeanors and eventually drove us back outside. I think we all removed our hats to let the breeze blow through our damp hair. No doubt the bank manager would have done the same had he not found our interrogation more odious than the dank air inside.

"So, do we still head to Washington to see the attorney?" I asked, knowing the answer but wanting to start the deliberations on a new footing since paying the monthly note was not going to be a solution.

Mr. Freeman ran the fingers of his left hand through his hair, sweeping it back while setting his hat in place with his right. "There won't be anything left by the time you got back."

Persimmon nodded slowly. "Yeah, looks like fate has stepped in. All I know to do is pay Mr. Jenkins a visit."

I knew what sort of visit Persimmon was likely contemplating and, short of Jenkins confessing to the theft, things were likely to happen that would not be looked upon kindly by the law. Getting mixed up in that was not a good career move and I began to consider how I might abstain.

Being far less familiar with Persimmon than I was, Mr. Freeman spoke up to offer an option of which he was clearly ashamed. Nevertheless, he cared more for the boy and Mrs. Sanchez than he did about what others might think of him, a rare trait. "I know it's not right by the law, but maybe you could offer to not turn him in for swindled money in exchange for the ranch?"

"It isn't right but maybe it would buy you time to visit the lawyer in Washington," the reverend added. "The Lord used deception against his enemies. We could look at it that way."

"Maybe." A single word but I could tell from Persimmon's voice that the idea appealed to him.

Maybe, I thought to myself, maybe I would go along with him if he intended to bargain with Jenkins. Maybe, if things got out of hand, maybe I could pull Persimmon back from the brink before he did something the law might make him regret. I had prevented Persimmon from shooting the American in the Key West saloon. Maybe, as then, I might be the one thing standing between Persimmon and a lawless act that would kill any chance of him finding happiness. Looking back, I see that I was hanging an awful lot of hope on maybe.

Mr. Freeman knew how to direct us to Jenkins' place. He occasionally did business in Leadville and had to pass the Jenkins spread. Persimmon and I set out up the valley the next morning. Conversation was light, but I did stealthily slip in a few statements about keeping his cool and reminding Persimmon that he had something worth returning to.

The mountain shadow was creeping across the valley when we reached the turn leading to the Jenkins ranch. As we neared the house, what stood out to me was the eerie silence. Anyone living in the area would tell you that Jenkins kept a platoon of men on his payroll to manage the properties he had acquired. The best of them stuck near his home as a guard detail. To see no one rattled my nerves more because seeing people gave you something in which to gauge the situation.

Persimmon did not tie off his horse. When I grabbed my horse's lead rope, Persimmon took it from me and made a simple loop around the rail which could be easily snatched free. It was a reminder to the horse to stay but one that would make for a quick exit. It unnerved me further that he thought a fast exit might be necessary.

Persimmon knocked on the front door and a Chinese man answered, opening the door and waving us inside as if he expected us. He led us through the main room and down a short hallway to a study at the back of the house where a man with corn silk hair sat at a sturdy oak desk. He was obviously Jenkins. Behind him was a wide window with lightweight curtains and to the right of the window, a screen door, which let in the late afternoon breeze.

What was curious about the room was a rope which passed through the ceiling and hung about halfway to the floor next to the desk. As we filed into the room, Persimmon veered to the right and I to the left.

Jenkins looked up at us and then reached for a crystal decanter on the desk. "Brandy?" he offered, not allowing time for either of us to accept. "How can I help you gentlemen?"

"Your men tried to burn the Sanchez home," Persimmon bluntly stated.

"Why not, it's mine?" came the asinine response of a bully within his rights.

"I'm here to pay the next payment for Mrs. Sanchez." Persimmon's stare was cold which meant he was still on a business footing.

"I don't want your money," Jenkins firmly pronounced, leaning back in his chair with a glass matching the decanter in his hand and an air of triumph about him.

A flame was being kindled in Persimmon's eyes. Maybe if I interjected, maybe if I could start a dialogue of more than curt sentences, something could be worked out and no one would get shot. Maybe I could have, but instead I asked the first thing that came to mind, "Why burn the house?"

Jenkins glanced at me and then back to Persimmon. "To get rid of you. I figure, if the woman has no house, she'll give up the dream of that ranch and move on and the two of you can drop your crusade."

"How did you get that loan?" Persimmon asked.

"That's my business but I guess it's no secret, I bought it from the bank along with some others," Jenkins answered warily.

"Yeah, but why did Mr. Sanchez take that sort of loan in the first place?" Persimmon countered. "And what happened to him after he did?"

"Well, I guess you'll have to ask him. That's his business." The smirk on Jenkins's lips meant he knew more than he was telling.

Persimmon stuck his thumbs into his gun belt and pushed. The leather groaned against the buckle, then he repositioned the gun belt and adjusted his pants, hoisting them a bit. I had never seen Persimmon fidget in uncertainty. When he spoke, I realized he had been preparing himself to choke down his pride. "We know you are the same Jenkins that swindled those fellas in Richmond. We'll make a trade with you. Our silence for the Sanchez ranch."

A wide, condescending smile stretched across Jenkins's face and he tipped his chair forward and propped himself on the desk. "What need do I have with your silence? The law has been here and photographed me and done their due diligence and they can't find any reason to arrest me. So, why should I be concerned with you?"

Persimmon leaned forward and spoke down to Jenkins. "Because there's still one more witness who knows the truth and can testify against you and I'm going to pay him a visit."

The smirk ran off of Jenkins's face and he pursed his lips in thought. "I was afraid you were going to say that." Then Jenkins calmly reached over and gave the rope a tug.

Through the screen door wafted the knell of what sounded like a ship's bell. Immediately, I knew that chime meant I was about to get shot. My suspicion was confirmed when bits of a confession began trickling into the conversation.

"Pinkertons couldn't get anything out of him. I don't know why you think you will," Jenkins said without first asking who the witness was Persimmon mentioned.

"I'm not hindered by the law like Pinkerton men," Persimmon smirked and turned to the door.

"Like you were unhindered with Grant? You see what good it did you," retorted Jenkins.

I saw the blaze growing in Persimmon's eyes as he turned back to face Jenkins. What was worse, I heard voices in the distance and knew men were surrounding the house.

The smirk returned to Jenkins's lips as did the air of control. "Want to know how my man found you in St. Louis? My attorney told me you were headed back from Key West with Grant in tow. In fact, he's kept me abreast of your entire adventure, telegraphing me the important parts then mailing me copies of the Richmond paper." Jenkins reached over to a table in the corner and retrieved a newspaper which he spread on the desk in front of him. "The serial your friend here has been writing has been very informative. Robert Grant," Jenkins laughed, "I bet you wish you had disguised your *characters* a little better. You didn't even bother to change Persimmon's name." Jenkins picked the paper up, spun it around and tossed it across the desk for Persimmon's perusal if he had any doubts.

By this time, Persimmon's convicting glare was on me, hot like the fires of hell. My neck and face burned. I ceased worrying about the men outside and turned my fears toward Persimmon. What a foolish thing I had done, so nearsighted, so destructive to our cause, so hurtful to a friend.

"I'm sorry, Persimmon. I—Watch out!" I screeched, flinging a finger in the direction of a man drawing a bead on Persimmon from a few feet outside the screen door.

Persimmon lunged at me, surely to kill me I thought, but it was only to avoid a bullet. The man outside fired but missed. Persimmon snatched his Schofield from its holster and swung it around, finding the attacker through the window behind Jenkins. Persimmon fired through the glass, knocking the gunman to the ground.

The stomping of boots announced another assailant in the parlor about to enter the hallway. Persimmon spun and fired but the attacker saw Persimmon's muzzle in time and ducked behind the corner. Persimmon fired into the wall and a painful yelp was heard. Rushing down the hall, Persimmon stuck his revolver around the corner and fired again for certainty's sake.

With the immediate threats eliminated, Persimmon turned his attention back to Jenkins. I had trailed close behind him and had to dive flat against the wall when Persimmon swung his gun hand around to shoot Jenkins. Jenkins was under his desk with his hand in the top drawer, blindly thrashing about for a pistol. Persimmon fired at his arm but splintered the top of the oak desk just short of his target. From the parlor all we could see in the back office was the desk, but we heard the screen door creak open. Persimmon raked an oil sconce from the wall with his pistol. The lamp crashed to the hall floor. Persimmon leaned forward and fired his last round into the puddle of kerosene with the muzzle an inch from the floor. The hallway burst into flames.

Persimmon darted into the parlor, breaking the Schofield's action across the small of his back as he ran. Empty casings clinked across the floor. I chased after him and then cowered in the parlor corner while he reloaded.

"Where's the pistol I loaned you?" he asked hastily.

Staring back sheepishly was all the answer I could give or needed to give. Persimmon rolled his eyes in disgust as he clacked the revolver closed. To my right, from the hallway, came the rhythmic thud of a cloth beating the roaring flames and the voice of Jenkins screaming for another man to swat them faster. Along the front porch, a man crept up to the window, not knowing where we were. As soon as enough of his torso was visible, Persimmon put a bullet in it.

As that man fell, Persimmon scurried across the floor to the second window in time to see a man grab my horse by the reins. Darting out the front door, Persimmon shot the horse thief in the ribs and then a rider as he rounded the corner of the house. The gunfire spooked my mare but the thought of being stranded amongst these killers frightened me into action. I jumped off the porch and grabbed my horse by the halter. She pulled away from me but I hung on. I let the lead rope slide through my hand as I slipped down her side, hoping to mount her before she trampled me or fled.

I managed to get a hunk of mane in my left fist and the saddle horn in my right and take one bounce with my foot in the stirrup before she bolted. Pure terror drug me into the saddle and I pulled on the horse's mane trying to slow her. The reins were dragging the ground and she was headed away from the house but not up the road. I heard more shots behind me and then thundering hooves, it was Persimmon.

My horse caught sight of Samson and turned to follow. Carefully, I stretched one arm at a time to reach the rein on either side and, by the time we were back to the main road, I was in control of my horse. Persimmon kept up a southward gallop as I pleaded with him for forgiveness.

"The reason I started riding with you was to tell your story," I yelled to him ahead of me.

"I thought you were going to write a novel half packed full of lies, not describe our plans in detail to the world!" Persimmon yelled back.

"I never thought the story would leave the east coast and I was flat broke. If I had had any idea that it—"

"Too late to think about that now!" Persimmon cut my excuses short. Just as well. What excuse can explain away getting your friend's father killed, even if he was a bad father?

The last sunlight slipped off the peaks of the eastern mountains and the road began to get dark in a hurry. I wanted to ask where we were headed, what Persimmon's plan was, could he ever forgive me, but I did not have the chance. Those Jenkins men who had not made it to the house at the sound of the bell, had organized themselves and the growing rumble of hooves meant they were nearly upon us.

Over my shoulder, I could see five men come into view around the bend, much closer than I expected. Persimmon and I spurred our horses. The posse continued to gain on us and began firing. Persimmon returned fire for effect but it was nightfall that saved us. We rounded another bend in the road and Persimmon came to a fast stop and ducked off the road into the trees. My heart was pounding, thinking any moment the posse would come into view and catch us before we were out of sight but we made it.

Far into the woods, Persimmon stopped and spun around to face in the direction of the road, waiting to see if the posse caught on to our deception. When he was satisfied he had outwitted them, he turned his horse, without a word, and headed down into the valley.

As my nerves settled, I began to feel weak. My head felt like it was falling off my shoulders. Before I knew it, I hit the ground. I heard the thud more than felt it. My horse pranced away but not far. I sat up and took a deep breath. My shoulder ached where I had landed on a rock. I called for Persimmon as his silhouette withdrew from sight. Trying to stand, I got dizzy and fell back on my rump. I reached over my right shoulder with my left hand. My shoulder felt wet and sore. As I rubbed it, my finger slipped into a hole and I winced at the sharp pain. Damned if I hadn't been shot!

XX
LOST FRIEND

I lay in the grass under a thicket of conifers for perhaps an hour, perhaps two. A distant owl and the occasional soft clop of my horse's hooves were all the sounds I can remember, except for the breeze. The breeze was crisp and firm and purred through the treetops. I slept some, only knowing if it had been for a minute, or possibly twenty, when I looked for a star I had been watching and found another in its place. At some point, I became aware of my mood and lay there trying to determine if it was my wound or apathy that held me to the ground. Maybe Richard Grant had been a bad father and a crook, and certainly he was to blame for the situation in which he placed himself but, more directly, it was my fault he was killed. It was my fault Persimmon's father was dead.

Maybe I would have lain there until man or God found me if it had not been for an itch. It began as an annoyance in the small of my back but grew stronger than my power to ignore it. Once the notion entered my mind that there might be a bug chewing on me, I had to scratch, but I could not quite reach it with my left hand without rolling onto my right shoulder, and nearly any motion with my right arm was painful. Eventually, I took my right wrist in my left hand and hoisted the bulk of my right arm across my body so I could sit up.

The pain was excruciating as I struggled to balance sufficiently on my left arm to hoist myself. Something in my shoulder clunked in unison with a sharp pain. I knew it had to be a broken bone. Once up, the pain changed. I do not want to say it dulled, for that might give the indication that it was a lesser agony. More, it became a blunt ache. I scratched my itch and then remained in the sitting position, not wanting to endure the pain of having to sit up again later. A few deep breaths were uncomfortable, but also reassuring that the bullet had not pierced a lung.

Where was Persimmon and how angry was he? He could have killed me for what I did, but he didn't. Then again, he did leave me bleeding in the woods. The closest thing to this attitude I had observed from Persimmon had been his treatment of his father.

Mountain nights can be cold in the summer but this one felt colder due to my condition. I knew I had to get help and waiting until daylight meant enduring the cold night as well as more of a chance that Jenkins's men would find me. Moving under the cover of darkness was my best bet. There was a small tree within arm's reach. I grabbed a low limb near the trunk with my left hand and pulled myself onto my knees. The weight of my arm tormented my shoulder so I tucked my hand and forearm into my shirt, between the buttons, as a makeshift sling.

Darting my eyes about let me better make out the silhouettes of trees and eventually my horse as I followed the sound of the last hoof stomp I had heard. Speaking softly to her, I approached her from the right and put my hand on her shoulder to calm her. There was a tree in front of her so I slid my hand along her side and around her hind quarters to let her know it was me behind her. As my hand glided over her right rump, I felt something gummy in her coat, it was blood. She too, had taken a bullet.

We were a few miles from town, more than I could walk in my condition. I hated to ask my wounded horse to carry me but her ability to do so likely meant the difference in my fate. Still, I had to mount her. Could I drag myself into the saddle? Taking her lead rope, the two of us wove through the maze of trees until I spied a large log. The only assistance I had was this log and the gradual slope of the valley. I brought her alongside the downed tree in such a way that I would be uphill from her.

With the reins in my left hand, I grabbed a hunk of mane, put my foot in the stirrup, took a deep breath and groaned through gritted teeth as I launched myself with my right leg. It was not enough. I clung to the side of my horse with a sufficient amount of my weight over the saddle to keep me from falling off but unable to pull myself up with my left arm only. Instinctively, I drew my arm from my shirt buttons and flung it over the saddle to grab its bottom edge. When I pulled, I heard the crunch of bone and felt the bullet hole snap open and blood trickle down my back. The dizziness returned and I slid back off the horse.

When full consciousness returned, I blinked to clear my vision and found a ceiling above me. I was in a bedroom I did not recognize. Rummaging through the fuzzy pictures in my head, I remembered entering a house and seeing Mrs. Sanchez seated in the parlor, but I knew this was not the Sanchez home. I remembered feeling my saddle horn in my gut and the horse's coarse mane on my cheek while watching her step below me. This, despite also remembering falling off the saddle before then. How had I mounted the horse in the first place?

The reverend's wife entered the bedroom and when she saw me awake, she rushed back out the door to fetch the reverend.

"I see you are still with the living," he joked to ease the tension.

"How did I get here?" I asked, but the words stuck in my dry throat and choked me.

The reverend's wife left again to fetch me some water. As I watched her leave, I realized I did not know her name and, being embarrassed about this and having other pressing questions, I decided to stick with calling her ma'am.

"You rode in on your horse a little after four in the morning. I heard a noise outside and found you on my doorstep," the reverend answered.

"What time is it?" Scanning the room, I could not find a clock.

"It's about one in the afternoon. How are you feeling?" asked the reverend.

Sliding my hand up, I felt the bandages wrapped around my chest and shoulder. "I feel heavy but I don't hurt. I guess it is amazing what ten hours of rest will do."

The reverend laughed and glanced at his wife who was smiling. "You've been in this bed for two days."

"Almost three," his wife added.

My expression of amazement must have been obvious.

"I went to the mine and rousted the doctor out of bed. After he quit fussing, he took your bullet out. Said it chipped your shoulder blade but missed anything vital. You lost a good deal of blood is all. He said it was a wonder you could make it back to town and on a horse."

"I remember falling off and I remember trying to get back on and falling again. I remember seeing Mrs. Sanchez somewhere," I rambled, as the few recent memories I had flipped by.

"She was here, but she's with the Freemans now. We only had the one extra room," the reverend's wife said.

"I'm sorry to burden you, ma'am."

"Don't you worry about that. We all know what you've been doing to help that poor woman." The reverend's wife spoke in a way that left me without a doubt that she meant what she said. There was a knock at the door and she left us to answer it.

"Have you seen Persimmon?" I asked.

"No. No one has, but the marshal is doing all he can to find him."

"Edwards?" I clarified.

"Yes. He found out you were here and wanted to talk to you but I wouldn't let him disturb you. I think it's best if we don't volunteer that you're awake. He's been on a tear. Says he is after Persimmon for shooting that man at the Sanchez home. When I told him I was a witness to that and that the man drew on Persimmon, Marshal Edwards said it didn't matter because Persimmon was also wanted for shooting up the Jenkins place. What happened up there?"

I was about to answer the reverend when his wife and Mrs. Sanchez entered the bedroom.

"Are you well? Is Persimmon safe?" Mrs. Sanchez spoke frantically.

Having people staring down on me while I was in bed was odd and I did not like it. Though they all tried to discourage me, I pushed myself up into a sitting position and when my head proved steady, I swung my legs off the bed. Discovering a little too late that I only wore my drawers, I flipped the covers over my lap but not before Mrs. Sanchez turned to hide her face.

Rather than prolong the embarrassment on both sides, I chose to ignore my attire and said, "Help me to a chair and I will tell you all about it."

Reluctantly they agreed. The two women left the room while the reverend helped me into my britches and then into the parlor. The reverend's wife let the curtains hang down, not closing them completely, as that would be suspicious, but allowing them to block about two-thirds of the window. According to the reverend, Jenkins men were watching the house. There was one chair which sat in the north front corner of the room, alongside the window. Anyone peering in to find me would not see me for the angle and the curtain. From that corner, I told the story of what really happened at the Jenkins ranch, making sure Mrs. Sanchez understood Persimmon got away.

"I cannot believe he would have left you lying in the woods," Mrs. Sanchez bemoaned.

"I wonder if he did?" replied the reverend from under a raised brow. "You said yourself you don't remember how you got onto your horse."

The thought that Persimmon might not have abandoned me after all made sense. I hoped it was the truth.

"We need to get the law here. Not Edwards, he doesn't seem interested in justice. He has formed a posse from Jenkins men and has sent them out in different directions, looking for Persimmon. Fifteen to twenty men, I'm not sure. I don't know if Edwards is blinded by his vendetta against Persimmon or if he knows who Jenkins is and is ignoring it. I don't think he is working for Jenkins because he did not try to take you and I am sure Jenkins wants you dead the same as Persimmon." The reverend's analysis was uncomfortably sensible and it meant one thing, at some point soon, someone would be out to kill me.

I was glad when Mrs. Sanchez changed the subject.

"Has Persimmon spoken of me?" she asked.

"In a way," I replied. In truth, Persimmon had said very little of her specifically but I remembered his lamentation to me on how I had made him think he might be happy here.

"You must think I am a fool," Mrs. Sanchez laughed, wiping her eye. "But he is a kind man, and a handsome man and why shouldn't a widow with a young son fall in love with such a man? Or maybe you are asking why a man like Persimmon would want a widow and a boy to take care of?"

"Actually, I'm curious how you have decided that Persimmon is a kind man?" I refrained from adding that there were a number of dead men that would disagree if they could.

"I see it in his eyes—"

"In his eyes?" I blurted. I had seen little better than the fires of hell in his eyes.

Mrs. Sanchez smiled, "Maybe it is something only a woman can see? I saw it most when he looked at Sancho. You might think me a fool, but I am no fool. I know Persimmon has killed many men, but he has worked for our happiness and I want to work for his if he will let me."

I told her exactly what I thought. "Persimmon is a difficult man to read but based on the few things he has said and done, I think he would very much like to get to know you, if only he can find a way."

"Maybe when the local sheriff comes, he can put a stop to this madness and Persimmon can come back to town then," was Mrs. Sanchez's hopeful reply.

"I don't mean find a way around these men. I mean he needs to find a way on the inside. There is a great deal of sadness in him," I clarified.

Mrs. Sanchez nodded.

"May I ask... what happened to your husband?" The appropriateness of such a question is often difficult to determine but since Mrs. Sanchez was focused on Persimmon, I figured the loss of her husband was far enough in the past to question.

"No one knows for sure. He took a loan with the bank to buy cattle. We purchased the ranch with about half family money and half a loan from the bank. We did well for a few years but each year left us in the same position as the last. Carlos learned of cattle he could buy cheaply to the south. He planned to buy them and bring them here, fatten them up on our ranch and then sell them to the mines and to the army. The bank would make the loan but only with collateral so the loan we had on our ranch was combined with the loan for the cattle. Carlos figured the money he made selling the cattle would come close to paying off the entire amount and make it easier to say no to Mr. Jenkins who kept trying to buy our ranch. Carlos set out with four men and the money to buy the cattle and hire more hands to drive them. When they got to Cimarron, they checked into the St. James Hotel. Carlos signed the register and people there saw him, but that night he disappeared, along with the money and one of the men with him who was his close friend."

"What happened with the other men?" I asked, anxiously.

"They testified that they were in the saloon all night and people there said this was true and that they only left occasionally to... to..." I nodded to save Mrs. Sanchez the unease of mentioning men relieving themselves. She smiled and nodded back. "The law decided that Carlos must have fled with the money, but I know Carlos would never have done such a thing. The other men now work for Jenkins."

No doubt, this was suspicious. I could see why the reverend felt like Carlos Sanchez had been murdered and why he suspected Jenkins had a hand in it. If Carlos Sanchez was not available to pay the note back, the bank would have incentive to sell the loan to Jenkins who then only needed to call it in to own the land that Carlos Sanchez would not sell to him.

A knock at the door came without the heralding clatter of hooves or wagon. The reverend strained against the window glass to see who was outside, then rushed to the door to open it. Mr. Freeman hurried inside with the reverend nearly closing the door on him in his haste.

"I heard that a couple of Jenkins men just returned from Pueblo and when they found out everyone was searching for Persimmon, they asked if anyone had looked at Persimmon's cabin. I guess no one else had known of the cabin because Marshal Edwards is down at the Bansheen now with about eight or so men. It's funny…" Mr. Freeman stopped himself and clarified, "I don't mean the situation is funny, I mean it is… well, funny, that Edwards must be scared of Persimmon because he is waiting on a few more of Jenkins's men to return from their search before he goes to the cabin." Mr. Freeman spoke excitedly, as if he was afraid any slower would be too late. "Oh, and I saw the deputy ride into town."

"Which deputy?" the reverend asked.

"That young buck, Jim," Mr. Freeman answered.

The reverend nodded, "Jim's a good man but not the man we need to go up against Edwards. Let's see if we can get him to fetch the sheriff. Does he know about Edwards's posse?"

"No, and I don't think he was planning to stay in town either. He probably stopped at McLaglen's place, though."

"Let's go get him," the reverend said, grabbing for the door.

"You stay here, I'll fetch him," Mr. Freeman commanded as he blew out of the house.

Scooting out to the edge of my chair to get my weight over my feet, I stood with little trouble. My limbs still felt heavy but my head was stable.

"What are you doing?" the reverend's wife cried out with more concern in her voice than was necessary.

"I have to warn Persimmon. After all, this is my fault."

"I know what you are saying but this is not your fault," the reverend assured me, taking me by the arm as if I needed help to stand even though I was already on my feet.

"Someone please fetch my horse while I get my overshirt. No matter what you say, I owe it to Persimmon to warn him."

"Your horse is at the livery with a bullet in his rump and you couldn't ride him anyway, not in your condition." The reverend tried to be firm with me but I could not be swayed.

"Then let me borrow your wagon. If I don't return, there is some money in my bag." I knew the argument wasn't over, but I tried to sound in control.

"If you go out of this house, you are sure to catch a stray bullet, one a bit better placed than the last one," the reverend scolded but when he saw how determined I was he offered to go in my stead.

"I'm going!" I cried.

"You don't even know if he's there," the reverend argued.

Like everything the reverend had said, it was a valid point but something told me Persimmon had not fled and that he could be found at the cabin. "I can't tell you how I know, I just know it. Leastways, I'm going to find out."

"Well then..." the reverend hesitated in reluctance, "I'll go with you. Let me hitch the wagon out back."

"No tricks!" I demanded. "I'm going with or without you."

The reverend nodded in capitulation and told his wife, "Get some cushions and take them out the back door to the wagon. He'll need to be covered with the canvas so that no one sees him."

While the reverend hitched the wagon, his wife lay down a pallet of cushions for my comfort, what little it would provide on the rough road.

"You know you might bust that wound open again. You ought to stay here," the reverend pleaded with me once more.

"I think these thicker cushions will save me injury... thank you for going with me."

As we rounded the house, the reverend driving and I hidden away under the canvas, Deputy Jim rode up and stopped us.

"Where are you headed? Mr. Freeman said you needed me," the deputy questioned.

"Where's the sheriff?" asked the reverend.

"Leadville."

"How about ride along and I'll tell you all about it on the way?" the reverend requested.

For the entire ride north up the main road, I lay in the back of the wagon, covered with a piece of canvas with only my head exposed but tucked under the seat so I could not be seen easily. The reverend was regaling the deputy with our story. The rough road often forced me to favor my left side which meant using my stomach muscles to hold the position, so I did not chime in on the telling of it. Based on the deputy's questions and occasional exclamations, he must have been shocked to hear all that was going on right under his nose. In his world, Jenkins had been a ruthless, would-be cattle baron and his men were questionable drifters he hired cheap. There was nothing illegal about that.

When I thought we were nearing the turnoff for the little road up the creek to the cabin, I raised up periodically to get my bearings. Seeing a small creek and overgrown road merge into the main road, I called out, "Turn here."

"What the hell?" Deputy Jim liked to have jumped out of his skin, twisting in his saddle in search from whence the disembodied voice came.

I raised my left hand and waved as the reverend pulled on the reins to bring the wagon to a stop.

Deputy Jim backed his horse up a couple of steps to get a good look at me. "You mean you've been back here all this time and haven't said a word?"

"It's tough to talk, get jostled about and hurt all at once," I joked, despite the pain on my face.

"Jenkins do that to you?" he asked me.

"His men did," I replied.

"We'd be obliged if you'd fetch the sheriff from Leadville while we try to find Persimmon and get him hidden," the reverend told the deputy.

"If everything you tell me is true, I think it is best if I take Persimmon into custody for his protection. Jenkins won't be able to touch him in the county jail. Mind you, he wouldn't be a prisoner but we could keep him safe until we can bring in another marshal and representatives from the Pinkertons, whoever we need to prosecute this case."

"Persimmon respects you but he doesn't trust lawmen in general. I wouldn't bet on him agreeing to your plan," I advised the deputy.

"I owe Persimmon my life. I want to return the favor. Let's ride up and if he's at the cabin, I'll try to talk him into coming with me. If nothing else, we'll let him know that I know and get him to a better hideout for the duration." There was honest concern in the deputy's voice.

The deputy followed the wagon up the rocky, unmaintained trail along the creek. The main road had been slow and every bump, to which a healthy person would pay no mind, had felt like a hammer against my shoulder.

Traversing the trail along the creek was slower still and a string of six-inch drops. I winced audibly more than once and the reverend tried to get me to let him turn back while the deputy went ahead, but I waved him onward telling him we were almost there.

The deputy saw the cabin in the clearing and rode up the hill as Persimmon and I had done before, but the wagon could not traverse the steep and overgrown incline. Instead, the reverend continued up the narrow trail to where it began to encircle the far edge of the clearing.

I lifted myself up onto my left elbow where I could peer over the side of the wagon. From this vantage, I could see the rear of Persimmon's huge horse under the shed roof out back. The deputy had not received an answer to his calls, despite announcing who he was, so he rode into the woods in search of Persimmon.

From the opposite side of the clearing, Persimmon broke through the tree line wearing his white Key West shirt and his shoulder holster. "Persimmon!" I yelled. He looked to me but continued to the cabin. Upon my call, the reverend spotted him and jumped from the wagon, but before he made it ten feet across the clearing, a large group of riders came into my view along the creek. Our impediments of wagon and wound had been enough to allow the posse to catch up with us.

"Run!" I cried out to Persimmon, but he simply stood in front of the cabin door, hearing the riders but not yet seeing them.

My yelling had alerted Deputy Jim who galloped from the woods as he deftly snaked his horse through the trees. He approached Persimmon to warn him and I could see the deputy pointing, pleading with Persimmon to flee whilst the deputy did what he could to slow the posse.

I never saw Persimmon open his mouth, he quietly stood there, watching for the riders to appear over the hill into the clearing. When they did, Marshal Edwards was up front and he bellowed across the meadow, "Persimmon Apricot, surrender yourself or be shot down!"

Persimmon made no attempt to reach for his pistol or say a word. He only turned, opened the cabin door, calmly walked inside and closed it behind him.

Marshal Edwards dismounted and began barking orders to the members of the posse, sending men all around the edge of the clearing to surround the cabin and cut off any chance Persimmon had of escape.

Deputy Jim slid off his horse and gave it a gentle slap on the rump to send it loping back to the wagon where I had submerged in hiding, under the canvas, and was now peeking through a crack in the side boards.

Marching up to Edwards, Deputy Jim boomed with authority as I had never heard from him. "Marshal, this is my county and my jurisdiction. Persimmon is my prisoner. You need to take your posse back down the mountain and let me handle this."

"Apricot," the marshal yelled over the deputy, "come on out here or we are going to pull you out." Then the marshal turned to the deputy, dismissively. "I have over a dozen men here and will likely have to take Persimmon by force, but you claim you and your posse made of one preacher are going to take Persimmon Apricot into custody? I know what this is all about. You've been listening to that preacher tell you how Apricot is some kind of hero and you already have a sweet spot for him so you want to get me to leave so you can let him go. Well, it's not gonna happen. I'm going to see to it that he gets what's coming to him, this time."

"See here, Edwards—"

"That's Marshal Edwards to you, kid," the marshal snapped.

"Well, I'm Deputy Jim Hayworth and I represent the law in this county and Persimmon is my prisoner."

Edwards laughed. "I'm U.S. Marshal Edwards and I'm the law everywhere. I'm taking Persimmon in, dead or alive, and anyone who interferes will get the same. Now stand aside."

I half expected Edwards to shove the young deputy, but he only stepped past him a few feet and yelled out to the cabin again. "Time's up, Persimmon. You're not escaping justice from me again. Get out here now or we will smoke you out!"

The reverend was already traipsing across the meadow and when he heard Edwards's decree, he let into him. "See here marshal, you start burning that cabin you are likely to set the entire side of the mountain ablaze and there are prospectors up this creek." The reverend lambasted as he walked until he stood directly in front of the marshal.

"Out of my way, Reverend. I don't make a habit of hitting men of God but don't think I won't." Then Edwards called out to those members of his posse along the right flank of the meadow who could approach the cabin without being seen, "You there, light it up."

The reverend was incensed and grabbed the marshal by both shoulders, "Stop it! You could kill innocent people, maybe burn down the town."

"Get away from me, I told you!" the marshal growled and shoved the reverend hard with a backhand swipe of his left arm.

The reverend stumbled sideways in the clumps of grass along the eroded edge of the meadow, falling hard across a tree stump.

Deputy Jim had had enough and drew his revolver. "There's nothing lawful about what you're doing so I'm placing you under arrest. Even if it means my job."

"It will mean your life if you pull that trigger. These men with me will chew you to bits. Besides, it's too late." Edwards pointed as one of the posse threw a makeshift torch onto the cabin roof and another man threw one against the thick plank siding.

While this drama played out before me through the crack in the wagon, I lamented not being of any help and of being partially to blame for the unfortunate turn of events which had swallowed us. I also remembered the last time Persimmon and I left this cabin and how Persimmon had been sure that anyone following us knew how to find us. He had set a trap for those men at the rocks and I hoped Persimmon was setting a trap now. I ruled out a Gatling gun since he had no way to fire it from within the cabin. Would he soon burst through the door slinging dynamite?

The weathered cabin caught fire quickly. Smoke billowed from its far side but in less than a minute I could see flames rising from the roof. For the first time, I saw Samson become spooked and he pulled free of the makeshift stable and bolted to the far tree line, still wearing his saddle. One of the posse grabbed at him but the big horse snatched the man off his feet and nearly trampled him. Before Samson was out of sight, half the cabin was engulfed in flame. Still, Persimmon did not emerge.

The reverend stood, and with his left hand clamped to his ribs, hobbled toward the cabin but before he could reach the door, the entire front wall was a curtain of flame. The reverend tried to kick the door open but the sturdy door and intense heat beat him back.

A few minutes later the roof began to collapse. I knew then, Persimmon was not coming out. The walls were swaying in the breeze, ready to crumble at any moment, when Marshal Edwards said, "Well, he made his choice. He's your prisoner now, deputy." Edwards then whistled to gather the remaining men who had trickled out of the tree line and into the meadow. They stood dumbfounded at what they had witnessed. None could get close to the cabin. The heat was unbearable and the wind blew cinders this way and that.

The rear wall was the first to go, tumbling inward from the extra weight of the shed roof. One by one, the men trickled after Edwards. Some were sickened but the meanest of them jested at the crispy state of Persimmon and other grotesque comments.

As the last of them rode from sight, I struggled to sit up in the back of the wagon, tears in my eyes. I could not believe I had lost my friend.

XXI
RUMOR

What could I have done to save him? While I struggled from the back of the wagon, my left arm exhausted from easing my weight along so as to not tear open my shoulder, I admitted to myself the answer was, nothing. There was nothing I could have done to save Persimmon this day, but that failed to ease my guilt over having been the source of Jenkins's informant.

The reverend hurried over to help me, still holding his ribs, but by the time he reached me, I was out of the wagon and steady on my own two feet.

"Broken?" I choked, nodding toward where he gripped his chest.

"Just bruised, I think," the reverend replied, somberly.

Together, we eased ourselves across the meadow to where Deputy Jim stood, gawking at the flames in disbelief.

"I can't believe he didn't come out. He didn't even shoot any of them. He just sat in the cabin and gave up." The deputy's thoughts mirrored my own.

By now, most of the cabin had collapsed in on itself, save for the left wall which was crumbling bit by bit from the top down. The grass around the cabin caught fire and the three of us began stomping around the blaze like wild men, trying to stamp out the flames before the entire mountain went up. In my urgency, I got carried away and made my shoulder ache. With my left hand, I squeezed where my shoulder met my neck which relieved the pain a bit.

I circled the cabin. Beneath the wall planks which leaned against the stove, nestled in bright red embers, I could see what looked like melted pewter and broken glass. It was the mirror which had been on the little table. Try as I might, I could not locate the matching frame with the woman's photograph or lamp painted in tulips but neither stood a chance in the heat. Morbidly, I looked upon every timber I saw as if it might be Persimmon's limb but I could not find his body.

The cabin had been a free-standing structure with its corner posts resting on flat stones. With no floor, each wall supported the others and were tied together by the roof. The roof had burned away quickly, having first the walls and later the stove to hold it up so that air could feed the inferno from underneath. Now that the walls were down, the pile of wood and coals was denser and would burn longer, certainly until after dark.

As if he read my mind, the reverend said, "There's no way we can find the body until all this cools down. I don't mean to be insensitive but if there is anything left of Persimmon, I don't think it will be anything the critters want. My suggestion is for you, Jim, to go fetch the sheriff. Tell him what's happened and that Pete's life is still in danger. Let's resolve this matter with Jenkins and as soon as we can, we'll return with a shovel to clear the coals and bury Persimmon. Maybe, by then, my ribs will quit hurting me."

"I'm going to do all I can to have Edwards stripped of his U.S. Marshal badge," Jim said, prompted by the reverend's injury.

Besides sorrow and guilt, the three of us left the meadow with good intentions and without a clue as to how to fulfill them. Deputy Jim stayed with the wagon as the reverend did his best to inch it down the mountain to save my shoulder and his ribs. Despite the reverend's denial, I was confident he had at least one cracked rib. At the main road, the deputy bid us to be careful, then galloped north to Leadville to find the sheriff.

I reclined on the pile of cushions in the back of the wagon, with the canvas pulled up to my chin, ready to duck beneath it at the first sign of a rider. It would be a lie to tell you I was not tearful or to blame it on my shoulder. In fact, my shoulder pained me very little on the ride back as my mind was adrift elsewhere.

As the wagon creaked to a stop behind the reverend's home, I heard him exclaim in a panicked voice, "Sarah!"

The wagon shook uncomfortably with the shift of the reverend's weight as he leapt from it. Without the caution I should have exercised, I shoved myself up by my left arm and snapped my eyes toward the back door in time to see the reverend disappear through it. The door jamb was splintered where the door had been kicked in.

Scrambling from the back of the wagon, I scooted off the tailgate until my feet were planted on the ground, then rushed inside after the reverend. In the front parlor, I found the reverend standing over his wife who was laying across the settee. She sat up, her dress torn, forehead beaded, hardly resembling the well kempt and elegant lady the few decent denizens of this rathole town had come to admire.

"I'm fine, George. I'm fine," the reverend's wife said nervously.

"What happened?" I asked, thinking I had missed the answer to that question by hobbling in late.

Sarah dabbed her forehead with a handkerchief, then pressed it firmly, hatefully to her eye and held it there a few moments while she gathered herself to speak. "There was a knock at the front door and when I looked outside, I didn't see anyone. Then the back door burst open and two men rushed in. One came at me, the other went to both bedrooms. They were looking for you." Her last statement was as a blade of guilt through my soul. How many more people would be hurt because of my poor judgement?

"Who were they?" the reverend growled, his fists clenched. I had never seen him angry before.

"I don't know. They had their heads covered with flour sacks."

"Your dress!" the reverend gasped, "It's torn... did they... did they..." The reverend sank to his knees in front of her, his rage shaken loose by panic.

"One of them snatched me by the dress and threw me into the chair. They tore it, that's all," was how the reverend's wife explained away the dress.

I was not sure I believed her. I knew some of the men in the Jenkins fold were pure trash and the rest were questionable at best. My doubt must have shown because as the reverend leaned in to hug her, she cut her eyes to me. The expression on her face was not the stern conviction of my guilt I expected, but one of fear, fear as though I might let slip a desperate secret that only she and I knew.

Growing weak in the knees, I sat on the edge of a chair whose cushion was still in the back of the wagon, and rested my head in my left hand.

"All this is my fault. I shouldn't have come here either," I bemoaned.

"Either? What do you mean, either?" the reverend's wife asked, eager to change the subject from her own ordeal.

The reverend hesitated a moment, reluctant to burden his wife further but when she pressed the matter, he told her of all that had happened at the cabin. As expected, she was horrified at the tale but she was clearly a strong woman and shook off the shock of it and immediately began trying to comfort me as the reverend left to get her a glass of water.

"You can't be blaming yourself for what bad men do. Those sins are theirs alone. I am very sorry to hear of your friend though. I could tell you two had become good friends. Losing a friend is never easy but—" Her words were well-intentioned but they were the same empty words that are always said when someone dies. In this case, they were made all the hollower by the fact that Persimmon was placed into that situation by my actions.

"I keep seeing Persimmon go into the cabin and shut the door without a word. Slowly, calmly, as if he was resigned to his fate." I spoke my misgivings aloud but my call for help drew no answers.

"Persimmon was a tortured soul. I know George had hope for him but then, that's George's business, hope," she said, referring to the reverend. "Some men have burdens so heavy that the only thing worse than dying, is living. Some burdens can only be shouldered by Christ but you have to ask for His help."

"I think Persimmon would have to forgive God first," I replied, having witnessed the depth of Persimmon's bitterness. "The other day, in Pueblo, Persimmon was in a sorry state and he told me how I had made him think he could be happy here with Mrs. Sanchez. It made me angry at those men who had taken that from him. Turns out it was me who stole it."

Oh, I had forgotten about Mrs. Sanchez but the reverend returned with the water and said, "I wish Frank would come by and let us know all is well at his place."

"Who's Frank?" I asked.

"Mr. Freeman," the reverend answered me, then turned to his wife, "I don't want to leave you to find out."

"Go make sure. I'll sit with the shotgun in my lap until you return," Sarah replied.

Before the reverend could refuse, there came a knock at the door which tightened our guts. The reverend looked at me, unsure of what to do. The knock came again, this time accompanied by a voice. "George, it's me, Frank."

I'm sure Frank heard the sound of the three of us sighing in unison. The reverend warily cracked open the door and finding only Mr. Freeman, yanked the door wide so Mr. Freeman could breeze through quickly, hat in hand.

"I heard what happened at the cabin," Mr. Freeman said, nervously threading his hat brim through the thumb and forefinger of his left hand.

The reverend looked puzzled. "How did you hear about it?"

"Some of the Jenkins men were shootin' their mouths off loudly when they got back. Mr. McLaglen found out and came and told us," Mr. Freeman clarified.

"Oh, I was hoping that maybe it was Deputy Jim who had slipped past us but he probably had to go to Leadville to fetch the sheriff. Is there any deputy in town?" the reverend asked.

Mr. Freeman shook his head.

"Well then, I guess I have to go to Marshal Edwards instead," the reverend groaned, unhappy with his own conclusion.

"Edwards? I thought Edwards was half the problem?" Mr. Freeman asked. "I heard he gave the order to burn Persimmon out of the cabin."

The reverend explained, "He had a grudge against Persimmon but he's still a U.S. Marshal and I intend to remind him of it. While we were gone, two men figured out that I wasn't home and broke through the back door looking for Pete. They roughed Sarah up too... Damnit, I shouldn't have left her!"

"George, your language. Don't forget, you set an example," the reverend's wife scolded.

Mr. Freeman shook his head. "I don't think you want to talk to the marshal, not now. Him and his posse are in the Bansheen and he's buying drinks. Guess it's his way of paying his volunteers. I don't know about the marshal, but some of those men are libel to eat you alive in the state they're in."

The reverend nodded and then asked, "How are things at your place?"

"We're safe, if that's what you mean," Mr. Freeman's response was less than reassuring.

"Mrs. Sanchez?" the reverend astutely asked.

Mr. Freeman nodded. "She's been distraught since we heard." Then Mr. Freeman laughed guiltily as he continued, "I had a choice of staying at home with her there like she is, or risk getting shot to come see you... Here I am."

The levity was welcomed by everyone, though no one could muster more than a quick huff through a smile.

Mr. Freeman raised his hat to punctuate his next statement. "I mean no disrespect to the poor woman. I know you had hopes of putting the two of them together but, well, she barely knew the man. Why is she bawling her eyes out, prostrate on my bed? I can understand shedding a tear or two but..."

When the reverend shrugged, his wife spoke up. "I can tell you why."

We all turned to face her.

"I know she had feelings for the man, because she told me, but that isn't the half of it. Mrs. Sanchez is a widow with a small child, living in an unforgiving land, with a ranch she can't work alone and without the money to hire help. Because of the lien against the property, selling the ranch would leave her with practically nothing. What she's lost isn't just a potential suitor, it's hope."

"I suppose you have a point," Mr. Freeman sighed and then glanced out the window in the direction of the saloons and changed the subject. "I tell you, if those men are going to be drinking like that, I hope they tie one on so good they sleep for a week." Frank Freeman's voice broke a little. His brow was crumpled and he had yet to stop spinning his hat. He was nervous, and rightly so.

"I sent Jim after the sheriff. If he finds him right off, they should be back here sometime tomorrow. I hope those men will still respect the marshal as a representative of the law and won't try anything foolish. If Edwards is still here tomorrow and the sheriff hasn't come, then I'll try talking to him. Pray God puts a lick of remorse in him." Anger began creeping back into the reverend's voice.

"Any ideas about what we do tonight?" Mr. Freeman asked.

"Not much we can do. There's no place to go. I guess we hole up in our homes and pray." The reverend's response sounded apprehensive to me and I have to say, I prefer a preacher to speak with confidence when turning to prayer as a last resort.

Wishing to ease Mr. Freeman's nerves, I spoke as he approached the front door to leave. "Be careful, of course, but I don't think you have much to fear. With Persimmon gone, Mrs. Sanchez is no threat to Jenkins. It is me he'll be wanting because I can testify against him in court."

Maybe I reassured Mr. Freeman, maybe I didn't, but I scared the hell out of myself. The realization that I was now the sole focus of murderous men ran through my middle like ice water. When Mr. Freeman was gone, I told the reverend I would go stay at the church but he argued. I told him to then take his wife and go to Mr. Freeman's but he argued with me again. I then begged him to at least take his wife to the Freeman's home so she would be safe but then she argued against it. One thing I knew of missionaries, they are a strong willed and hardheaded lot. So, I quit suggesting.

In the bedroom where I had been left to recuperate, the curtains were drawn for safety. In the gloom, I found my bag. From it, I dug out the Smith & Wesson Model Three. For a few moments, I held it and stared. Wouldn't Persimmon have been confounded that I went to the cabin, amidst bloodthirsty Jenkins's men, unarmed? Confounded maybe, but not surprised. In retrospect, perhaps it was foolish. In most of the civilized world, being armed meant being prepared for a threat that likely would not materialize, but there were still places where it meant staying alive. I wedged the revolver into my waistband and then rifled around in my saddlebag until my knuckles bumped something hard, wrapped in a cloth.

The cloth was an old shirt I dared not wear anymore for the worn spots in conspicuous places but I had been fond of the yellow plaid material and repurposed it. Taking hold of a button, I unfurled it, lifting it higher until my cap and ball Colt tumbled from it, onto the bed. At first, I thought to load it with fresh powder but seeing as how I had no powder and only one good arm, and since I had never shot a man, nor fired at one who was shooting back at me, I decided to keep the Colt available and pray the powder in it lit. If it came down to that Colt, prayer would likely be all I had to live on anyway.

The reverend retrieved his shotgun from above the mantel, loaded it and handed it to his wife. Then he set out to secure the back door. As he was driving the first nail, his wife called out for him to get the cushions. Mumbling to himself, he pried the plank from the door casing, brought the cushions in from the wagon, and then returned to boarding the back door.

The rest of the day I sat out of sight, coiled in a chair in the front corner of the parlor. Every passing rider was a frightful moment, every shadow an enemy. From my vantage point at the edge of the front window, I could see up the street to McLaglen's saloon. The Bansheen Saloon was just out of frame. Hour after hour I stared up the road, expecting at any moment a horde of Jenkins men, uninhibited by booze and lathered up by rhetoric, to barrel out of the Bansheen, storm down the street and drag me from the reverend's house.

The reverend and his wife sat with me a while, she with knitting needles in her hand, he in the dark with a book. I do not recall a single page or purl being turned. As dusk set in, she went to the back to find what she could to make us supper. The reverend told her not to make a fire in the stove, then he went to lend her a hand. Half a small loaf of bread, some three-day-old cake and a little jerky was all the meal available without a fire but I was glad to forego a hot meal not to draw attention.

At my urging, the couple went to bed but only after my impassioned reminder of how much we would all need them the next day. It was the truth and they knew it. Whether they slept a wink is doubtful. As his wife pushed the bedroom door nearly closed, I saw the reverend kneel by his bedside in prayer.

Though I could not see the Bansheen, as the sun went down the road began to glow with the light from its windows. McLaglen closed his doors by midnight but I could hear the raucous sounds from the Bansheen into the wee hours of the morning. That long night stuttered by through a fitful sleep. I slept because I could not help it. I stayed awake because I could not help it. Exhaustion drug me under. Panic jerked me awake. Much of the time I stared at the glow on the road but it was the ghastly scene at Persimmon's cabin that I saw.

As the moon rose across the valley, its light trickled through the thin forest, casting shadows of the trees on the back wall of the parlor. The mountain breeze tickled the leaves of a stand of aspens, making the wall shimmer. Getting lost in this spectral canvas for a few minutes at a time was all the relief I received.

With the sun came the promise of security, no matter how empty a promise it might be. Quiet were the small cluster of buildings, graciously referred to as a town. The late-night revelers at the Bansheen had done as Mr. Freeman had hoped and all were somewhere sleeping it off. I was very thankful for it.

The sun also brought the reverend and his wife from their bedroom. With the two of them to keep watch and the false notion of security the quietness gave me, I decided to go into the dark bedroom and lay down. I never expected to sleep, I only wanted to stretch out for a bit, but my muscles gave way and I fell asleep without knowing it.

I woke again in the early afternoon to find the curtains half drawn in the parlor. As I emerged from the bedroom, the reverend caught me by the elbow. "Stay away from the windows. There are men watching the house."

Despite the warning, I carefully peeked from various windows. Across the street there was a group of men without business, mulling around where there was no business to be had. They were huddled in conversation, as if they were fooling anyone, but from their vantage they could see three sides of the reverend's house and the mountainside out back.

"Anyone have any suggestions?" I asked, despairingly.

"Looks to me, the only option we have is to sit tight and pray the deputy returns soon, with or without the sheriff," the reverend said in a voice more optimistic than my own.

"I can do that alone. The two of you should go. It is me they want and you could get killed in the crossfire." I knew I was wasting my breath.

"My being here is the only reason they haven't stormed the house already. If I left, it would be as though I offered you up for sacrifice. I'm staying." The reverend was adamant.

"And I'm not leaving you," Sarah firmly told her husband.

The couple trailed off in an argument while I kept an eye on the huddle of men. Up the street, there was more movement. Men coming and going from the Bansheen. A few minutes later I thought I heard a light tapping on the back door. The three of us were staring at each other when the tapping came again. The reverend and I eased into the small kitchen, he with the shotgun and I with Persimmon's pistol in my left hand. As we crept to the door, I saw a face dart into the window, it was McLaglen's son. The reverend hurriedly opened the window.

"I was sent to tell you that Marshal Edwards is asleep on the pool table in the Bansheen. Jenkins's men are watching the house and we think they are waiting for the marshal to leave. You need to get out of here the first chance you get." The young man might have been his father's messenger, but he spoke as his equal.

"How did you get here without being seen?" the reverend asked the teen.

"Slipped down the mountain. When it gets dark, you need to leave the same way."

"Thank you for taking the risk to tell us," I told him.

"It's not me they're after," the young man replied.

"When the sheriff or deputy show up, tell them what is going on and send them here," the reverend instructed.

I had no doubt that Deputy Jim would return. The question was whether he would arrive in time? Around five o'clock, I saw the marshal appear in the street. He looked hungover as he slowly made his way to the livery. I was anxiously watching his every move. Would he leave town so late in the day? The shadow of the mountain was already creeping across the road.

My attention was still on the marshal when I heard the clatter of a wagon. A cruel flash of hope hit me but faded as soon as I saw its occupant was a miner, not the sheriff. The miner stopped and spoke to the group of men, then went on his way to McLaglen's saloon.

Two of the men from the huddle ran to the Bansheen. It was the beginning of a rumor sweeping through town and before long, McLaglen himself was knocking at our front door, in spite of the two remaining men across the street.

"Get in here," the reverend commanded as he hid himself behind the half-open door.

McLaglen squeezed through, barely retrieving his arm before the reverend shut the door on it.

"Jenkins has been killed!" McLaglen nearly yelled.

"Who says?" the reverend dubiously snapped.

"Someone returning to the mine from Leadville. They say you could see the smoke for miles. The house and bunk house were both burned to the ground and someone found Jenkins laying up against a well with his throat cut." McLaglen's delivery was frantic with joy and an up-to-no-good grin was strung across his face.

We all stared at him, dumbfounded. Struck by a welcomed shot of hope, I said, "How do we know it's true and if it is, what does that mean?"

"I don't know what it will mean to us," McLaglen replied, shaking his head, "but I can tell you who, or rather what, they said did it. The rumor is, it was the ghost of Persimmon Apricot."

XXII
RETRIBUTION

"Nonsense. I've seen some strange things in my time but I haven't ever heard of a ghost taking revenge," reflected the reverend.

"True or not, a handful of Jenkins's men got spooked and headed south," McLaglen countered. "The rest of them will stick around. They are too busy trying to prove to one another that they aren't scared. After some goading, two of them volunteered to ride up to the Jenkins ranch to verify the story and prove their manhood but I wouldn't be surprised if they didn't skip down to the river and follow it out of the valley as soon as they were out of sight," McLaglen added with contempt.

"We both watched the cabin burn to the ground and Persimmon never came out," I foolishly reminded them. Not exactly believing in ghosts, I didn't exactly not believe in them either and if a man ever lived who had enough meanness in him to defy the grave and seek revenge, it was Persimmon Apricot.

"Yes, but that doesn't mean it was Persimmon who killed Jenkins, or if the rumor is true in the first place. If it is true, I am sure a man like Jenkins has made plenty of enemies with his sort of dealings... Nevertheless, maybe the rumor will keep them busy until the sheriff gets here." The reverend made sense but I would have gladly traded his logic for some soothsaying that could tell us plainly what we should do next.

We watched as the two bravest scoundrels tore out of town, racing to verify the rumor. By my estimation, if they could find fresh horses for the return trip, the pair would ride back into town around midnight.

The reverend asked Mr. McLaglen to check in on everyone at the Freeman house and to try to alert us if anything changed. The afternoon wore on and to our surprise, the two men watching us held their post. We speculated amongst ourselves and decided that by definition, these two men must be peons in the gang to have been assigned this duty and were timid enough not to argue. The two of them would likely remain there until relieved or at least until the rumor could be substantiated.

Meanwhile, the sun was setting and still no sheriff. My gut said tonight would be the night. When I mentioned my premonition to the reverend, I expected him to dismiss it as anxiety getting the better of me but instead, he nodded with a dire look on his face. He then took his wife aside and gave her stern orders to go to the Freeman home. When she began her squabble against the idea, the authoritative set of his brow squelched it. The two men across the street were getting antsy with the creeping darkness and kept pacing up the road and back. Each time they moved closer to the Bansheen than the last. It was during one of their nervous strolls that Sarah darted away unseen after climbing out of the bedroom window. Unboarding the back door would have been too loud.

We watched as she crossed the road and slipped along the roadside to the Freeman's home, down the hill. A few minutes after she left, the reverend went to the back of the house. I heard a scratching noise coming from the reverend's bedroom, then what sounded like the dull clatter of a thin board. A moment later the reverend returned with a bottle in hand.

"The missus doesn't like me drinking. She thinks whiskey will turn any man into the likes of those up the street but I thought we could both use a shot of tonic to soothe our nerves," the reverend said, smiling as he pulled the cork.

He took a swig then handed me the bottle. After a couple of good-sized swallows, I handed it back to him, gasped a little from the burn in my throat, then asked, "So, what do we do now?"

The reverend scurried hunched over along the back wall, away from the window, and crept up to the chair I had sat in the night before. Pressing the curtain to the window with the back of his fingers, he stared up the street for a minute before answering me.

"Well, I'm praying for the wisdom of Solomon in my deduction but here is what I'm thinking. Since he didn't get here today, I would expect the deputy to return with the sheriff by early tomorrow. Even if the rumor is true, Jim knows we're sitting here with Jenkins men still after you and he knows that Jenkins's men might not know that Jenkins is dead. I say we hole up here as long as we can and try to wait for Jim and whoever comes with him." The reverend took another small sip from the bottle.

"Whether Jenkins is dead or not, what do you think those men up there are going to do?" I asked, having my own speculations but hoping the reverend had some that were more reassuring.

"If he isn't dead, then we are in the same position we were. If Jenkins is dead, I'm not sure. Those aren't saints up there in the Bansheen. If Jenkins is dead, I suspect those of them that are hired guns will move on to find another paycheck. I don't know what the rest of them will do but it could depend on whether they get the notion that they are owed something. Either way, I don't think any of them will leave before morning. Some will wait until light for the practicality of it. Some will wait because they fear what's out there in the dark."

The reverend's estimation of the situation did not provide the level of comfort I wanted but it made sense. Yet, what I really wanted to know was what we were going to do if Deputy Jim did not return in time? I had been shot and did not want to be shot again. "What if the rumor isn't true and Jim doesn't get here in time? We can't stay here."

The reverend pressed his fingers against the curtain again to see up the street. "Those two fellows watching us are spooked by the shadows. If I was a gambling man, I would bet you that they will eventually go up the street and stay there. The woods get thicker as the lower ridgeline pulls away from the road to the south. That makes that end of town darker. They probably won't go into the Bansheen because they don't want their boss to know they aren't down here doing as they were told, but they will likely stay close to the light from the window. When they do, I am going to unboard the back door so we can get out fast and easy. Then we'll keep watch and if men pile out of the Bansheen and head this way, we'll flee up the mountain and hide out until Jim does show."

Could I scramble up the steep mountainside behind the house? The sheer cliff that began at the Bansheen tapered in height until it was spent not far beyond the reverend's home, but a mountain is still a mountain. At least we had a plan in which to cling.

The reverend's prediction of what those two men would do proved true. Within the hour, both were nervously fluttering like moths around the edge of the glow spilling from the Bansheen window. We suspected they did not want to get too close so no one in the Bansheen would see them. Once they were gone, the reverend pried the board off the back door. Since it had been kicked in, the latch would not hold the door closed, so the reverend wedged the board under the doorknob.

We sat in the parlor talking for several hours, I in the chair by the front window with Persimmon's pistol in my lap, the reverend in the back corner of the room with his shotgun, our posts cautiously outside of the faint light which trickled through the windowpanes. I think both of us wanted to discuss Persimmon but neither of us could bring ourselves to mention him. Instead, we discussed a wide variety of useless topics such as Wabash, Indiana becoming the first fully electrically lit city in the world, and how Denver had recently added a telephone exchange along with speculation as to when the telephone might replace the telegraph. All of these were things that civilized places could concern themselves about.

The rising moon cut silhouettes against the parlor wall as three riders trotted past the reverend's house. It was difficult to tell in the dim but I felt confident two of the riders were the men who rode for Jenkins's ranch. If so, they had picked up a third. Could he be a survivor? Looking across the room at the clock, I could not make out the hands in the gloom, so I pulled my pocket watch from my pants pocket and held it to the window. The moonlight reflected well on its white face—it was half-past eleven.

I watched as the riders spoke first to the two men who guarded us from outside the saloon. Whatever was said between them made our guards feel they could enter the Bansheen with the others. Wanting the sage conjecture of the reverend, I spoke to him but he did not reply. His figure was swallowed by the darkest corner of the room and I could not see his face but when I spoke a second time, the reply he gave was a light humming snore. Knowing he had not slept any better than I had the night before, I let him be. Instead, I deliberated on the evidence I had and determined that if the two guards had gone into the Bansheen, they must have assumed that watching for me was no longer important. That could only mean that the rumor must be true. Jenkins was dead.

That conclusion, and probably the whiskey, relaxed me to the point that I began dozing too. Never having been one to sleep while sitting up, I woke every time my head dropped. I could not stop this cycle but because of it, I did not stay asleep and lose time. I think it was a few minutes before midnight when the clop of a large hoof on the rocky street drew me back from the brink of slumber. I leaned forward, breathed deeply and blinked, trying to regain full control of all my faculties.

There came two more clops, one dulled by sand, the other sharp against stone. Something was slowly drawing near. On the back wall of the parlor emerged the silhouette of a horse and rider. It was a familiar figure but one that could not be. I feared looking out the window. What if it was the ghost of Persimmon? Might he take revenge upon me?

The rider was slipping from the moonlight as I mustered the courage to peek. All I could see was a dark figure riding against the glow of the Bansheen. The reverend was still snoring so I left him to rest. With my courage up, I had to know if that was Persimmon's ghost and what he was up to, and I did not need to waste time arguing the point with the reverend.

Easing out the back door, I rounded the back of the old assayer's office next door so that I avoided the moonlit end of the road. The horseman stopped in the darkest part of the street, near Mr. Freeman's store. Remembering that Samson fled the burning cabin, I wondered if maybe one of Jenkins's men found him? Whoever it was dismounted in the middle of the street. All I could discern were the shapes backlit by the glow from the Bansheen. I could see the flap and belt of a saddlebag as they were flipped open. They jostled as the figure dug into the bag.

When he had retrieved what he was after, I heard the firm but gentle slap of his hand against the horse's rump, sending the huge animal trotting behind the buildings across the street. Following the outline of the figure's hat, I watched as he squatted down and set what sounded like two separate items on the rocky street. Next came the rake of metal on glass and then the sizzle of a match. In its meager light, I could see the hand holding it as it was touched to a lamp on the ground.

The wick caught and a short flame stretched across the burner. Beneath it, I thought I could make out tulips on the font. The figure did not replace the chimney. Instead, he cranked the wick up until a tall, golden flame bounced on it. Picking the lamp up in his right hand and what looked like a kerosene container in his left, he stood and in the flicker of puffing lamplight I saw a face I recognized. It was Persimmon.

With deliberation, Persimmon marched up the street until he was close enough to toss the kerosene container onto the porch, beneath the windows of the Bansheen. It came to rest on its side and I could see the glint of kerosene pouring from its open top into a large puddle. Before anyone inside could react to the noise, Persimmon hurled the lamp against the Bansheen's door, shattering it and throwing up a wall of flame.

Persimmon jerked his pistol. Someone snatched the door open and yelped at a face full of flame. A man leapt through the engulfed doorway and Persimmon fired, sending the escapee sailing face first into the street. A second man was about to follow but thought better of it. He ducked back inside and began shooting aimlessly through the emblazoned doorway. The door had taken the fire inside with it. Through the flames, I could see Peabody, the bartender, running up with a bar towel and pitcher but before he could attack the flames, the burning door became too much and someone kicked it closed in a vain attempt to hold back the conflagration. About that time the puddle of kerosene reached the flames. Fire rushed across the fuel-soaked planking and began climbing the rough lumber walls. Persimmon backed into the undulating shadows next to McLaglen's saloon, then onto its porch, kicking in the saloon door in case he needed to take cover. By then, the entire window of the Bansheen was enveloped in a curtain of flame.

Someone burst from the Bansheen door, it was Peabody, panic-eyed and still clutching the bar towel with which he uselessly beat at the flames as he fled. He had enough wits about him to duck to his left and make for the seclusion of the darkness but Persimmon shot him as his boot hit the dirt.

I do not know if it was curiosity or guilt that drove me to get closer but I darted across the darkest part of the road and up against a building, immediately regretting it as soon as my wounded shoulder hit the wall. A moment later, one of the local miners came running up the street with a bucket in hand, yelling, "Fire!" When the miner broke into the light, Persimmon put a bullet through the wooden bucket. The stunned miner stopped fast and stared at Persimmon while water poured from the hole onto his stocking feet. The clacking of the hammer as Persimmon cocked his Schofield jolted the man back to his senses and he dropped the bucket and fled. In the distance, I saw a couple of other spectators who were too far away to see exactly what was going on but with no intentions of getting any closer.

Gunfire roared from inside the Bansheen. Bullets tore through the window glass, sending Persimmon scrambling into McLaglen's saloon. Persimmon fired back methodically, two shots through the window and another through the door. Whether he hit anyone, I could not tell from my vantage.

When most of the glass was shot from the panes of both saloons, my ears focused on the thwack of bullets slapping the front wall of McLaglen's place. Someone began yelling above the others in the Bansheen and when I looked to the Bansheen's rear corner, I could see flame licking the eave from inside. The booze had caught fire.

The dead sound of bullets against the plank wall ceased, but the gunfire had not. The shooting continued sporadically, accompanied by loud banging. There was no window on the right side of the Bansheen Saloon because the bar took up most of that wall. Neither was there a back door on the Bansheen and what good is a window on the other sides when the building sat tucked into the corner of a cliff? The ruckus the trapped men were keeping up was from them trying to break through the back wall.

On the outside, the blaze had climbed atop the roof, spreading quickly up to the ridge. The entire front and right side of the saloon were consumed. This flame was mirrored inside and the men in the Bansheen were soon cut off from their only exit.

My attention was on the blaze and horrid sounds from within it that grew fainter. Persimmon broke open the action of his pistol and the clatter of empty casings raining down on the porch drew my attention in time to see a second figure breeze from the shadows and wheel around the front corner of Mc Laglen's saloon, gun in hand.

"I knew when I heard about Jenkins that it was you, and not no ghost either," I heard the voice of Marshal Edwards say. "I don't know how you did it. I saw you go into that cabin and never come out. I watched it burn slap to the ground with you inside."

"Edwards, you're a coward," Persimmon said, firmly, calmly. "You couldn't face me alone. You had to get the likes of them to go with you." Persimmon motioned with his hat brim to the band of murderers and thieves in the Bansheen. "Even now you had to wait until I reloaded to face me."

"You can go back to hell. I don't know what kind of devil you are to have made it out of that cabin alive, but I told you I'd get you. This time I'm not going to depend on a jury to see it my way and there aren't going to be any magic tricks either. Let's see how you survive a bullet between the eyes."

Edwards cocked the hammer of his revolver and aimed it at Persimmon. Blam! A muzzle blast boomed from under the porch roof. Persimmon's entire body twitched and Marshal Edwards seemed to freeze in place. A moment later a cloud of smoke encircled the marshal's shoulders. He let out an excruciating groan and sank to his right knee, crumpling half off the porch, dead. As he fell, Persimmon could see behind him a tiny thread of smoke swirling from the muzzle of the revolver in my left hand.

I was standing in the middle of the alley and, though I could not hear it over the roar of the flames across the street, I could see in Persimmon's shoulders as he half laughed, half sighed with relief. Stepping onto the porch, I placed the pistol atop my right forearm which was cradled in a sling.

Persimmon continued to reload as if nothing had happened, letting out a loud whistle in the direction of Samson as he dropped the bullets into the cylinder. Then he snapped the revolver closed and holstered it before looking me square in the eyes.

"No matter how many times they ask you, no matter how many different ways they ask you, you didn't do this," he instructed me, like a father trying to impress a point to his son. Then he looked down at the pile of marshal laying half in the street. "That son of a bitch ain't worth hanging over."

From behind me, up the alley, I heard again the deep clops of huge hooves as Samson trotted up to Persimmon. With the toe of his boot in the lower stirrup, Persimmon swung himself onto the magnificent beast. Then, from his towering perch above me, Persimmon thrust his left hand at me. I reached into the sling and retrieved the Smith and Wesson by the barrel and handed it back to him. Persimmon drew his hand back a bit and cocked his chin then thrust his empty hand at me again. I understood that time. I stuck the revolver back in my sling and took his hand in mine. He shook it but when I thought he would let go, Persimmon looked away before giving my hand a firm but gentle squeeze. A knot tightened at the base of my throat. It was the most powerful handshake I've ever known.

Without another word, Persimmon Apricot rode out of my life from the same place he rode into it. Despite the roar and crackle of blaze across the street, the town seemed still. There were no more sounds of the living coming from the Bansheen. It will remain a mystery, whether or not anyone managed to claw their way out the back wall and scramble up the fifteen feet of near vertical mountainside to safety. As I stood there, the front wall buckled and the roof swung down with a crash. A whoosh of flame and embers shot skyward.

Looking down at the marshal, I felt sick. Not because I had killed a man, because he would have shot Persimmon if I had not shot him. It was because I had killed a U.S. Marshal, shooting him in the back no less. I had to do as Persimmon told me. No matter what, it wasn't me. First, I had to get back to the reverend's house, unseen.

XXIII
LAWS OF GOD AND MAN

I have often thanked God that the breeze that night was light and blew in from the northwest. Had it not, the stench of cooking flesh would have overtaken us. Any stronger and the town or the entire mountain would have been engulfed. Despite my worry about being charged for shooting the marshal, I slept some that night. I was too exhausted not to. In the early daylight, McLaglen came knocking on the door, followed closely by Mr. Freeman. The commotion woke me and I crept from the bedroom, my shoulder sore from my clandestine escapade and the revolver still tucked into my sling.

In the parlor, I found the two men in conference with the reverend and when they all looked my way at once, I figured they must have known what I did. To my relief, McLaglen asked, "Did you hear what happened to Marshal Edwards?"

I shook my head slowly at an odd angle which I am sure McLaglen took as an inquisitive gesture. The real reason was I had slept funny due to catering to my shoulder, and an ache rose up my neck into my skull.

"Someone shot him dead on my porch! I know you know about the Bansheen burning, everyone knows about that. They say the ghost of Persimmon Apricot did it and shot the marshal too."

I needed to patronize McLaglen's gossip so no one would become suspicious, but not being a good actor, I rubbed the back of my head and scrunched my face in pain, playing up the headache and my sore shoulder as I sat down in the corner where the reverend had slept.

The reverend knew I had left the house the night before. He had not seen me leave and I slipped in through the back door while he and Mr. Freeman were in the middle of the street watching the Bansheen burn. Still, he knew I had been missing for a time and now his eyes gave me the impression he was trying to piece things together. I knew that if I kept looking at him, he would see the guilt in mine, so I tried to play ignorant and keep my attention on the ramblings of McLaglen and Mr. Freeman who were chattering away, excitedly.

The arrival of Deputy Jim with the sheriff took the reverend's attention from me. McLaglen saw them riding into town and ran outside to meet them. I could see him pointing up the road, no doubt to the dead marshal's body crumpled on his porch where it had lain all night. McLaglen discovered him at first light but the local undertaker had recently moved to Leadville where business was booming after the local mine had hired on a live-in wheelwright which cut into the undertaker's primary profession.

No one else wanted to touch the body. As for those poor devils in the Bansheen, their bones would have to wait to be plucked from the ashes after it cooled a bit more. McLaglen jogged up the road in pursuit of the sheriff and his deputy. In the meantime, I sat with the reverend and Mr. Freeman as they discussed and speculated on the repercussions of all that had happened.

A little more than an hour later, the sheriff and Deputy Jim came knocking at the reverend's door.

"Morning, Reverend," the sheriff said as he and Jim entered the parlor. "Seems y'all had a crazy night."

"It was definitely not what I expected, I can tell you that," the reverend replied as he shook the sheriff's hand, "but we're alive. I wasn't sure we would be."

The sheriff raised his brow and nodded. "Not what I expected either. Young Jim here came charging in as I was having supper with a neighbor, telling me we had to get down here immediately because Marshal Edwards had burned a man alive and Jenkins's men were out to kill your friend here. The next thing I knew I was sending Jenkins's dead body to town and now I find the Bansheen burned to the ground and a dead marshal laying half in the street and swelling up. And if that wasn't enough, there's talk that a ghost did all this. There's a man who says the ghost of Persimmon Apricot shot a hole in his water bucket. What do you have to say about it, Reverend?"

"Honestly, I don't know what to say about it. Jenkins's men were after Pete there," the reverend explained, throwing an index finger up in my direction, "but what happened last night, I really don't know. I was awakened by the sound of gunfire and watched the chaos from this end of the street."

The sheriff continued nodding in acknowledgment and contemplation. "Well, I have sent a telegram to the U.S. Marshal's office. They'll be sending another marshal right away. I want to interview everyone in town before then and see if I can get to the bottom of all this before the arriving marshal gets to meddling." The sheriff turned to Mr. Freeman, "Pretty much everyone in town passes through your store, don't they?"

Mr. Freeman nodded.

"Do you think you could introduce me to everyone so I can find out what they know? I ought to be able to speak to everyone still alive in this wide-spot-in-the-road you call a town." The sheriff's words were contemptuous but his tone was not.

Mr. Freeman agreed and headed out the door. The sheriff took the open door by the knob and turned back to say, "I'm going to leave the kid here to take your full statements. Tell him what you know and what was going on with Jenkins. I'm sure someone is going to want to know why he was killed. I want to hear about this ghost too."

Jim stepped to the door and bid the sheriff good luck then stood there, watching him until he and Mr. Freeman were several yards away before closing the door slowly and turning his attention to me and the reverend.

"You know, I don't think we've ever had a chance to talk at length... not without someone around who would likely address me as, 'kid.' Did you know I'm twenty-seven years old?" Jim asked and we shook our heads. "I reckon I have a bit of a baby face and I'm the youngest deputy and the one with the least number of years in the job. All that adds up against me but I've grown used to it."

The reverend and I sat quietly. There was something peculiar about the conversation and neither of us knew how to enter into it.

Jim looked at me. "I bet you would also never guess why I became a deputy. It was because of my fascination with firearms," Jim said with a slow nod as though confirming his statement against a question we had not asked. "I love the mechanical design of them and the artistry of the fancier ones. I guess that means I ought to be fascinated by clocks too, and they do interest me, but you can't shoot a clock. A clock is useful but comparatively it is like having a pet dog that is stuffed rather than a live one you can pet and interact with."

It was during Jim's story that I noticed his rig sported what looked to be the same model of Smith and Wesson as I had tucked into my sling.

"Anyway, I couldn't afford to feed my curiosity. I wanted to be a gunsmith but the gunsmith in my hometown already had an apprentice. When I came out west, I found myself needing to eat. I also discovered that the office of the sheriff often had a variety of weapons. Plus, being a deputy gives me a certain standing in the community so shopkeepers tend to let me try new models when they arrive."

Jim was walking toward me while he was talking. He must have spied the grip of the Model Three peeking from my sling because he went straight to it and fished it out. Since it was identical to what he carried, my gut told me that his interest in mine was not good.

Jim held the pistol up as though presenting it in a lecture. "I believe you and I are the only ones in the area that carry an original American Model Three." Jim slowly rotated the pistol in the air, back and forth as if examining one for the first time. "I bought mine used after a few paychecks. I know Persimmon toted a Schofield and I seem to recall a fella' passing through who had one of the Russian models and there are a couple of men in Leadville sporting the New Model Number Threes. The sheriff carries a Colt Single Action Army. He thinks it's pretty, and it is. They are tough guns too and I'd love to have one, but if I have to be in a gun battle, I like the idea of how fast I can reload one of these. The sheriff likes to joke that if all hell breaks loose, he will just send me and my pistol to deal with it."

Having mentioned the gun's quick reloading, Jim sat in the chair by the window and slowly broke open the action so as not to launch the bullets from the ejector. Of the six, there was the customary empty chamber for safety and next to it a single casing with a dent in the primer from being struck by the firing pin. My chest grew tight and I could hear my heart thumping. Why had Jim not asked us a single question?

"Looks like you've got a couple of empties here," Jim commented, matter-of-factly. "You know, our guns are special. This was the first large caliber handgun and..." Jim pulled the empty casing from the cylinder by his fingernails and held it up, "it used a brass casing instead of copper—Takes the heat better."

Feeling the need to interject into the conversation and hoping to divert Jim's attention, I said, "I don't have any more bullets for it. Persimmon loaned me that pistol the day he saved... followed you up to the Jensen gang's cabin."

I knew my diversion had failed when Jim wiped the tip of his index finger over the muzzle of my revolver and came away with a black streak across it. Pulling a handkerchief from his pocket, he wiped the smudge from his fingertip and then fully ejected the remaining rounds into his lap. Carefully, he piled them close to his torso, in the folds of his britches where they would not fall, then he laid the pistol on his thigh and began twirling the handkerchief around his left finger.

"Yeah, if Persimmon hadn't followed us that day, I doubt I would be sitting here talking to you." Jim took the tightly twisted point of the handkerchief and stuffed it into the muzzle, twisting and threading it into the barrel until it emerged from one of the cylinder chambers. Grabbing both ends, he began to slowly saw the handkerchief through the bore as he talked.

"Edwards never should have been a lawman. A lawman has to have grit, but he also has to have compassion and a lawman must always try to take his suspect into custody. A lawman can't be executioner too. That skips judge and jury and we don't operate like that in this country. I bet Edwards got pushed into being a lawman and before long that was all he knew how to do." Jim pulled the blackened handkerchief from the barrel, folded it the opposite way, to show its mostly clean side, and rethreaded it.

Nervously, I watched him, wondering when and how his rambling was going to lead to an accusation. The reverend sat quietly near the kitchen door. The perplexed expression on his face told me that he wondered much the same things as I. Had the reverend figured out that I killed Edwards? Had Jim?

"The same thing happened to my father," Jim continued. "He was the son of a farmer and when you have a family farm, it is expected that one of the sons will take it over some day. By the time my daddy figured out that he didn't want to be a farmer, he already had a family depending on him and nothing else to fall back on. Now, there's nothing wrong with being a farmer, you understand, but some folks just aren't cut out for it. I figured out early on that I wasn't cut out for it either and one day I told my brother the farm was his and I headed west."

Jim pulled the filthy handkerchief from the barrel, wadded it up and stuffed it back into his pocket and then, with the pistol and bullets laying peacefully in his lap, he looked at me and said, "The thing about Edwards is, he was shot in the back."

My gut went queasy and I held my breath.

"The miner whose bucket got shot, testified that he later saw a second figure on the porch with Persimmon but that they were facing off." Jim dropped the four bullets back into the cylinder and then added, "You know, there is something else unique about this revolver." He reached behind him and pulled a shiny new bullet from a loop on his belt and held it up with his thumbnail near the top of the brass casing. "See here how the bullet is the same diameter as the casing?"

I nodded, sheepishly.

"This is the original Smith and Wesson .44 American round. The heel of this bullet is smaller in diameter so it can fit down inside the brass and leave the bullet flush with the casing. The .44 Russian, and other large caliber rounds, use a bullet that has straight sides and the casing is crimped on. There's no mistaking a .44 American bullet, even after it is fired, as long as it doesn't hit anything too hard, like a rock." Jim dropped his demonstration round into the cylinder of my revolver and then reached behind him again for a second bullet off his belt. Dropping it into the last empty chamber gave my pistol a full complement of six.

Jim stood and softly clicked the pistol closed and, to my surprise, handed it back to me and said, "It was good of Persimmon to give you a fully loaded pistol for protection." There was an uncomfortable pause and Jim looked out the window and up the street before continuing. "I suspect when the new marshal arrives to investigate, he'll probably want the bullet taken out of Edwards. In fact, I'm sure the sheriff will get someone to do it as soon as he can find someone." Jim turned back to me. "The marshal will want to interrogate everyone in town, so expect a visit. However, other than this Jenkins matter, I don't think they will waste much time with you... seeing as how you were too injured to leave the house."

Jim stared at me with a hint of a wry smile on his lips, then he turned to the reverend. "Wouldn't you say so, Reverend?"

"Uh, um... yeah. I would say so. Yes," the shocked reverend guiltily but eagerly agreed.

On his way out the door, Jim glanced back at the reverend and added, "It's good that Pete had you here to look after him." Smiling, Jim closed the door and headed up the street.

The reverend and I looked at each other in amazement but the reverend never asked me anything about it. Two days later, a U.S. Marshal arrived and, like Jim suspected, the marshal interrogated everyone. I got the impression the new marshal had known Edwards and was not all that broken up over his death. Still, a U.S. Marshal had been killed and a thorough investigation was made. Without a viable suspect and desiring not to leave the case unsolved, the final verdict was that a stray round had either been fired from within the Bansheen or set off by the blaze, striking Marshal Edwards who was unlucky to be in its path.

The new marshal did not believe in ghosts and Persimmon was listed as wanted for the murder of the men in the Bansheen and a few men at the Jenkins ranch, including Jenkins.

When the next stagecoach hit town, on it was a package wrapped in brown paper, addressed to the reverend. In it were land deeds, liens and instructions for the reverend and I. The first item on the list was to check with the local bank about the Sanchez ranch. There was also a copy of a letter Persimmon sent to the men in Richmond. In it, he gave instructions to the Richmond Consortium that once they had recouped all the money they could from Jenkins's holdings, they were to split the reward money, half to Mrs. Sanchez and a quarter each to the reverend and I. The letter was signed, "Or Else, P.A."

As long as Persimmon was free, I was sure that eventually the reward would be paid but sifting through the evidence in the courts would take time. The letter also reminded me of the shyster attorney in Washington. I wondered if some night he would not wake in his bed or be walking down an alley on his way home and meet a dark figure with a revolver?

The reverend checked with the bank about the Sanchez lien but the deed had been taken by Jenkins when he foreclosed. Persimmon included it in the package to the reverend and no remaining evidence of the loan existed. The reverend would need to check with the state to see if the property had been placed in Jenkins's name but if not, then Mrs. Sanchez would own her ranch free and clear and without a court battle.

Over the next week my shoulder healed well. Certainly, it helped to not be sitting up all night in a chair or chasing ghosts through town in the wee hours of the morning. As I recuperated, I pondered. Persimmon had not left the burning cabin. Was Edwards right, was Persimmon some sort of devil? Or was it really a ghost who shook my hand in the hellish glow of the Bansheen that night?

When I felt I could make the trip up the rough road sitting on the seat, the reverend and I returned to the meadow where the charred remains of Persimmon's cabin lay. We parked the wagon as before, and tread solemnly through the grass and little purple flowers as if approaching a grave.

"Something that amazes me is how quickly everything turned against us," I commented to break the silence.

"That is usually the way it goes. One, seemingly innocent mistake, can flip your world upside down." The reverend spoke as if he had experience in the matter. Then he added, "I've seen it happen to many men."

Rummaging through my thoughts, I lamented, "I really thought the two of us were going to put Persimmon and Mrs. Sanchez together. Maybe it was a foolish notion to begin with but we'll never know because I messed it up."

"Don't be too hard on yourself. You might have put the two of you on the wrong side of Jenkins but not on the wrong side of the law. It was Persimmon who killed those men." The reverend paused as we stepped up to the rectangle mass of charcoal and ash, tamped down by the dew. "Vengeance is mine, saith the Lord. He doesn't give us that command because He is selfish and wants to keep it to Himself. It is because vengeance harms us. Sometimes it only hardens our hearts but, as we've seen, it often puts our very lives and the lives of others in jeopardy. Persimmon put his and Mrs. Sanchez's well-being in jeopardy when he took revenge on those men."

Putting my left hand on the small stove which stood amid the ash, I steadied myself to step into what remained of the cabin. Carefully, I began to toe through the debris, flipping the small chunks of remaining timber and raking away the ash. I had no idea what I sought. As I did, I was thinking about shooting Edwards and whether or not that had been revenge. Yes, I had prevented him from murdering Persimmon but shooting the marshal felt satisfying like revenge always promises to be. Then again, I did not shoot Persimmon to prevent him from bottling up those men in the fire. Did that make me equally guilty in the sight of the Lord? Should I add hypocrisy to my list of sins?

The reverend must have taken my silence as disapproval or perhaps he felt the need to be completely honest. "Please don't get me wrong. I owe Persimmon my gratitude and maybe far more."

"For what?" I asked, keeping my eyes at my feet.

"When I found my door kicked in and Sarah laid out in the parlor, first I panicked until I knew she was ok. Then my blood boiled. I wanted revenge too. I could lie to you and call it justice but when you are the victim, justice is only a polite word for revenge. I don't know what I would have done, if anything, if I ever found out who broke into my house but what Persimmon did prevented me from getting myself into trouble. Yes, I should have turned it over to the Lord, and maybe I would have after I stewed on it a bit longer, but I am a man too."

Glancing up at the reverend, I gave thought to what he said. I guess people usually do not allow for the fact that men of the cloth are still men. They struggle with temptation the same as any of us. I nodded, "Yeah, I think I understand you. Seems there is plenty of sin to go around."

My boots and the cuffs of my pants were clad in grey. The ash that was still damp clung to my heels in clumps. Near what would have been the left side of the cabin, I noticed what felt like a large flagstone under my feet. I scraped back the piles of ash atop it. Befuddled and disgusted that I had not learned the secret of Persimmon's escape, I was ready to accept that Persimmon's return was supernatural. To shake off as much dust and clumped ash as I could, I stomped my feet on the flagstone a few times. It sounded hollow and then I heard it crack. I leapt off of it, not knowing what would happen if I broke through.

The reverend saw what happened and knowing I was still nursing my shoulder, he knelt down beside the stone where he could pry it from the hot soil. Beneath it, a shaft fell away into the darkness.

"It's an old mine!" blurted the reverend, excitedly.

The shaft was tight and a limbed aspen trunk, about as big around as my arm, leaned against one side. I was not physically able to shimmy down the tree and the reverend did not seem keen on dropping into a dark hole and without a lamp, but it struck us that this ventilation shaft must lead to a mine entrance somewhere. Not having seen a mine along the trail, we eagerly scrambled down the mountainside which began to slope off a few feet into the tree line behind the cabin.

After several minutes of zigzagging through the woods, we found where the gentle slope was cut back into a short but steep drop and at the bottom was a mine entrance, covered in limbs and old autumn leaves. It was

Persimmon's tunnel to freedom. Marshal Edwards had encircled Persimmon, but it was Persimmon who had laid the trap.

I think what I found most interesting is that he had built the cabin over the shaft. What does that say about a man's life that he has the notion to plan ahead for escape?

The idea of revenge and the reverend's words on the subject stuck with me. Marshal Edwards had sought revenge over embarrassment, for which he blamed Persimmon. It had made him a bitter man and ultimately cost him his life. Then there was Persimmon who bowed to revenge rather than justice, and in doing so, traded peace and potential happiness for a handbill.

Of course, I had thus far dodged a murder charge but I would carry the weight of that worry for the rest of my days. The Lord forgives, but the law holds a grudge, especially in the case of murder.

Despite this, despite nearly being killed on several occasions, despite having been shot and hunted like a wounded animal, those few weeks were like no other in my life and I do not regret the days I spent with my friend, Persimmon Apricot.

EPILOGUE

Gathering my serial submissions and the additional notes I had made, I managed to bring this book together. It took time though, what with the serial being popular and demanding additional, more fictitious tales to satisfy newspaper editors. It also took time for me to modify a few details as not to do more than bruise the truth a bit while keeping myself out of jail. Once I was done, I could not bring myself to publish it at first due to the worry of what repercussions it might bring.

To that end, I consulted attorneys and even a judge, going so far as to file an affidavit with the judge as to my innocence. So, if any lawman reads this tale and decides justice behooves them to track me down and question me in a court of law, I imagine you can guess which portions of this story I will testify to as being fabricated.

More to the point, my hesitation to publish proved fortuitous. About two years after I said goodbye to the reverend and continued my search for new stories across the West, I happened into a saloon in Denver. Without Persimmon around, my imbibing had been curtailed dramatically but my habit was to order a beer, or if beer was not available then a whiskey, to sip on at my table while I observed the crowd or read the local paper. It was a prop that helped me to fit in.

When the barkeep in the Denver saloon slid down the bar to serve me, we locked eyes and I think both of us tipped our heads sideways a bit, like a mutt does when puzzled. The bartender asked me who I was and I gave him my pen name. To this day, I am not comfortable giving my real name when connected with this story.

The barkeep kept pondering and said, "I recognize your face but I can't place it in that suit or with that name."

My income had much improved since the day I met Persimmon Apricot and so had my wardrobe. I had a well-made but inauspicious suit along with new boots and hat, but among my new accoutrements, I was most proud of the holster hanging under my left arm and tucked inside my coat. Never would I go looking for a fight but Persimmon could be proud that I was prepared if one found me. I knew the barkeep must remember me a bit more tattered and trail worn so I asked him his name.

When he told me his name was McLaglen, memories flooded back and a smile stretched across my face. "Pete. You know me by the name Pete," I exclaimed, ripping his hand off the counter and shaking it vigorously.

McLaglen's face lit up when he recognized me. "Drinks are on the house. What will you have, my friend?"

Given the circumstance and the conversation I knew I was about to have, I asked him if he had any good brandy? He poured two glasses and between waiting on other customers, we talked of old times. Two hours we talked. For him it was gossip, for me it was reminiscing.

We discussed the railroad which was laid up the valley, to Leadville. I had known of it being built but McLaglen told me that it had done nothing to boost the little town because soon after, the mine played out. McLaglen had taken what he had saved and moved to Denver but he made a point to credit Persimmon for his good fortune. With the burning of the Bansheen went the only competition McLaglen had in the little town. Even more miners came than before because the Jenkins gang was no longer there to intimidate them.

Of course, we discussed the events of that night. McLaglen described all the soot and blood he had to clean from his saloon's porch. The wind that carried away the smell had also carried ash and embers into McLaglen's place. Luckily for him, none of the embers were able to get a good bite. The bloodstain, where Marshal Edwards fell, became an attraction. Anyone new in town would hear of it and seek out the saloon to see it and have a drink in the place where it all happened. I did not volunteer that McLaglen really had me to thank for it.

Eventually, McLaglen asked, "What is Persimmon doing these days?"

I thought it odd that he would assume I would know. Sadly, I did not. I explained that I had not seen nor heard from Persimmon since then. As far as I knew, Persimmon was far away, where he could avoid U.S. Marshals. "It is too bad, too. I grew fond of Persimmon. He had had a tough life and I had hoped he would get to settle down with Mrs. Sanchez on her ranch," I explained, with a heavy heart.

"Mrs. Sanchez left," McLaglen replied.

My chin scrunched in thoughts of pity for the widow. "I guess she couldn't make the ranch go, then?" I said, stating my assumption more than asking for an answer. "That's a shame. Was she able to sell the ranch for much?"

"No, no, she still owns the ranch. At least she did, last I heard," McLaglen eagerly corrected me. "About a month after you left, she leased the land to another rancher for grazing land and disappeared."

"Disappeared?" I asked, both surprised and concerned.

"Yeah, she just picked up and left. No one knows where." McLaglen was animated as he spoke, overjoyed to share mysterious gossip.

"Didn't she tell the reverend where she was headed?" I challenged him.

"Nope. Her boy did not come to the hardware store that Saturday and then she and the boy didn't show for Sunday worship so the reverend and Fred got worried and went out to the ranch to check on them." McLaglen propped himself on the counter and I leaned in anxiously. "They found the house empty and swept clean. All that was left was the furniture."

With raised brow, I leaned back with my hands on the bar. Was she safe? Had she gone back to her family? Why would she have left without any notice to the reverend who had helped her so much?

Then McLaglen remembered a final detail. "Oh, I forgot the oddest part. On the table, they found a pewter frame with a picture of a beautiful blond woman. Strange, huh?"

I shook my head slowly. "Maybe not as strange as you might think," I answered, a huge grin stretching across my soul.

ABOUT THE AUTHOR

Jason S. Litz is a lover of history, in particular American history. The stories he writes are painlessly doused in historical fact. Having traveled extensively throughout the United States, Jason strives to take his readers to a variety of locales along history's timeline. Jason's interest spans many topics including the great outdoors, mechanics, woodworking and billiards. He also has a master's degree in Computer Science.

NOTE FROM THE AUTHOR

Word-of-mouth is crucial for any author to succeed. If you enjoyed *Persimmon Apricot, Gunfighter*, please leave a review online—anywhere you are able. Even if it's just a sentence or two. It would make all the difference and would be very much appreciated.

Thanks!
Jason

Thank you so much for reading one of our **Western** novels.
If you enjoyed the experience, please check out our recommendation
for your next great read!

Pokeweed by Brian L. Tucker

2019 Best Book Awards Finalist – Novella

"Brian has my permission to write."
– Chris Offutt, best-selling author of *Country Dark*,
writer for HBO's *True Blood* and *Weeds*

View other Black Rose Writing titles at
<u>www.blackrosewriting.com/books</u> and use promo code
PRINT to receive a **20% discount** when purchasing.